Praise for JANE ISENBERG's
BEL BARRETT MYSTERIES

"Bel Barrett brings killers to justice with her wry
sense of humor and handy estrogen patch."
Bergen Record

"Jane Isenberg delivers a well-plotted, light mystery
peopled with likable, realistic characters and
skillfully served by sharp wit."
Ft. Lauderdale Sun-Sentinel

"Bel Barrett is distinguished even among a crop of
increasingly diverse fictional detectives by punctuating
the discovery of clues with bouts of hot flashes."
New York Times

"The gifted Jane Isenberg writes with wit and
compassion about life transitions that range from
menopause to murder."
Susan Conant,
author of the Barker Street Regulars mysteries

"Bel's sleuthing is frequently interrupted by personal
concerns, but seeing her deal with them is nearly as
compelling as watching her unravel the mystery."
Publishers Weekly

Bel Barrett Mysteries by
Jane Isenberg
from Avon Books

JANE ISENBERG

A BEL BARRETT MYSTERY

HOT ON THE Trail

AVON BOOKS
An Imprint of HarperCollinsPublishers

This is a work of fiction. Names, characters, places, and incidents are products of the author's imagination or are used fictitiously and are not to be construed as real. Any resemblance to actual events, locales, organizations, or persons, living or dead, is entirely coincidental.

AVON BOOKS
An Imprint of HarperCollins*Publishers*
10 East 53rd Street
New York, New York 10022-5299

Copyright © 2004 by Jane Isenberg
Excerpts copyright © 1999, 2000, 2000, 2001, 2002, 2003 by Jane Isenberg
ISBN: 0-06-057751-7
www.avonmystery.com

First Avon Books paperback printing: November 2004

Avon Trademark Reg. U.S. Pat. Off. and in Other Countries, Marca Registrada, Hecho en U.S.A.
HarperCollins ® is a registered trademark of HarperCollins Publishers Inc.

Printed in the U.S.A.

10 9 8 7 6 5 4 3 2 1

To dear friends in Massachusetts, with love

Acknowledgments

For generously and patiently sharing his considerable expertise in raising and racing pigeons, I offer many heartfelt thanks to David Maldonado of Williamsburg, Massachusetts. I'm also indebted once again to the Jersey Room of the Jersey City Public Library for information about Hoboken pigeons and pigeon fanciers. It was Elaine Foster who steered me to David and who put me up while I visited the Jersey Room, so thank you, Elaine. Also for hosting me in New Jersey, I'm grateful to Maureen Singleton, Arlene and Mike Silver, and Ruth and David Tait. Joan Rafter slipped some pigeon-related reading under the door, for which I thank her as well.

My faithful writing group, Susan Babinski, Pat Juell, and Rebecca Mlynarczyk, sent perceptive suggestions and welcome support across the continent by snail mail, e-mail, and phone. I also appreciate the insights and accessibility of both my editor, Sarah Durand, and my agent, Laura Peterson. Grace Ingersoll, too, deserves thanks for her encouragement as I worked to finish the book, and so does Susan Tompkins for suggesting the title.

I wrote *Hot on the Trail* during a year when my husband and I moved across the country from Massachusetts to Washington. Just before we left, Daniel Isenberg and Shilyh Warren lent their formidable party planning skills to make my adult bat mitzvah celebration run smoothly, and Rachel and Brian Stoner put their shoulders to the renovation wheel to make sure our new home would be ready for us. Their combined efforts left me more time to write. My husband Phil Tompkins, whose modest demeanor belies a chilling understanding of the criminal mind, provided useful advice on every aspect of this book. Thank you.

HOT ON THE Trail

Chapter 1

To: Bbarrett@circle.com
From: Florag@juno.com
Re: Papa
Date: 01/21/03 16:04:04

Dear Professor B,

I'm so upset about Papa. I have to remember to breathe while I'm typing. I know you were worried when he didn't show up yesterday. Papa really likes your memoir-writing class and there was no way he would have missed that session, not with it being his turn to read. Wait a minute. I have to breathe again. Okay, I'm okay now. You probably figured Papa was having one of his weak spells that he gets when his pressure goes down and that I decided to stay home with him. Let me tell you, professor, I almost wish that was true.

What really happened is Papa just disappeared. I swear to God, none of us seen him since he went up to bed Monday night. When I hollered to him yesterday to get ready for the class, he didn't answer. And he had made me promise to get him up early so he could practice reading his essay, you know? He wanted to read good in front of the class. So I went up to see if he was okay, you know? I have to take a deep breath when I get to this next part. He wasn't in his room. The gray slacks and blue plaid shirt I got him for Christmas that I put out for him to wear to the class were still on the chair. His galoshes and his navy blue down jacket with the hood were gone. He wasn't in the bathroom either. My brother Leo lives downstairs from me and my daughter, Mary, and Papa. Leo came up and we looked everywhere, even on the roof, you know, where his pigeons used to be. Remember I was telling you how sometimes he would go up there and just walk around. But Papa wasn't there. Papa wasn't anywhere. He was just gone. Like them damn pigeons.

Finally me and Leo reported Papa missing. I was crying the whole time we talked to the officer. He said Papa must have wandered off, so they're putting his picture in the paper and in stores in the neighborhood and sending out his description. That detective made it sound like Papa has Alzheimers. Like I told you Dominic Tomaselli can be a pain in the butt and he does get depressed sometimes. But demented he isn't. So anyway I'm supposed to stay home in case he calls or wanders back. I'm trying not to think about how cold it is outside. Anyway I'll be missing my Cultures and Values class with you today too. Hopefully Papa'll show up soon, and I'll make it to the next class. I'll let you know. Meanwhile, I have to remember to breathe deep and pray hard.

Flora Giglio

"Poor Flora. She has stress related asthma, but she hyperventilates even when things are going well. This might push her over the edge. Where could that sweet old man have gone?" I muttered. I had addressed this query to myself, but, seated at her desk not two feet away from mine, my officemate Wendy could not help overhearing.

"What sweet old man? Listen Bel, now that you've finally weaned yourself off estrogen, if you're going to start babbling to your computer, we're going to have to rethink this cozy arrangement." She looked up from the business section of the *New York Times* and gestured around her at the claustrophobic cubicle that she and I had shared since the seventies when we'd both joined the English Department at River Edge Community College in Jersey City, New Jersey. We also shared this "closet" with Thelma and Louise, two feisty philodendrons that thrived on our windowsill despite decades of sporadic watering and long outgrown pots. Their vines meandered over Wendy's cluttered desktop and would have encroached on the pristine surface of mine except that they knew better.

Ignoring her dig, I passed Wendy the jar of M&M's I kept on my side of the divide, and she helped herself to a handful. "Better than estrogen, right?" she quipped. "Maybe if I eat enough chocolate the fact that my IRA has been shrinking like cotton undies in the dryer won't seem so important," she said. The curve of her grin softened her drawn features. "Jeez, Bel, you've completely interrupted my efforts to calculate how old I'll have to be before I can retire on what's left of my portfolio." She pushed the newspaper away as she spoke. "So, what sweet little old man were you just ranting about?" Without waiting for me to answer, Wendy continued. "I hope nothing bad has happened to that old charmer in your memoir class, the one who was bragging about having been an extra in *On the Waterfront*." I'd invited Wendy to a session of "Tell It Like It Was," my memoir-writing course for senior citizens, because she was considering teaching it in the fall.

"No. That 'old charmer' is Sam Simon, ex-war hero and ex-convict." I was gratified to see Wendy's eyebrows lift as she registered Sam's criminal record. "He started his memoirs while he was in jail for taking bribes when he was head of Hoboken's ABC, you know, the Alcoholic Beverages Control Board. You're right, though. He's a sweetheart." I shook my head at the irony I saw embodied in Sam Simon. The man was undoubtedly a rogue, but a rogue who radiated comfort spiked with charisma. "But I'm worried about the other guy in the class, Dom Tomaselli, the one who wasn't there, the one whose piece about the pigeons I talked about, remember? I assumed he was sick, but actually his daughter just e-mailed me that he's missing." I pictured Dom's serious gray eyes and weather-beaten face blotched with age spots. I hoped that, like the racing pigeon he wrote about in his memoir, Dom would find his way home fast. Meanwhile, I empathized with poor Flora. I too was responsible for an aging parent. Thank God, Ma did not wander off. But she could be stubborn at times, and she had been depressed as well.

Wendy's voice brought me back to our conversation. "The guy who wrote that piece about the pigeons that you were talking about? I never got to meet him." She had swiveled her chair around so her back was now to her desk and the columns of stock market figures she had been studying. The whereabouts of my missing student vied for her attention along with the failing economy. Poor Dom appeared to be winning.

"Funny, but it's on account of Dom that I ended up

teaching that course," I said with a sigh. "I don't usually teach continuing ed courses."

"I know. But I thought Amelia Norcross was supposed to teach it, and then when she bagged it at the last minute, you offered to take it over because of your mom," said Wendy, swiveling her chair from side to side, a nervous habit she'd refined over the years. I'd gotten used to talking to her while she was in motion. Wendy was caregiver to her own aging mom, and we had become an ad hoc caregivers' support couple, sharing problems, solutions, and resources just as we had when our children were growing up. "I thought Sadie was depressed and you got her to sign up for that course to distract her."

"You're partly right. Dean Smithers was going to cancel it, but I'd convinced myself that Ma's sanity depended on her taking that course, so I offered to teach it in spite of the negligible pay and the fact that I already had a full course load." I shook my head as I remembered how upset I'd been when I'd learned of Amelia's last-minute defection.

"I first heard about 'Tell It Like It Was' from Flora Tomaselli. She's in my Cultures and Values class, and she's doing a research project on attitudes towards aging in our culture." I liberated a few M&M's from the jar and began ingesting them two at a time. When I wasn't dieting, I ate them by the fistful. Wendy was not the only one in our office with a nervous habit. "In her introduction, Flora explained that her dad had been depressed and had retreated into the past. She enrolled him in this course at the Senior Center, hoping that writing down his memories for his grandkids would reconnect him to the present. I thought she was on to something, so I persuaded Ma to enroll. It helped that

Sofia thought it sounded like fun. You know those two are joined at the hip." Wendy nodded, aware of the close bond between Ma and her housemate.

"I do remember over the holidays you were worried that Sadie was kind of down," Wendy said. What she left unsaid was that most people were down then. Our country was on the brink of waging a historic preemptive war, our economy was in the toilet, and our white Christmas had heralded a long white winter during which orange-level alerts from Homeland Security had flared through our frozen world. But Ma had been even more down than the rest of us. She had stayed home from a Senior Center trip to her beloved casinos in Atlantic City so she could "rest." She hadn't even responded when Sofia tried to engage her in a bet on when it would stop snowing. Ma hadn't returned her grandson's calls or added the latest photo of her great-granddaughter to the others on her fridge. Desperate to banish Sadie's blues, my partner Sol had even asked for her advice about how to organize our upcoming nuptial ceremony.

"Do what you want. You two are certainly old enough to plan a wedding," Ma had responded, in a tone more disinterested than peevish.

"She really had us all worried then. She'd lost her zest for life, and she wasn't eating much," I said, recalling how Ma's cheekbones had seemed to surface just beneath her skin, like skeletal signals of something amiss.

"No wonder you were worried," said Wendy. "It makes me nuts when my mother doesn't eat. Did you ever figure out what triggered her depression?"

"Sol was convinced she was having a delayed reaction to 9/11 or she couldn't bear the thought of another war. I thought she was upset because she has to use her walker more and more or maybe because she has to pay so much for her arthritis meds. Sofia thought maybe it was because Ma had cashed in some CDs and invested in a tech company she read about that later went belly-up." I shook my head. "Who knows, really? Jeez, was I relieved when she agreed to enroll in that course."

"Well, it was a stroke of genius to get her to do it. Her childhood sounds so interesting. I swear, Bel, she practically had me in tears when she was talking about how she had to leave her best friend, the little Irish girl, on the Lower East Side when the family moved to Brooklyn. Besides, I always thought your mom was born in Brooklyn."

"She pretty much grew up there, but she was born on Delancey Street," I said. "I like that anecdote too. But the best part is, she's a lot more upbeat since she's been taking that course. Writing and talking about her life energizes her. She's even learning to use the PC now." I smiled, picturing my mother hunkered over the keyboard, cursing the machine every time she inadvertently pushed the wrong key. I glanced at my own PC, where Flora's message begged for a reassuring reply.

I definitely knew where Flora was coming from, and my heart ached for her. In her fifties, Flora was a full-time student with a 3.7 GPA, at long last getting the education she had always wanted. At the same time, she not only acted as caregiver for her dad, but she had raised a daughter as a single parent and was still keeping house for three generations of her extended family. No wonder she was having trouble breathing. Compared to Flora, I had it easy. I had a job I loved, my kids were long gone, my mother lived a few blocks away with Sofia, and I shared housekeeping and care-giving duties with a live-in partner who couldn't wait to make an honest woman of me. I was reliving my un-orthodox proposal of marriage to Sol when Wendy's voice recalled me to the present and our conversation about my mother.

"Go, Sadie," said Wendy. "Meanwhile I've got to stop counting what's left of my money and put some articles on reserve for my Children's Lit class. I hope your pigeon-loving student hasn't flown the coop for good." She stood and began gathering the books and papers that were scattered all over her desk.

"Me too," I said, clicking on REPLY. I was deter-mined to respond to Flora's distressing message with some words of comfort.

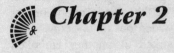

Chapter 2

Dominic Tomaselli, Sr. (con't.)

. . . like when I was a kid coming up
in Hoboken we didn't have no computer
games, no team sports, no after school
programs, no nothing that's what we
had. And we didn't mess with girls so
young neither, not like my Leo with a
girlfriend in junior high school. So
it was something to have the birds and
to go up on the roof and feed them
and train them. It was a real good
hobby, kept a lot of us off the
streets, out of trouble, you know? The
older guys would start us off like my
old man, he gave me two breeders and I
was on my way. Every day before and
after school rain or shine I was up on
that roof taking care of them
birds . . .

At home early Friday morning, I had begun to reread Dom's memoir in the hope of finding in it some clue as to where the missing man might have gone. But this time the description of the pigeon coops on his Hoboken rooftop was crowded out of my consciousness by the image it evoked of another Hoboken rooftop dovecote. In this one, the young and brooding Brando tends the pigeons of his dead friend Joey Doyle while strains of Leonard Bernstein's score charge the background. Before I could get too caught up in the next scene of my mental replay, the one in which *I* replace Eva Marie Saint in Brando's arms, the phone rang. I slipped the memoir into Dom's folder and took the call. "Hello," I answered as politely as I could in view of the fact that the caller was intruding on my tryst.

"Yo, Ma Bel, good morning." It was my son, Mark. And this time he was not logging in from some remote global hot spot he had chosen to visit as part of what he now called his "twenties' adventure." No, this time he was calling from Ma's house three blocks away, where he had spent the night during a surprise visit I had orchestrated as part of my plan to raise Ma's spirits. My daughter, Rebecca, was living her own version of *Sleepless in Seattle,* juggling school, work, and parenthood, so I hadn't even considered trying to spring her and Abbie J. But Mark was living in Maine with his girlfriend, Aveda, and his job was "winding down," so he was able to come. Although I had summoned Mark for Ma's sake and encouraged him to stay with her and Sofia, I was pretty happy to see him myself. Too many months had passed since his visit at Rosh Hashanah last fall.

"Listen up, Ma Bel. Grandma Sadie and I want to

make Sabbath dinner tonight for you and Sol, okay? But we want to do it in your rockin' new kitchen because it's way more cool than the Odd Couple's." He was right. The Odd Couple, our nickname for Ma and Sofia, lived in the brick-front row house Sofia had shared with her late husband. She had not changed anything she didn't have to, with the result that the place resembled a time capsule from the seventies, the last time they had redecorated.

Sol and I had gutted and remodeled our kitchen only a couple of years ago. Most of the work had been done in the immediate aftermath of 9/11 while I was looking into the killing of a neighbor and colleague. But even so, the new kitchen did, as Mark said, "rock." I looked around, taking in the state of the art appliances, cherry cabinets, and sleek, low-maintenance counter space. They fulfilled Sol's Wolfgang Puck meets *This Old House* fantasies. He was so taken with the remodeled kitchen that I hardly got a chance to cook, a deprivation I had no trouble adapting to at all. While men of all ages, as well as college students and celebrities of both genders were discovering the joy of cooking for the first time, I was discovering the joy of their doing most of the cooking along with the shopping and dishwashing. The thought made me grin. It was a lot easer to thank God it was Friday now that I didn't have to be solely responsible for pulling together a Shabbat meal after work. "So leave the door unlocked when you go. Don't forget. While you're in class, we're going to buy a few groceries and a little vino and bring them to your house and make magic. You and Sol won't have to do a thing. Hold on, Grandma Sadie wants to talk to you."

I waited, wondering if it had occurred to Mark that

he'd done all the talking in that conversation. Mark was one of the few people I knew who could outtalk me. "Sybil?" My mother's voice sounded so vibrant and excited that I almost forgave her for her insistence on using my full name. "You should have seen what Mark made Sofia and me for breakfast. He didn't even go shopping. Just took the leftovers out of our fridge and in two seconds there was an omelet you would not believe. It was delicious, and it looked gorgeous. Sofia took a picture of it. Don't work too hard today, Sybil, dear. See you later."

"Ma, before you hang up, please invite Sofia to dinner tonight." I said. I doubted that this suggestion was necessary, but I wanted to make sure we asked Sofia because Sofia's family included Ma in everything they did.

"We already asked her. She'll be there. After that omelet, she wouldn't miss one of Mark's meals. See you tonight, Sibyl." I heard the click of the phone and pictured Ma's smile of satisfaction.

With the evening's feast and festivities to look forward to, I went off to work quite cheerfully in spite of the frigid temperature and soot-frosted snow that greeted me as I trudged from the house to the car and later from the car to my office. My classes went well, although I was sorry to note that Flora Tomaselli did not show for Cultures and Values. I took this to mean that her dad had not yet found his way back home. Or, more likely, he had turned up and was ill. How far could an old man wearing only a down jacket over his pajamas have gone in this weather? I was willing to bet Dom had materialized in an area hospital suffering from exposure. I scrawled myself a reminder to e-mail Flora about him over the weekend and slapped it onto the dashboard of my car. It stayed there with about five other small lilac squares reminding me about everything from Ma's next dentist appointment to the due date for turning in the minutes of the RECC English Department meeting, which it had been my turn to take last month.

Rarely has any family welcomed the Sabbath with a tastier meal than the one we shared that night. In fact, the whole evening was memorable. We were only five, but a very convivial five. Ma arranged the royal blue silk shawl she wore so it partially hooded her head. Then she intoned the blessing and lit the candles, circling her arms and hands repeatedly above the flames as if to gather in the very spirit of the Sabbath. Sol blessed the challah and wine. As he did so, I inhaled the scents of cinnamon, garlic, and another spice, less familiar but no less delicious, perhaps ginger. My old black tabby Virginia Woolf, hardly immune to the pleasures of our table, positioned herself beneath it and favored some of us by rubbing up against our legs.

Mark's cooking had advanced well beyond the basic dishes he had learned at my table and now reflected his extensive and exotic travels. He had arranged our feast buffet-style on one of the gleaming new counters. There was a roast capon, rubbed with a mélange of aromatic spices, accompanied by a tangy apricot salsa. I recognized Ma's potato kugel, golden brown and garlicky, long a favorite of Mark's, and a large green salad. Sol filled plates for Ma and Sofia, but I opted to fill my own, eager to admire Mark's presentation from up close.

Sol raised his wineglass and said solemnly, "To world peace." We all raised our glasses and echoed his words, knowing as we did so that with the memory of 9/11 ever raw and the invasion of Iraq imminent, peace was possible only in our dreams and prayers. For a few minutes there was little conversation as we all sampled our food. When Sol spoke again, his tone was lighter, "My compliments to the chef."

"My compliments to the kugel maker," said Mark, ever the adoring grandson.

"My compliments to my lovely bride to be," said Sol, his voice deep and mellow as he winked at me across the table. I returned the wink, knowing that his toast was Sol's way of acknowledging the success of my full-frontal attack on Ma's depression. Like me, he was relieved and happy to see her once again animated and eating well.

"To the chefs and to the happy couple," said Sofia, her voice thin and chirpy in contrast with Sol's. "So tell us, you two, what are your wedding plans? Is it time for me to start shopping for a new dress?" She put down her glass and picked up her knife and fork again.

Mark didn't wait for either of us to reply before he said, "I think you guys should have a small private service in the synagogue and then a blow-out party back here. I'll cook. I'm sure Rebecca and Keith will help. And Alexis and Xhi." It was sweet of Mark to include Sol's daughter and her husband in his scenario. "We could get a keg, and I bet I could round up a few other musicians. You always let us rehearse here. The old band might just come through for you two," said Mark, his eyes ablaze with the image of his mother's wedding as a live rock keg party thrown by Iron Chef.

Sol and I exchanged glances. Again before either of us could fashion a tactful response, Ma chimed in.

"That's a possibility, but I've been thinking we should all fly to Vegas for a long weekend." In the brief silence that greeted Ma's bombshell, I saw Sol reach for the bottle of wine and pour himself a generous refill. I held out my glass and held my tongue. If Sofia and Ma had not been inveterate gamblers, I'd have laughed off her suggestion as a joke. But Sadie Bickoff would bet on anything, and she had very happy memories of her one visit to Las Vegas, a trip she had made with my dad to celebrate her fiftieth birthday. She had paid for that trip and another one to Bermuda with her winnings at roulette. "Sofia and I could pay for the whole thing with one good night at the tables. And it wouldn't be so far for Rebecca and Keith and little Abbie J." I had to marvel at my mother. When she wasn't clinically depressed, she thought of everything and made everything seem easy. I reached over to squeeze her hand.

We passed another hour in pleasant conversation, trying to honor the spirit of the Sabbath by dwelling on our blessings and deferring all mention of work, war, and other realities that might violate the evening's otherworldly mood. Sofia, Ma, and I were still at the table lingering over tea and the excellent devil's food cake Mark had made. "I snagged the recipe from the Hershey's cocoa can," he said, sloughing off our compliments. Mark and Sol were putting leftovers away and loading the dishwasher when the phone rang.

"I bet that's Rebecca." I leaped for the phone as I spoke. "She knows Mark's in town, so maybe she decided to call tonight. She can make unlimited free calls evenings and weekends." Eager to hear my daughter's voice, I pounced on the phone before the third ring.

"Professor Barrett, I'm so sorry to bother you at

home." The breathless rasp was a woman's voice, but not Rebecca's. I felt my shoulders sag with disappointment, and I shook my head. Ma's expectant glow faded a little. The voice was familiar, though, and her term of address marked her as, most likely, a student. I had no idea which one. Very few of the 120 people who filled the five classes I taught each semester called me at home anymore. They preferred to use e-mail to make their excuses, ask for clarification, beg for extensions, and, occasionally, share their news. I was grateful, preferring to reserve the telephone for personal use and retain the semblance of a private life. The caller's failure to identify herself immediately annoyed me. For all I knew, she wasn't a student at all but a falsely apologetic telemarketer. Just as I was about to inquire, she went on, her words rushing out between inhalations. "I wouldn't have bothered you but I thought you'd want to know. They found Papa."

Of course. The voice belonged to Flora Tomaselli. My hostility evaporated. "Oh Flora, I'm so glad. Thank you for letting me know. I've been worried too. I was rereading your father's memoir to see if it offered any clues as to where he might have gone. Where did they find him? Where on earth did the man go?"

"You don't understand, Professor." Flora's voice softened, but then broke on the last word. I felt a chill that had nothing to do with the chill of our winter, and I pulled the dinner napkin still in my hand close up against my chest as if that white linen square could protect me from what I guessed was coming. My other hand tightened on the phone. Ma and Sofia, aware that something was wrong, stared at me over their teacups, their eyes wide with questions and concern.

"Tell me, Flora," I said, spacing my words and keeping my voice low.

I heard Flora inhale before she spoke again. "What I mean is, they didn't find him. Not really. Not Papa. They found his body. Frozen. Papa's frozen to death."

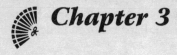

Chapter 3

To: Bbarrett@circle.com
From: Lbarrett@squarepeg.com
Re: Your wedding
Date: 01/28/03 09:24:56

Bel,

Rebecca tells me you and Sol plan to marry. It's about time he finally proposed. So like you to get involved with someone with commitment issues. Anyway, I figure you'll expect Cissie and me to show up for the ceremony because whenever one of the kids hits me up for tuition or a loan, you lecture me about how, when you and I divorced, our marriage ended but our family continued. That's how you guilt-tripped me into canceling a meeting with a big client to go to Mark's graduation, and then the kid refused to wear a tie to the Dean's reception.

Of course, Cissie and I won't be visiting the house in Provence this summer. No point spending my hard-earned dollars in a country opposed to America's crusade to rid the world of weapons of mass destruction in the hands of an off-the-wall tyrant. No way. After I get through tax season we'll be traveling domestically. Our first stop is Cissie's 15th college reunion. Attached is a list of dates that work for us. Let us know as soon as you and Sol make up your minds when.

Lenny

Before going to Dom Tomaselli's wake, I returned to the office to drop off my books and pick up student folders. I checked my e-mail as I did several times a day in what had become a routine effort to keep up with messages from students and from members of the countless committees I served on. Finding a communication from Lenny listed among the incoming mail was like finding a spray of poison ivy in a bag of mixed salad greens.

"Can you believe this?" I sputtered. "Wendy, you have to read it for yourself. This man's impossible. I can't believe I stayed married to that overgrown brat for so long." I practically pulverized the mouse with my index finger, so emphatically did I click on the print icon.

"Easy, Bel," said Wendy. "You're upsetting the plants." She nodded at Thelma and Louise in their clay pots on the windowsill. "Let me see it." She reached over my desk to snatch Lenny's e-mail as it emerged from the printer.

Wendy scanned the printout and put it on my desk. "It's kind of sad. Lenny still can't handle your relationship with Sol, can he?" she asked. Before I had a chance to reply, she continued. "I guess he doesn't know that Sol's been trying to get you to marry him for years."

"How can you feel sorry for Lenny? He's so arrogant. I can't believe that he really thinks he's coming to our wedding let alone that we should schedule it at his convenience." I reached for the jar of M&M's, helped myself to a handful, and passed the jar to Wendy.

She shook her head. "No thanks. Bel, you haven't even had lunch yet."

"And that little rodent has the nerve to say Sol has 'commitment issues.' " Anger tightened my throat, forcing my words out in a series of squeaks. "Lenny's the one with commitment issues. He ought to be committed. And wouldn't you know he'd use the word *issues*? I can't stand the way people use that word when they mean *problems*." I inhaled through my nose into my abdomen, the way we learned in yoga. I needed all the prana I could get to recover from my e-mail encounter with Lenny.

"Bel, don't let him get to you." Wendy spoke soothingly. I half expected her to reach over and pat me on the head.

"Don't let him get to me?" I was sputtering again, trying to keep my voice low so colleagues in the next cubicle would not be privy to my outburst. I was about to berate Wendy for her lack of empathy when I reminded myself that she was among that rare breed of woman who had been married for over three decades to the same nearly perfect man. Thoughtful, witty, generous, and romantic, Jim O'Conner never failed to flood our office with floral tributes to mark their wedding anniversary or Wendy's birthday. He was a great lover and father, enjoyed his work, and shared housework. He also shared Wendy's overdeveloped passion for the outdoors. How then could I expect Wendy, long married to this paragon of modern manhood, to understand the rage inspired by messages from the puerile, pompous, and tightfisted narcissist who was my ex? As my friend, she'd just have to try because I wasn't about to stop ranting.

"I'm sorry, Wendy, but it *does* get to me. Lenny earns enough to fund a palazzo in Provence but makes Rebecca beg for half of every semester's tuition money even though he committed to ante it up in our separation agreement." Wendy looked as if she wanted to respond, but I didn't give her a chance. "And it also gets to me that ten minutes after I finally divorced him, he married his teenybopper receptionist, a trophy bride if there ever was one."

"But, Bel—" Wendy began.

"And you know what? I don't care about his newfound Francophobia or his pitiful politics." Wendy swiveled her chair back and forth, frustrated at not being able to stem my tirade and get in a word of her own. That was her problem. I was on a tear. "He's probably got that house rented out so he doesn't lose a penny. And you remember what I had to go through to get that jerk to go to Mark's college graduation?" Wendy nodded. I'd made that phone call from our office, so she'd heard my half of the conversation. "That turkey was actually going to miss it because of a fishing trip with a client."

"Feel better now, Bel?" Wendy asked in the pause that followed my last words. She was gathering her books. She smiled at me, and I had to smile back. I did feel better. "You know, you have serious ex-husband *issues,*" she said as she darted out the door on her way to class. I smiled again as I began packing student folders into my book bag to take home. After I had my coat on and my book bag in place, I picked up the printout, compacted it into a small ball, and pitched it neatly into the circular file.

So therapeutic had my hissy fit been that by the time I collected Ma and Sofia, Lenny's words were a fading memory; and a few minutes later, when we arrived at the Failla Funeral Home, I had refocused my thoughts completely.

Chapter 4

Dominic Tomaselli

Hoboken—Dominic Tomaselli, 83, of Garden Street was pronounced dead on arrival at St. Mary's Hospital on January 24, 2003. Born in Hoboken on October 24, 1920, he was the son of Dominic and Flora Tomaselli. He attended local public schools and served in the military during World War II. Stationed in Fort Monmouth, New Jersey, in the Pigeon Service of the U. S. Army's Signal Corps, Sergeant Tomaselli trained messenger pigeons there until he was shipped overseas to England to train carriers transmitting messages from behind enemy lines in Europe. He received a commendation for his contribution to the war effort by General Eisenhower in a ceremony at Fort Monmouth in 1946.

After the war Sgt. Tomaselli returned to Hoboken, married Renata DeFranco of North Bergen, and found work as a custodian in the Hoboken Public Schools. He was a founding member of the Hoboken Chapter of the School Custodial Workers of America.

He continued to raise pigeons and was an active
member of the Hoboken Racing Pigeon Club, serving
as Secretary and Treasurer of that organization repeatedly over the past fifty years. He achieved national recognition in 1956 when one of his birds,
Hoboken Harry, flew 600 miles in 10 hours and four
minutes, to win the National Derby.

Mr. Tomaselli leaves a daughter, Flora Giglio, a
son, Leo, and two grandchildren. There will be a funeral Mass Saturday, February 1 at 10 AM at Hoboken's Sacred Heart Church followed by burial at Holy
Cross Cemetery, 874 West Side Avenue, Jersey City.
Calling hours are from 2–5 PM at Failla Funeral
Home, 533 Willow Avenue, Hoboken. Memorial gifts
may be made to the Hoboken Racing Pigeon Club, PO
Box 446, Hoboken, NJ 07030.

From across the room, Flora appeared to be holding court at her father's wake. She was seated in an
armchair against the wall next to her daughter,
Mary, a young woman with brown hair, her mom's
padded cheekbones, and Dom Tomaselli's gray eyes.
Next to Mary sat a dark-haired man in a rumpled
gray pinstriped suit. I assumed he was Flora's brother,
Leo. They were greeting a procession of relatives
and neighbors, so Ma and Sofia and I took our place
at the end of the long queue. While we waited our
turn, I glanced at Flora. Her graying hair cropped
short left her face unframed, so her tear-stained
cheeks and red-rimmed eyes were especially prominent. "Poor girl, looks like she's been crying for a
year," said Sofia.

"What do you expect?" said Ma. "It's hard enough
losing your dad, but to have him fall off the roof and

freeze to death. . . ." Ma shuddered beneath her coat.
"Poor Dom."

"Maybe that's better than to have him live long
enough to lose it with Alzheimer's," said Sofia, articulating the worst fear of many of us. "It said in the paper
how he was up on his roof where he used to keep those
birds when he fell. In his PJ's yet." I wondered how
Sofia knew this until I remembered that Sofia was
B&R, born and raised in Hoboken, a lifelong member
of the town's close-knit Italian-American community.
If pressed, she could probably tell me what Dom had
eaten for breakfast the day he died too. She shook her
carefully coiffed head and furrowed her brow as if to
imply that Dom's fall might have been less fatal had he
been more appropriately dressed. "I know the family
was worried about him going off the deep end, especially lately," Sofia continued. "But, you know, even if
he was a little loopy about those birds, Dom was a nice
old geezer." Sofia was apparently unaware that the man
she was calling an "old geezer" had actually been a
few years younger than she was.

Concealing a smile, I said, "Let me take your coats
and put them on a chair over there. It's too hot to keep
them on in here." I helped Ma and Sofia remove their
heavy woolen coats and deposited them on an empty
chair not far from where the Tomaselli family was
seated. I was pulling their scarves through their coat
sleeves when I heard a voice say, "Professor, allow
me." I looked up into the discreetly smiling face of
Sam Simon.

"Why thank you, Sam," I said. Still I hesitated,
wondering if the octogenarian with the distinctive limp
would be able to manage the heavy coats.

"Now don't you worry, Professor. I get around

pretty good, you know, gimpy but good." With that he commandeered the armful of sodden wool, and we walked together to a cloakroom in the vestibule. There he handed off the coats to the cloakroom attendant, and turned to say, "And now for your coat, Professor. Allow me." He stood behind me and helped me wriggle my arms out of the sleeves like an attentive father delivering a toddler to preschool. I was very relieved to be rid of my heavy red down coat. It was one of those shopping mistakes that I forced myself to wear when it got really cold, but the damn thing always made me feel like a walking barn.

"Thanks, Sam," I said, smiling at the old man who clearly took pleasure in being useful. As we turned to rejoin the line of mourners, I added, "I know you and Dom go back a long time. I'm sure his death is a loss for you."

"Well, yeah, Professor B. Dom and me, we go way back. Way back." Was that the glimmer of a tear I saw in his eye? Before I caught him in a display of feeling, he said, "Oh, excuse me, Professor. I gotta take care of something. Be right back." Sam left my side, made his way across the room, grabbed a chair and returned with it to where Ma and Sofia stood. "For you, Madam," he said with an exaggerated bow to Ma. "Your turn now, Sofia," he said. And indeed in a moment he reappeared with another chair for Sofia.

Ma and Sofia sank onto the chairs so fast that I realized I should have seated them right away. What had I been thinking? While the two women were bantering with Sam about which one of them should give up her chair so he could sit down, I was chastising myself for denying my mother's increasing frailty.

When I next looked up I recognized several other

faces from our memoir-writing course in the group milling around the viewing room. There was Ana, a Puerto Rican matriarch who still returned to "the island" every Christmas. Ana was writing about moving, something she and her family had done often. Chatting with Ana was Ellen, whose writing centered on a reunion with a childhood friend from County Donegal. Hilda, her high cheekbones flushed from the cold, stood in the doorway, scanning the crowd. When she spotted the people she knew, she strode purposefully toward them. She walked the way she wrote, deliberately, economically, energetically. Her memoir was a detailed room-by-room description of the country home she had recently and reluctantly abandoned in favor of a condo near her children and grandchildren in Hoboken.

I enjoyed their writing. They all had a lifetime of stories to tell and they told them in relatively readable prose. Unlike my younger students, who also hailed from far away places and who also had begun life speaking different languages or nonstandard dialects, most of these folks, all of whom came of age before television, had long ago mastered standard English, and most of them wrote smoothly and grammatically. Ana's English would have needed work if she were intent on earning a degree, but at eighty, she sought only to capture her memories for her grandchildren. Her English was eminently readable if not always grammatical. Even Dom and Sam, neither of whom had much formal education, made only a few grammatical gaffes, which seldom prevented me from understanding what they meant. It was actually a relief to read papers whose authors did not contract *back in the days* to *backintheday* or use the ubiquitous slang term *phat,* which translated roughly as "good." I welcomed papers written by those who reserved the word *awesome* for religious experiences and whose lexicons did not include the monosyllabic *"duh."*

Another way the seniors differed from their younger counterparts was their relationship to the work world. Most students in my credit-bearing classes were working full-time, and many were parenting as well. They struggled to find the time to attend classes and complete assignments. But the memoirists had long ago retired from active parenting and work outside the home, so they had time to write, and write they did, often at great length and in considerable detail. One or two of them used a word processor, Hilda typed her work on an old Smith Corona like the one I'd used at Vassar, and the rest, except for Ellen, wrote their memoirs in the unembellished but highly legible longhand they'd learned in school. A retired elementary school teacher, Ellen *printed* her work on lined paper. At the thought of her neat letters marching across the page, I felt grateful. What a treat it was to work with these late-blooming authors, to read their inspiring stories! I was so glad that I had agreed to teach the course. They were dears, all of them. They had bonded while exchanging memories of the past and comparing current symptoms related to age. And that day they had come, as we had, to offer condolences to the family of their classmate.

As I gazed fondly at them, my eye caught a glimpse of the coffin through a space between Hilda and Ellen. My neck muscles tensed, and that tension triggered a slight and predictable flush. Like millions of other ex-estrogen addicts, I was having a postmenopausal hot flash. Deprived now of even artificial estrogen, my body had once again become a barometer for my anxiety level. The prospect of viewing Dom's body on display in an open casket made me anxious. It didn't help that the several stands of white roses and crimson carnations shaped into hearts and crosses triggered the memory of my colleague Vinny Vallone's wake. Vinny's fluid-filled suited body had lain in an open coffin that had been nearly obscured by a deluge of flowers. Maybe Vinny's death had brought forth so many flowers because, unlike Dom, Vinny had been murdered.

Willing myself to approach the coffin, I saw with relief that the dark wooden box was closed. At once my neck muscles relaxed and my face cooled. Sam followed my eyes and said, "The family wanted the coffin closed. That's good 'cause, you know, Dom kinda kept to himself, and he wouldn't want nobody staring at him."

I nodded. That made sense. Dom had been a quiet, unassuming man, more at home with pigeons than with most people. He had confided to me that reading his memoir aloud in our class was to have been his first public address. "I didn't say nothin' at my retirement party or even at Flora's wedding reception" was how he had put it.

Standing there staring at Dom's classmates clustered around his coffin, I noticed a small but distinctive floral arrangement off to the right of the others. This one was crafted of white, purple, and blue flowers into the shape of a bird, a tribute no doubt from Dom's fellow pigeon lovers. Suddenly I felt very sad. I did not share Sofia's rationalization that Dom was better off dead because he might, someday, "lose it." Rather, I thought he was missing out on the rewards of a long life, including the lately come courage to try new things like memoir writing and oral reading. I knew he had been enjoying his family, his friends, and his memories. I didn't think he was better off dead at all.

When I looked over at Flora, I saw that the line of mourners advancing on her had thinned, so Ma and Sofia and I walked over to pay our respects. Her years as a court stenographer and her innate warmth served my mother well in most ceremonial situations. Ma took Flora's hand, leaned over it, and planted a kiss on the grieving woman's cheek. "Your dad was a dear new friend. I'll miss him. He was a real gentleman. He was nice to everybody, no matter who. And he was so proud of you and your brother and his grandchildren." I saw her press Flora's hand again before stepping aside so Sofia could approach Flora.

Before Flora could even respond to Ma, Sofia spoke. "I knew your father before he got, you know, a little depressed, before he took this class even." She was determined, I could tell, to offer her interpretation of Dom's death to comfort his grieving daughter. "He was a good man, a hard worker, a good husband and father. That's the way I'll remember him. Not moody like he got lately. You know, Flora"—Sofia pressed on, reaching out with her bony index finger to raise the seated woman's chin—"maybe this is for the best. Maybe this is God's way of saving Dom from something worse." Two new tears slid down Flora's cheeks as she stared at Sofia. "Remember, if there's anything I can do . . ." Sofia added. I knew that before the weekend, one of Sofia's signature lasagnas would have found its way to Flora's fridge.

"I know, Mrs. Dellafemina, I know. Thanks." Flora brushed away her tears and looked at me expectantly.

Following my mother's lead, I gave Flora a hug and then took the empty seat at her side. "I'm so sorry, Flora. You must be in a state of shock. I know I was when my dad died suddenly. I still miss him. I think about him several times a day."

"How long ago did he die?" Flora asked, clearly interested in how long it takes the heart to heal.

"It's been a few years," I said. "But it does get easier." I squeezed her arm. "Tell me, how is your daughter taking Dom's death? And your brother?" I nodded in the direction of the man seated on her right who had been talking to Father Santos for several minutes.

"Leo's a mess like me. Maybe worse." Flora shrugged. "Look at him." I cast what I hoped was a discreet glance at the disheveled figure huddled in the now empty chair where Mary had been seated. Father Santos was leaning over him and whispering in his ear. "I gotta remember to breathe when I look at my brother. Men don't take these things as good as we do. Besides, we were, I mean, we are . . ." Flora paused and inhaled deeply, "a very close family, you know? Papa was good to both of us, and we all lived together all these years. Father Santos has been coming to the house for days now, even before they found Papa—" Flora's voice broke.

"I'm glad he's been so supportive. But tell me how Mary is doing. This must be very painful for her too."

Flora pointed across the room to where Mary stood talking with a few other young people. "My Mary's okay, but I don't think it's really hit her yet, you know? Since she's gone to medical school in Newark, she's hardly ever home any more, not like me and Leo." Flora's tongue lingered over the clause introducing that sentence, and her chin jutted out just a bit as she uttered it. It seems that even grief could not diminish her pride in Mary's acceptance to medical school. "But my Mary's smart and tough, you know? She'll be all right." Flora sighed. "And so will I, Professor. I'll be back in class next week, you'll see." She took a deep breath, squeezed my hand, and turned to recognize Sam, who reached to clasp her other hand in both of his. "Sam, thanks for comin'. And thanks for the flowers. Papa would've loved them." Flora paused to take in more air. "They mean a lot."

As I stood and moved away, leaving him to speak privately to her, I overheard Sam say, "Well, Flora, me and Tommy and the boys from the old loft, you know, we wanted to send something special . . ."

Chapter 5

Son Finds Frozen Corpse of Missing Dad

Leo Tomaselli was digging out the storm drain behind the house in his downtown Hoboken backyard Friday morning when his shovel hit the frozen corpse of his eighty-three-year-old father, Dominic Tomaselli. The elder Tomaselli became the object of a police search Tuesday, January 21, after he was reported missing by his family. Pronounced dead of exposure by the medical examiner at St. Mary's Hospital, Tomaselli was wearing only a jacket over pajamas. His distraught son told police, "My Papa he was up on that roof a lot, especially lately. It's where he used to keep his pigeons." Police conjecture that Tomaselli, who family members said had suffered from depression, wandered up to the snow-covered roof, slipped, fell, lost consciousness, and froze to death. According to police reports, during an earlier search of the rooftop and the yard, newly fallen snow had concealed Tomaselli's footprints as well as his corpse.

33

I'd missed this article when it first appeared in the *Jersey City Herald*, but Flora had clipped it to a draft of the introduction to her paper on attitudes towards aging in America. I scanned the column of newsprint, remembering again the self-effacing old gentleman I had liked so much. I imagined that the kids in the schools where he worked would have liked Dom, and I could also see how his soft-spoken and gentle manner would have been soothing to his birds. I tried to picture him as a young veteran, dashing in his uniform, courting Flora's mother, a Jersey bobbysoxer. But try as I might, I couldn't conjure up the younger man. The old one, sun spots, soft Dr. Scholl's, wisps of gray hair, and sad gray eyes got in the way. A knock on my office door interrupted my reverie. It was Flora.

A week had gone by since Dom's funeral. Flora had been back to class twice, but I had refrained from scheduling a conference about her paper until she'd had a chance to begin processing her loss. So I was surprised when I saw her name on the list on my door where students could sign up for conferences. I interpreted her interest in a conference as a sign that she was refocusing on her schoolwork, and that pleased me. "I didn't know your dad was a military hero until I read his obituary," I said by way of welcome once she had settled herself in Wendy's chair. "I hadn't gotten that far in his memoir."

"Well, he was." Flora's reply was almost terse. She had clearly made an effort to pull herself together since the funeral. Today her salt-and-pepper hair spiked out around her face, softening her features. Deftly applied eyeliner defined the perimeters of her eyes, making the circular smudges beneath them less noticeable. She wore a pair of black jeans and a black sweater accented by a loosely knotted scarf patterned in rust and black. "Thanks for comin' to the wake," Flora said. "And the funeral." She took a deep breath before she went on, the only obvious sign of her distress. "Me and Leo, we appreciate it. His boy John and my Mary too." Flora inhaled again, and we sat in silence for a moment.

I took the paper clip off her folder, letting the article settle on my desk, and began to rifle through the pages of her draft. Just as I was about to compliment her on the amount of research she had done, she inhaled deeply and said, "I need your help."

"Actually, Flora, you need very little help with this. You just have to make up your mind how many of these sources you want to include in your text. You don't want it to be too repetitious. You need to figure out which facts and quotes are the most convincing, and use only those. You can list the others in the 'works cited' section. Let's look at a few of your references, and I'll show you what I mean." Pen poised, I spread out her paper on my desk.

"Professor Barrett, I didn't schedule this conference to talk about my paper." When my face registered surprise, Flora sucked air in and squared her shoulders. "I want to talk about Papa." It wouldn't be the first time I counseled a grieving student. I glanced at the box of Kleenex that had become a fixture on my desk since 9/11 and prayed that Wendy and I had not depleted the jar of M&M's. It had been my experience that the younger students tended to need Kleenex while the older ones like Flora found solace in chocolate. "Professor, you saw that damn newspaper article." Flora pointed at the copy of it on my desk. I nodded. "That reporter said my brother went out to knock the icicles off the gutters and found

Papa lying there. He made it sound like Papa just fell from the sky."

"Well, didn't the investigating officer decide your dad's death from exposure was an accident?" I asked.

Dismissing my question with a smirk, Flora rushed on. "That reporter, he didn't come out and write that Papa was a nut case, but everybody could tell that's what he meant." Flora certainly had a point. The word *dementia* did not actually appear in the story, but rather lurked between every one of its lines with the result that Dom Tomaselli was reduced to an errant elderly and senile PJ-clad pigeon fancier, literally a frozen stiff, DOA at St. Mary's Hospital. "So now everybody thinks Papa lost it and either fell off our roof or went psycho and jumped." That was certainly what Sofia thought, I remembered, realizing that she had probably based her opinion on this very article rather than on hearsay from her friends.

I waited, beginning to sense where Flora might be leading our conversation. "Professor, Papa knew his way around up there. And anyway, there's a retainin' wall, you know? It's low, but still." Flora inhaled audibly and continued, staring at me out of Dom's gray eyes. "He'd have had to climb on the wall to jump. Why would Papa do that?" Before I could remind her of her dad's history of depression, she spoke again, her chin jutting forward, one hand fingering the ends of her scarf. "I'm sorry, Professor, Papa was not demented." Then as if somehow privy to my as yet unspoken thoughts, she added, "And he wasn't depressed anymore either. You know that, Professor. He was his old self again. Besides, even if he was depressed, he wouldn't ever kill himself. Not Papa. He was a good Catholic." This time when Flora took in air, I found myself inhaling too, an involuntary show of empathy.

"Have you shared your thoughts on this with the police?" I asked, keeping my voice gentle.

"Yeah. It's like I said. They're just like everybody else. They think Papa lost it. They think he wandered up there because he hallucinated that his pigeons were still there, and he lost his balance and fell or jumped. One of them even joked that maybe Papa thought he was a pigeon," Flora said. "They talk like he was just some old geezer who forgot to take his meds." She was speaking more rapidly, taking a short gulp of air at the end of each sentence. This made her words come out in the spurts associated with sobs, but her eyes were dry and focused on mine. "Professor B, if you could get the guy who killed Vic Vallone and the one who killed poor Louie Palumbo, you could nail the monster who pushed my 83-year-old papa off that roof. Especially if I tell you who he is." Flora leaned back in Wendy's chair and let out a long sigh, as if, having said what she came to say, she could rest.

It was my turn to take a deep breath.

Chapter 6

. . .our apartment on Delancey Street
was never big enough for us all, especially since my mother did piecework
there sometimes, and my father also
brought sewing home. The kitchen was
where we cooked, ate, and where my parents sewed. It was also where we cele-
brated the Sabbath and other holidays.
In winter it was the warmest room in
the house, but that same fire was our
enemy too. I remember when I was a
child, my mother was haunted by the
terrible Triangle Shirtwaist Company
fire of 1911. She was always worrying
that one of us would start a fire or
get burned on the stove. As a little
girl I had long hair, and she was very
afraid that it would catch fire.
"Sadie, stay away from the stove!"

```
"Sadie, watch your hair!" It's a mira-
cle that it didn't. When we moved to
Brooklyn, I thought our four-room
apartment was a mansion. . . .
```

Even though I'd heard about Ma's tenement days, I had read the latest installment of her memoir with interest. I didn't remember ever hearing her talking about her mother's fear of fire. The act of writing had triggered Ma's memory, and I looked forward to discussing her childhood with her. But as I made my way to the memoir-writing class, where I planned to return Ma's draft, I was distracted by thoughts of Flora's request. I was seriously tempted to look into her father's death. I had liked and respected Dom and hated to think of him as a victim of murder or suicide. I sympathized with Flora's discomfort with the police's slapdash search and the newspaper's cavalier implication that her dad had killed himself. But I was, as usual, overcommitted at RECC. And Sol and I had a wedding to plan.

Still debating, I took the bus to Hoboken from my office in Jersey City. When I got off, I picked my way over the partially shoveled and semi-salted sidewalks. Treacherous as this was, it was preferable to digging out our car and searching for a rare parking spot between the waist-high piles of curbside snow. I wondered if my students would be able to get to class and was pleasantly surprised to discover that the city van had collected them and delivered all but Ellen. She had sent word with Ana that she was nursing the beginnings of a nasty cold and would stay home rather than risk sharing it with us. "She got her head over a kettle of esteam," said Ana when I expressed concern. "I brought her some *sopa*. She'll rest. She'll be okay."

Pleased that Ana had looked in on the fragile Ellen, I shed my cumbersome coat and took from my book-bag the copies I had made of a passage from Dorothy Allison's early memoir *Bastard Out of Carolina*. I usually began each class with a short reading from a published memoir to demonstrate the variety of writing styles and subject matter found in the genre as well as to help my students reconnect with their own life events. I was eager to listen to them as they shared memories triggered by the reading. Surely their poignant recollections would distract me from my nagging inner debate. But before I could pass around copies of the text, I noted that everyone was already engrossed in reading another handout.

"I copied Dom's obituary for the group because a few people said they didn't get the paper that day on account of the weather," Ma explained. "Here. I made one for you, too." Ma had liked Dom. Was she trying to get me to figure out what had happened to him? I wouldn't put it past her. "I copied that other article as well, the one about how he died. It made me so mad. It's on the bottom." So much for being distracted from thinking about Dom's death. Leave it to Ma. I tried not to picture my frail elderly mother trudging through the snow with her walker to get to a copy shop. She must have persuaded somebody in the office at the Senior Center to Xerox the articles. Sadie Bickoff was no slouch in the persuasion department. After all, she'd persuaded me that at fifty-three I wasn't too old to study for a doctorate. Less happily, she'd almost managed to convince me not to divorce Lenny. I shuddered at the memory and returned to the moment at hand.

"Listen to this, Professor," said Ana. "It say here that Dom was een the war, you know? With them pigeons.

He got a medal. My Juan was een the war too. But he didn't get no medal. I guess our Dom, he was a hero." Ana made this pronouncement in a hushed voice.

"Well, maybe he was. But this other article makes him sound like a suicide or a dottering old geezer," said Hilda.

"Suicide?" Ana sputtered, recoiling into her purple fleece jacket as if in retreat from even the concept of such sacrilege. "He was Catholic. He went to church. Every Sunday." She stressed the last word by hissing it through clenched teeth.

"No, normally Dom wouldn't kill himself," said Sofia. "But he was losing it. There was even talk once that they were going to have to, you know, put him in a home." At this, every head in the room turned towards Sofia. Not only was she tapping into each of their worst fears, but her roots in Hoboken's Italian-American community lent credibility to her assertions. Encouraged by the attention, Sofia continued. "He was always going up on the roof mooning over those birds. He'd spend hours up there. And he'd started wandering. Once he got as far as the PATH station. His family was really worried about him. And remember he didn't talk much, and he hardly ever smiled." She shrugged, the dismissive gesture implying that people guilty of not smiling frequently were capable of anything.

"Just because a man don't run his mouth all the time don't mean he's senile or suicidal, Sofia." Sam's gruff interjection made him the center of attention. He disappointed his audience, though, because, having uttered his uncharacteristically sharp defense, he sat back in his chair without elaborating. Sam was not usually this laconic, so it took the group a few seconds to realize that he wasn't going to say any more.

"I know you and Dom go way back with the pigeon club and the neighborhood, and I didn't mean any offense," said Sofia simply. "I just think Dom may have had a touch of Alzheimer's and depression, that's all."

"That's all? That's enough," said Ma who, like Sam, had been unusually quiet throughout this discussion that she had instigated. Her voice was high-pitched and strident now. "A touch of Alzheimer's is like being a little bit pregnant. Every now and then I get lost, forget something. Does that mean I have Alzheimer's? Besides, Dom did smile but mostly when he talked about his grandchildren. I liked Dom, and I don't think he was losing it so much as he was a little down in the dumps sometimes. You know, before I took this class I was pretty down in the dumps. Was I suicidal ?"

Not for nothing had Ma spent all those years as a court stenographer. She used to entertain my father and me with imitations of some of the more flamboyant trial lawyers. That day she fired her questions at the group, but Sofia knew they were meant for her, and she had the good grace to lower her eyes in tacit acknowledgment of Ma's point. Enjoying herself, Ma leaned forward and, looking at each of her classmates, repeated her final question, "Was I suicidal?"

"Homicidal's more likely," said Sam, alluding to Ma's take-no-prisoners stance. The tension that had been building dissolved when Ma grinned at him. There were smiles all around. Leave it to Sam to be the peacemaker.

"What do you think, Professor Barrett?" Hilda asked. "Did it seem to you like Dom was losing it?"

I paused before replying. In those few seconds, I decided against telling them of Flora's insistence on her dad's sanity. Her view could be biased, and, more important, our conversation had been confidential. "He was always on task here, and his writing was very clear. That's all I have to go on. But now we need to turn our attention to our own writing and this handout."

While they read Dorothy Allison's dramatic account of her birth, I walked among them, noting their bony fingers following the printed words, Hilda using a magnifier to compensate for the inroads of age on her eyesight. Slight as an eight-year-old, Sofia seemed lost in her bulky cardigan. And Ma, her walker behind her chair, was so thin that her eyes gleamed like headlights above her permanently pinched cheeks. What if she disappeared one day and turned up dead? What if somebody did her harm?

Ma had gotten to me. Then and there, I decided that I would make time in my busy schedule to find out more about how Dom Tomaselli had died. But first I'd have to make sure Sol had no problems with my getting involved in yet another investigation. And of course I'd have to talk my good friends Illuminada Guttieriez and Betty Ramsey into helping me. Fortunately, I had inherited Ma's talent for persuasion.

Late that afternoon Sol and I were outside shoveling away the snow that passersby had knocked onto the path we had dug out the day before. Actually, Sol was shoveling while I followed, scooping salt out of a ten-pound bag with an empty coffee can and sprinkling it behind him. I had the advantage because the exertion of shoveling had winded him, making conversation a challenge. After recounting the story of Dom's death, I summarized. "So anyway, Flora, Dom's daughter, doesn't believe her dad slipped and fell off the roof. She claims he was pushed."

"Let me guess," Sol gasped, leaning on the shovel. "She wants you to find out who pushed him?"

I nodded. "Do you want me to shovel for a while?" I asked, suddenly recalling that snow-shoveling in-duced heart attacks in out-of-shape middle-aged males. For an answer, Sol turned his back on me and resumed shoveling, heaving the snow to the top of the old snow heaped beside the narrow path.

When he spoke, I could barely hear his reply. "When are you going to find time to help me plan our wedding? You're so busy now we practically have to make an appointment to have sex let alone dinner." That last zinger was a snide reference to the fact that I'd had either a class or a conference every evening for the past few days.

But wedding planning was a sore point. Somehow since we'd agreed to marry over a year ago in the af-termath of 9/11, I'd put off actually planning the cere-mony and attendant festivities. I was no longer ambivalent about marriage. I just could not picture the event itself. I couldn't get any further than the guest list. How could we afford to include all our friends and relatives? The plunge in the stock market and our ill-timed kitchen renovation had decimated our savings account. But how could we exclude them? Just think-ing about the guest list wearied me. The planning that should have been a prelude to a joyous ritual had somehow become an arduous homework assignment.

"This investigation will be a piece of cake, over practically before it starts. Flora says she knows who is responsible for her father's death. I didn't want her to tell me whom I suspected unless I decided to pursue it, but once she does, I'm sure we can wrap up the whole thing pretty fast." I shouted at his back. I was relieved when we had worked our way to the steps because we were able to talk face-to-face. He leaned his shovel on the banister and pulled me to him. "Did you hear what I said?" I asked when he didn't respond.

Sol nodded. "Love, I don't care if you solve all the murders in New Jersey as long as you make time to sit down with me and plan our wedding. I'm too old to be kept waiting much longer."

Chapter 7

Odrxntrh4@earthli . . . My fat is smothering me . . .
   wtnbptcgro
Wz89hd@earthlin . . . Increase semen and shoot further
bjyqnesxjx@yahoo . . . PENIS enlargement, grow longer
   and wider
3jmovixsi@lycos . . . zzl chose life instead of fat iq
xolcnlna@amne . . . add 3 inches naturally
wtrpsvxns@jun . . . With Viagra you'll have sex like a porn
   star

How had I, a female English prof in her fifties, managed to convince the medical miracle people that I might be in the market for a penis enlargement? Or for Viagra? Perhaps it had happened during my investigation of the murder of a colleague who had moonlighted as a stripper. I vaguely recalled having checked out the website of the club where she danced. Damn. But then, how had so many would be émigrés from developing nations gotten my e-mail address? And who had broken my cover to the weight-loss mafia, who now besieged me with cruel offers of firm thighs and a flat

46

belly? As I automatically deleted my daily dose of spam, I recalled long ago days when I logged onto my computer and found only the occasional and always welcome e-mail from a friend.

There was no time to indulge my nostalgia for a less connected era or to dwell on the fact that, according to a recent survey, many Americans spend more time each week deleting spam than they do reading to their children. I spotted the e-mail message I was looking for between one suggesting that I refinance my house and another offering me credit counseling. It was from Illuminada, and she was agreeing to meet Betty and me for a quick lunch at the RIP, the diner near RECC where students and faculty ingested calories and caffeine. The RIP wasn't fancy and their food wasn't particularly good, but lunching there was vastly more appealing than depending on the vending machines that spit out week-old sandwiches, snacks, and beverages, RECC's version of collegiate food service.

I picked up the phone and punched in Betty's number. "President Woodman's office. May I help you?" Betty's telephone voice, cheerful and at the same time imperious, the voice of Cleopatra ordering a slave to fan her, was perfect for her job as executive assistant to RECC's president, Ron Woodman. It was the voice of a tall, aristocratic woman with blue-gray hair in a bun and, perhaps, a lorgnette. It was not the voice of a short, stocky, dark-skinned woman with a retro, slightly silver Afro and a Palm Pilot. Visitors to RECC's executive suite were not always able to mask their surprise when they met Betty.

"Yes, your highness. You can help me. Be at the RIP at one. Illuminada can make it."

"Okay, girlfriend, but this better be important.

There's a board meeting tonight." I understood at once what my friend meant. President Woodman often needed a lot of reassurance and coaching before facing the Gang of Twelve, as he privately referred to the RECC Board. Even the antianxiety meds that he had been taking since 9/11 had not enabled him to completely overcome his concern about those meetings. On board days, Betty had taken to ordering in lunch for herself and the president and walking him through the agenda, explaining new items to him and reminding him of those he had forgotten. Betty explained that it wasn't that Ron Woodman was old or slow or uncaring, but rather, as she put it, "The dude is just a nervous wreck when it comes to that board. And you know, sometimes I don't blame him." I knew what she meant. The RECC Board was a motley crew of mostly underqualified but politically connected people, each of whom seemed to have an astounding number of unemployed relatives eager to consult at RECC. But Betty didn't argue the point that Woodman's anxiety sometimes came between him and understanding, and that's when she stepped in. For Betty was controlling to a fault and relished her role as backstage manager. Illuminada and I were only partly joking when we teased her about being the shadow president of RECC.

I was not surprised to see Illuminada waiting at our favorite table at the RIP. It was a corner booth in the section of the diner that was usually reserved for overflow. From there we could see who entered and left but at the same time enjoy at least the illusion of privacy. She was looking at her watch as I approached. "Where's Betty?" she snapped by way of greeting. The curt nature of her inquiry did not surprise me either because I knew how Illuminada obsessed about time. The

PI agency she had started years ago had taken off and my friend, who had aspired only to track deadbeat dads who opted out of child support, now found herself running a thriving full-service investigative agency with thirty employees in two locations. To further complicate her schedule, Illuminada had been teaching part-time in the Criminal Justice Department of RECC for years. A petite woman with a black blunt-cut made more striking lately by a single streak of silver, Illuminada was always counting minutes, always overbooked.

"Well, hello yourself. Good to catch up with you again. It's been awhile. I'm fine thanks, and how are you?" This had become my ritual response to my friend's brusque hellos. Illuminada grinned and tried to envelop me in a hug made awkward by the table between us and by my bulky down coat. "*Dios mío,* why don't you rent a fire house for that thing and park it," she cracked as I took off the coat and struggled to balance its mass atop Illuminada's sleek wool car coat on the unoccupied seat.

"I'm not sitting next to that," said Betty, who arrived as the coat slipped to the floor for the third time. "Here, give it to me." Never one to argue with a control freak, I handed her the coat, which she flung over the back of the booth. She motioned me to sit down in front of it. I did and, of course, the arrangement worked just fine. The thing about Betty was that when she took control, she usually knew what she was doing. Or, as Vic, her lover of several years, once joked, "Betty's not really controlling, she just knows how to do things better than everybody else and she doesn't mind telling you."

"Well, you finally made it," said Illuminada to Betty, who was exactly three minutes late.

"Uh-huh. And glad to be here too. It's rough up there. Our boss has got to deal with these projected budget shortfalls and the hike in enrollment at the same time. And he's totally terrified that if we attack Iraq, we'll provoke more terrorism here. Sometimes he just sits and stares out the window at where the Towers used to be. It's all too much for him. I'm afraid I'll have to get his doctor to up his dosage again." She sighed an exaggerated sigh, but Illuminada and I both knew that Betty thrived on the tension that so paralyzed her boss. "So what brings us here, Bel? You must have some reason for getting us together at the last minute. I know it's not just that you miss us."

"*Chiquita,* you wouldn't make me postpone an interview with a promising new office manager for some frivolous reason, would you?" Illuminada had been looking for an office manager for over a month and had yet to find someone who met her stringent requirements.

"Remember I told you I was teaching that memoir-writing class at the Senior Center? The one my mother's in?" Both women nodded, and Illuminada signaled a passing server. When she arrived, we all ordered chicken soup and tuna melts, standard cold-weather fare that wouldn't unduly challenge the RIP chef du jour. "Well, it's really working out well. The students are self-selected, so they're all articulate and highly motivated and they have such—"

"Bel, save it for your self-evaluation." Betty's curt reprimand was echoed by Illuminada, who was making a cranking motion with her hands and pointing at her watch.

Aware that sometimes I do make a short story long, I said, "Well, one of my senior students died. The cops think he fell off his roof and froze to death. His daughter thinks he was pushed. She wants me to look into it. I will if you will."

Illuminada was the first to respond. "*Dios mío,* what the hell was he doing on the roof in this weather? Was he demented?"

Betty was not far behind. "Did he jump?"

Turning towards Illuminada, I said, "He used to raise racing pigeons in a rooftop loft. You know, like in *On the Waterfront*." Illuminada nodded. "He trained pigeons that were used in World War II. And even though his pigeons are all gone now, he still went up there sometimes to reminisce about them, I guess." It sounded pretty lame until I added. "Don't tell me you haven't gone into Lourdes's old room and just sat there thinking about when she was a little girl." I saw Illuminada blink. I knew I'd hit home with that one. Empty-nesters all, we missed our kids no matter how liberating it was to have them grown. Betty was nodding too. Randy had recently moved to Connecticut, where his company relocated after 9/11, and Betty was not taking his defection well.

"So maybe he jumped?" Betty repeated. "Maybe he found out he had cancer or something, and he just jumped. Maybe he had a heart attack and fell because of that. You know, if you teach older folk, you've got to expect attrition." I winced at her reality check. But the scenarios she described were interesting. I knew little about the health records of my students other than what I could observe. And cancer was a stealth stalker often unseen and untreated until it was too late. Heart attacks too were often fatal surprises. I resolved to ask Flora about Dom's medical status.

"His daughter is also taking a course with me. She's

a returning student in her fifties, very enthusiastic and nice. She claims he did not jump. She insists her father was not demented although she knows that, prior to taking my course, he had been depressed." I tried to keep the pride out of my voice, but my friends heard it and smiled. They understood my enthusiasm for teaching and indulged my need to pat myself on the back every so often.

"Like your mom," said Betty. She and Illuminada had been aware of my concern for my mother.

"Oh, *chiquita,* I wish I could get my mother to take that class," said Illuminada. "The woman is driving me crazy. Since her friend Luisa died in Havana, she just sits around the house all day by herself watching Spanish soaps and imagining she has this disease and that disease."

"I'll suggest that Ma talk it up to her next time we're all together. Who knows? She might not resist going if someone else makes the suggestion," I said, empathizing with Illuminada's concern. Her mother occupied the apartment above Illuminada and Raoul's, and Milagros Santos believed in sharing her misery.

"Thanks, but it won't help. She's too self-conscious about her English. But she's making me nuts. When she's not watching TV, she's calling her Obeah. It's a tragedy. She used to be such a bright and vibrant woman." Illuminada paused. As soon as she stopped talking, she checked her watch. "*Chiquitas,* I can't believe you let me run on about my mother again. Look at the time."

"That's the problem, Bel," said Betty, refocusing the conversation back to my request for help. "Time. We're all so pressed as it is. You're always complaining about how overloaded you are. And now you're teaching an extra course plus you've got a wedding to plan, remember?" When I didn't say anything, she glanced at Illuminada. "And you, girlfriend, are always too busy to breathe. Maybe it'll be easier for you when you get an office manager, but lately even Raoul is complaining." This was a notable comment because Raoul seldom had anything but praise for all that his wife did. Since Illuminada's lumpectomy a few years ago, he had become even more solicitous, more protective.

"And you? Is your plate full too?" I asked. I didn't want Betty to miss her turn to complain. I had long ago observed that we all need to vent about how hectic our lives are.

"Well, we do have an accreditation visit next month and you know who's going to end up coordinating that whole thing again, don't you?" Betty shook her head. "And I'll probably have to write his self-evaluation again too." This time her sigh was an exaggerated exhalation, the kind emitted by all experienced martyrs. "And then there's the beach house." She paused, and her expression brightened. Betty and Vic had responded to the stock market's downturn by investing in the last remaining handyman's special in Ocean Grove, a gentrified shore community less than an hour from their Jersey City home and known for its Victorian houses, pristine boardwalk, and strict blue laws, a legacy of the town's Methodist founders. They spent every spare moment there now, trying to render their retreat habitable. "What's your stake in this man's death? Why do you want to bother?" Leave it to Betty to ask that.

"I liked him. He was a sweet, gentle soul, devoted to his grandkids, and trying to come out of his depression. He was enjoying writing his life story. And I like his daughter. She . . ." At this point in my narrative, Illuminada, who had little patience for capsule oral histories of my students, was imitating a violinist. I turned to her and shifted the focus of my argument. "Well, okay, look at it this way. Suppose somebody pushed your mother off her porch, and she hit her head and froze to death? How would you feel?" Illuminada stilled her bow hand and lowered the one that held the imaginary violin. "I mean, that's elder abuse, and it could happen to any of our parents. Hell, in a few years it could happen to us."

"What does Sol say?" asked Betty. Betty still remembered my love's violent objections to my second sleuthing effort when I had insisted on finding and exposing those responsible for the murder of an adjunct faculty member at RECC who happened to be Vic's brother. That's how Betty and Vic had met. Illuminada and Betty and I had met even before that when I recruited them to help me track down the killer of RECC's first woman president.

"Sol says I can solve all the murders in New Jersey as long as I make time to plan our damn wedding," I replied with a grin. Sol had resigned himself to my occasional forays into detection, and his eagerness to rush me to the altar was well known. "And that's the beauty of this situation," I said. Anticipating their objections, I had saved my strongest argument for last. "Flora Tomaselli, my student and the victim's daughter, says she knows who did it. So all we have to do really is help her prove it. It'll be a piece of cake, over before it starts."

"Unless she did it, the daughter, I mean," said Illuminada. "Did he have any other kids? In-laws? Sibs?"

After a few years of PI work, Illuminada's take on domestic life in millennial America was grim. But I could see that she was hooked when she added, "I keep telling you, most child abuse is committed by relatives of the victim. Do you suppose it's any different with elder abuse? Think about it, *chiquita*."

I thought about it for perhaps one second. "Not Flora," I said. "But she has a brother. He's the one who found the body." Betty's eyes widened slightly. "Here, read about it for yourselves." My two friends were poring over the Xeroxed articles I handed them by the time our chicken soup came. I knew I could count on them.

 **Chapter 8**

To: Bbarrett@circle.com
From: Sandig@calgal.com
Re: Wedding bells
Date: 02/05/03 08:06:45

Hi Roomie,

Sorry it took me so long to get back to you, but I've been recruiting at every college between here and LA. It's about time you and Sol tied the knot! Mazel-tov! I hope you are planning to have Rabbi Ornstein-Klein come to Vassar in the spring to perform the ceremony in Shakespeare Garden. Remember my wedding there the day after graduation? It was beautiful, wasn't it? What a gorgeous bridesmaid you were in that electric blue Yves Saint Laurent mini-chemise with the cut out midriff and those white boots! All your guests could stay at Alumnae House. But reserve now for a spring or summer weekend because you know how booked they get during reunion season. Come to think of it, maybe you could plan to combine it with a reunion weekend. Let me know as soon as you set the date so I can save it. Wouldn't want to miss this one! Let's have dinner soon.

Love,
Sandi

The "gorgeous" wedding my college roommate referred to with such nostalgia had been the campy foreplay to a grim marriage that lasted fewer than five years. Besides, getting married in Poughkeepsie would add two hours to almost everyone's journey. But I adored Sandi and couldn't imagine getting married anywhere without her there to bear witness. I figured calling Flora to tell her I would look into Dom's death would distract me from dwelling on Sandi's e-mail and the ever-growing wedding guest list. I picked up the phone and punched in Flora's number. After two rings, she answered. At first her voice was muted, but when I told her of my decision, she replied in what can only be described as a highly audible gush of gratitude. "Oh, thank you, Professor, thank you! I was prayin' that you would do this for Papa. Thank you." Her effusive professions of appreciation troubled me. What if I couldn't live up to her expectations?

We agreed to meet later that afternoon at her home, the place where Dom had lived and died. I wanted to see the lofts on the roof, the aerie that had drawn an old man out of bed on a wintry night to his death. In spite of Illuminada's conviction that one of Dom's relatives had done him in, I suspected that his death was somehow connected to his lifelong involvement with racing pigeons. On the walk across town, I continued to speculate. Maybe Dom had had a longtime rival or, better yet, an associate, perhaps even from his war days, with a long-festering grudge. My curiosity made me want to walk faster, but Hoboken's sidewalks were too slippery. At the corner I looked up from the pavement and noticed that one half of the street had just been cleared. I stepped onto the swath of plowed pavement and quickened my pace.

Striding down the middle of the street, I was struck by the quiet. Repeated snowfalls had succeeded in stifling the machines that were gradually transforming the area into a series of huge apartment buildings, each complete with underground parking, workout room, concierge, and other amenities essential to the yuppie market. In the few years since I had walked these same strangely silent streets in pursuit of the killer of Frank Sinatra impersonator Louie Palumbo, the whole area had been developed. The mile-square blue-collar burg filled with four- and five-story row houses that I'd moved into years ago had been gentrified almost beyond recognition. Maxwell House, Levelor, and Bethlehem Steel had given way to Starbucks, Barnes & Noble, and Wolfgang Puck.

Dwarfed by a monumental cube of condos on the corner, Flora's house was third in a line of two-family row houses. The slate gray aluminum siding looked new, and the walk had been carefully shoveled and heavily salted. The stoop steps were also clear of snow. I rang the bell, and stood there stamping snow off my boots. Within seconds, Flora appeared in the doorway. Wearing jeans and a heavy gray turtleneck sweater, she looked somber. Her small smile of welcome appeared to be painted on her lips, a polite afterthought. "Good to see you, Flora," I said, handing her my coat.

"I really appreciate your comin' today, Professor. It's pretty mean out there," Flora said. I leaned down to take off my wet, salt-crusted boots, and she said, "Oh, don't bother. It don't matter."

One glance at the sparking tile floor in the kitchen and the pristine beige carpet told me she was lying. It did matter. I slid my feet out of my boots. "Not a problem, Flora."

"How about we talk over some tea in the kitchen? You don't mind the kitchen, do you, Professor?" Before I could answer, she hugged herself and added, "It's got sun this time of day. See?" I followed her, and we were immediately bathed in late afternoon sunlight. The kettle whistled on the stove, and I spied a promising bakery box on the counter.

"The kitchen's fine, Flora. I'm a kitchen person, actually. And that sunshine is lovely." To show how at home I felt, I plopped into a chair at the table and looked around. Nothing jumped out at me except for a pile of what looked like condolence cards on the counter and an elaborately framed photo on the far wall of a young man in uniform and a woman in white. I couldn't swear to it from across the room, but I was willing to bet it was Dom's wedding photo.

"Tea's okay, isn't it, Professor? I know you always drink tea in class." I nodded, and Flora poured hot water over teabags in cups she had laid out. While she opened the box and plated the miniature Italian pastries from Giorgio's, Flora said, "I noticed you got a sweet tooth, too." I was touched by her efforts to entertain me, but I wished she'd stop playing hostess and sit down and tell me what she knew. I wondered if she had changed her mind about confiding in me. To test this hypothesis, I asked, "Flora, your dad was in good physical health for a man of his age, wasn't he? I mean, he didn't have cancer or some other disease?"

"No. He had slowed down some, and he took pills for his pressure, but otherwise he was okay," Flora answered. "It was just that he couldn't do what he used to do, that's all, just like the rest of us." She carried a plate of miniature Italian pastries to the table. Finally satisfied that she'd welcomed me adequately, she sat down at the table herself and took a deep breath. "No, it wasn't nothin' to do with his health that made Papa fall if that's what you're thinkin'," Flora added. "You see, Professor, my Uncle Emilio, my mother's kid brother, well, he gambles." Flora reddened and shrugged, embarrassed no doubt by having an uncle with such a vice. Later I would tell her that as the daughter of a woman who would rather bet than breathe, I had some understanding of what it is like to have a gambler in the family.

"I mean my uncle *really* gambles," Flora continued, breathing in again. I nodded and leaned closer because Flora's voice had lowered to a whisper. "I don't want Leo to know what I'm thinkin' about all this. He's still real upset, and besides, he's tight with our uncle. When you get something on good old Uncle Emilio, that's when I'll tell Leo." She inhaled again as if the very thought of telling Leo threatened to suffocate her. "So like I was saying, Emilio's always in debt. But about twenty years ago he got in way over his head, played with people he shoulda known better than to mess with. Like Papa said, he just hadda be a big shot, you know?" Flora shook her head and rolled her eyes at the recollection of her uncle's hubris.

"Emilio said if he didn't get the money . . ." Flora made a low whistling sound with her breath and then raised her chin and slid her finger across her bared neck. I got the message. "My mother, she was frantic."

At the memory of her mother's anxiety, tears pooled in Flora's eyes. She brushed them away with the back of her hand and inhaled two or three times before going on. "My mother begged Papa to help Emilio, to save her kid brother's life. So my Papa lent him the money he got from a lawsuit he filed after he was in a car accident. It had been in CDs all through the seventies and it was over a hundred thousand dollars. Papa was savin' it for the kids' college, ya know." Flora swatted away another tear. "Emilio promised to pay him back, but he never paid him back nothin'." With these words, Flora's lips tightened and she raised her eyes to meet mine.

I smiled at her, reached across the table and patted her arm, then raised my teacup to my lips. There were a lot of questions I wanted answered. Had Dom tried to collect the money? Was there any tangible evidence to support Flora's conviction that her Uncle Emilio had killed her dad to avoid paying his debt? Were there, perhaps, other grievances between them? Did Emilio have an alibi for the night that Dom had disappeared? But I'd learned long ago from conferencing with students to save my queries until I was sure the person had said all that she had to say.

On the other side of the table, Flora had shut her eyes and was breathing deeply. After a few breaths she opened her eyes and smiled apologetically. "I gotta keep breathin' or I get like, ya know, panic attacks," Flora explained. I resisted the impulse to direct her to the nearest yoga studio. Instead I nodded, patted, smiled, and sipped.

"So like I was sayin', what makes me sure Uncle Emilio pushed Papa is that last fall when my Mary started medical school at Newark Rutgers, she was

gonna have to live here at home because her grant
didn't cover housin'. Papa said he didn't want her
goin' back and forth at all hours, and he gave her thousands of dollars to cover room and board. Just like that
he handed her fifteen grand." Flora paused a minute
and then continued. "Now, Professor, you remember I
told you once, Leo and I had power of attorney for
Papa. I paid all Papa's bills. I could read you his bank
balance in my sleep. All the money he had was the little he let me and Leo pay him in rent, his Social Security and a small pension from Uncle Sam." Flora
inhaled and asked, "Where did he get that money?"
With a shrug I professed ignorance.

"Here, let me warm that up for you." Flora leapt up,
filled the kettle at the sink, and turned the gas on.
While she was busy, I sampled a cannoli and walked
over to the photo for a closer look. It was eerie to see
Dom's serious gray eyes staring out from the face of
the smiling young soldier with the full head of wavy
dark hair. Flora's mother, a voluptuous raven-haired
beauty, wore a smile like Flora's used to be.

In a few minutes the kettle whistled, and Flora refilled our cups. I waved away her offer of a fresh
teabag and resisted having another cannoli. I opted for
a biscotti instead. Seated again, my hostess resumed
her tale. "When Mary came and told me about the
money Papa gave her, all in cash, I was real worried
about it. So I went to Papa, and I asked him straight
out. You know me, Professor. I'm not one to beat
around the bush." I nodded to affirm her directness. "I
just came out and said, like, 'Papa, where did you get
so much money?' I know Papa never wouldna done
nothin' wrong, but still I was worried. So ya know
what Papa said?" Flora inhaled before she answered

her own question. "Papa said, 'Don't worry, Flo. Let the kid take the money. She earned it. There's plenty more where that come from.' So I figured Uncle Emilio finally come through."

Flora took a sip of tea and went on. "But then Leo's boy John, you know? He's some kind of genius, like my Mary," Flora lowered her eyes modestly, but she was clearly proud of her daughter and her nephew. At the thought of their achievements, she smiled the first real smile of my visit. "John got accepted early decision to Princeton with a scholarship. But the financial-aid package they give him, it wasn't enough. He didn't want no loan, so John figured he'd go to Rutgers. They offered him a bigger package. And it's a great school, right? So what does Papa do now?" Flora lowered her teacup, closed her eyes, took a deep breath and with her eyes squeezed shut, said, "Papa handed John fifteen thousand dollars just like it was nothin'."

Looking at me with eyebrows raised, she continued in a less dramatic tone. "Papa told John to go to Princeton. He said he'd have enough money for all four years without no loans." Flora looked across the table at me and said, "Last year, my uncle sold his house, a three-story brownstone with a lot of original detail. He's rentin' a studio now from the DeGennaros up the block." Not for the first time I marveled at how quickly the average B & R Hobokenite had learned that the ornate ceiling moldings, marble fireplaces, and recessed parlor doors that they had once thought outmoded and had often spent lavishly to alter or remove entirely were now prized as "original details." Flora was saying, "He got a bundle for that house. So I figure my Uncle Emilio must have been payin' my Papa back with interest like he promised, and my Papa was using the money to help his grandkids."

I decided to break my silence. "You think your uncle and your dad argued over the debt?" Now it was Flora's turn to nod. "But why meet on the roof? How would your uncle get up there at night without one of you seeing him? Wouldn't he have to go through here?"

Flora said, "No. He could just climb over a couple of low walls between here and the DeGennaro's roof." An image of the young Brando vaulting over such a wall to visit the loft of his dead friend threatened to distract me. It triggered the memory of the teenaged Rebecca and her girlfriends sunbathing on adjacent roofs and of Mark returning from the house of a buddy down the street by way of our unlocked roof hatch. That reminded me of how Sol and I came home one night to literally catch a burglar by the legs as he tried to leave the way he'd entered, via that same roof hatch. After that we secured it. Flora was right. Hoboken row-house roofs were often accessible. "They could meet up there without no one knowin' their business."

"That's for sure," I said, shivering at the thought of the cold, snow-covered rooftop. "Flora, there's lots I still want to ask you, but I'm going to have to head home soon. Before I go, I wonder if you could show me the roof and the lofts? I just want to get a feel for the place where your dad spent so much time. Do you mind? I could go up myself if it's too cold out for you."

Flora looked grim but resolute. "Sure. Let me get our coats. And you're gonna want your boots now," she added.

In the back hall we bundled ourselves into coats, boots, and gloves and climbed the back stairs. Flora played tour guide on the first landing saying, "This was where Papa had his room. We made the other bedroom into a little TV room for him. Me and Mary, we slept downstairs. We continued to climb past the doors leading to the third and fourth floors. "Leo and John, they got the whole upstairs apartment." In between each floor there was a niche in the wall in which the statue of a saint had been carefully placed. I knew those niches were morbid reminders of the days when funerals happened at home, and pallbearers had to maneuver coffins around corners while going down the narrow stairwells of these row houses

I was shivering before we mounted the wooden staircase leading to the roof hatch. "Papa built this stairway himself so it would be sturdy, not one of those cheesy things that looks like it wouldn't hold a flea," Flora commented. I hauled myself and my damn red coat that probably weighed ten pounds all by itself, up the backless stairway, clambering after Flora. I hate backless stairs and didn't look down. Flora pushed open the hatch and climbed through. I heard her gasp and then cry out, "No, Leo, no!"

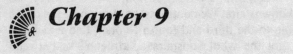

Chapter 9

Dominic Tomaselli (con't.)

. . . I always had three coops on my
roof. Sometimes more. One was for pairs
of birds incubating eggs. Them birds
mate for life you know, not like people
nowadays. And they take turns sitting
on the eggs. Then I had another coop
for the fighters, the ones who just
couldn't get along without making trouble, like my boy Leo. You know the
type. And then I had a coop for the
birds I was training and racing.

Them coops on my roof are old now. I
remember building some of them with my
old man when I was a kid. We used
scraps of wood and wire we found on the
street or that "fell off the trucks" at
construction sites. We used to hammer
out bent nails we found and use them
over again. Believe me back then we

never threw nothing out, not like nowadays . . .

When I heard Flora's anguished scream, the rush of
adrenaline triggered by her cry propelled me onto the
roof, where I stood blinking and sweating in the thin
sunlight for a fraction of a second, taking in the tableau
vivant just a few feet away. Leo, clad only in gray
sweats, was swinging an axe while Flora, now ap-
pended to his arm, attempted to stop him. "No, Leo!
Don't! Please! Not Papa's loft! Don't"

They were the same height, and for a second Flora
appeared to have stayed his hand. But in the next in-
stant, Leo twisted his shoulder, raised his arm, lifted
his sister off the ground, and flung her aside. She
landed in the snow a few feet away. I moved to where
she had stood, grabbed Leo's arm with both hands, and
leaned on it with all my not inconsiderable weight.
"Drop the axe, Leo," I ordered in the voice I reserved
for confronting students with evidence of plagiarism.
"Drop it now." While praying that Leo was not a total
psycho, I was also hoping that his frenzy would be
overcome by the shock of having a stranger intervene
in what he had, perhaps, envisioned as a family affair.
It is one thing to swat your sister away as if she were
an irritating insect, but quite another to raise your hand
to an unrelated woman several years your senior. I
hoped that he was enough his father's son to draw the
line at hacking me to bits.

When the axe fell to the snow, I was standing close
enough to smell the beer on Leo's breath and hear his
muttered, "What the fuck? Who the hell? . . ." With my
eyes glued to his contorted face, I bent down, picked
up the axe, and stepped back. The sweat that had

beaded all over my estrogen-deprived upper body when Flora had first cried out began to dissipate now that Leo was disarmed. In the wake of the media reports that hormone replacement therapy for postmenopausal women was not only useless but also risky, I had stopped wearing even my low-dose estrogen patch. So now I suffered not just from increasingly annoying stress incontinence, but also from increased stress-induced hot flashes. Grateful that at least I hadn't peed in my pants, I stood there with the axe in my hand.

"Leo, baby, you promised. Drinkin's not going to bring Papa back. And it's not gonna help to mess with these lofts either." Flora was on her feet again. As she spoke, she put her arm around her brother, who stood there, sweating and shivering, his eyes down. He leaned into her. Was he crying? I couldn't see his face. The two of them walked towards the open hatch. Casting a glance at me, Flora called over her shoulder, "Professor, I'm gonna help Leo downstairs and run a hot tub for him. Please pull the door closed after you, okay? Take your time."

Alone on the roof in the fading light and still gripping the axe, I took a few deep breaths and let the tension drain from my body. I glanced around at what was left of Dom's lofts. Before our arrival, Leo had reduced one of the large wooden coops to a pile of splintered slats, weathered gray, like bones against the white snow beneath them. Thanks to our intervention, the other two coops stood as they had when they were home to the birds Dom had nurtured and loved. Empty now, the wood-framed, wire-screened structures looked soulless and forlorn. I tried to picture Dom up here, reminiscing about favorite birds, his daily care of

them, and races won and lost. How he had enjoyed
writing down those memories! The hours he spent on
this forsaken rooftop had no doubt helped him to keep
his recollections alive and fresh, accessible to the
memoirist he was becoming.

I forced myself to look down at the spot where he
had either fallen or jumped or . . . or what? I shivered
again, thinking of Leo's drunken rampage. What pas-
sions moved that man? Was his rage fueled by alcohol-
inflamed grief or was it something more sinister, the
emotional aftermath of patricide? Why would he destroy the things that had given his dad the most pleasure? Illuminada would certainly be gratified to hear
that there were now at least two relatives who might
reasonably be considered suspects.

The snow near the low wall at the roof's edge was
tamped down with footprints, some undoubtedly
Leo's. I forced myself to peer down into the backyard
four stories below. There unmarred new snow covered
the ground with the result that the yard now resembled
a Christmas card rather than a crime scene. But just
beneath where I stood, I could make out an indenta-
tion in the snow. I shuddered, aware that I was probably directly above the patch of ground where Dom's
body had landed. Had no one seen him fall? I studied
the walls of the buildings whose yards backed onto the
Tomaselli's. There was the overgrown condo on the
corner and next to it a two-story building and then five
or six attached houses similar to Dom's. Rows of windows stared blankly back at me, lights already gleaming from some of them. Who lived in these? Had
there, perchance, been an insomniac at the window
that night? What might he or she have seen? A house-
to-house inquiry I made had helped smoke out Vinny

Vallone's killer years ago. Would it be necessary to
visit all these apartments? I sighed at the time and energy that would take. In spite of Flora's information,
this case was not going to be the walk in the park I'd
expected.

Hugging myself against the cold, I took a last look
at the concave spot on the ground below and the buildings across from where I stood. Then I reentered the
roof hatch and pulled it shut behind me. I descended
one backless step at a time, clutching the damn axe and
trying not to look down. Flora had left a light on in the
stairwell, so I had no trouble navigating once I reached
it.

"Professor B, thanks for helpin' me out up there. I'm
so sorry about Leo." Flora closed her eyes and drank in
air. When she opened her eyes, she said, "He don't
usually drink. He's just not himself since Papa died."
She exhaled. "I'll get Father Santos to stop in again to
talk to him. Can't figure out why he'd want to wreck
Papa's lofts." Flora was shaking her head as she spoke.
Her customary exaggerated respiration aside, she
might have been describing someone with a headache
rather than an axe-wielding demon who had flung her
part way across the roof. "Can I fix you some more tea,
Professor?" Flora bustled over to the range while I
shed my boots prior to reentering the kitchen.

I'd been holding the axe behind me. While Flora had
her back to me, I found my bag where I had left it and
stuffed the axe inside, grateful that, as Sol often teased,
my tote was big enough to hold a pregnant elephant.
Leo's outburst might have been an aberration, but I
wasn't taking any chances. "I understand. I'm glad Father Santos is seeing him often. I hate to leave you with
him in such a state."

"Leo's fine, really," Flora said, putting her hands on her hips. "Just had a few too many beers is all," she insisted. "He's not used to drinkin'. He's soakin' in the tub now. A little later I'll fix him some soup and a nice steak for supper. Maybe Father Santos will eat with us." She sounded hopeful. "Now about that tea . . ." Flora picked up the teakettle to pour.

"No thanks, Flora. Another time. I'm running late as it is now. We'll talk again soon. See you in class." As I spoke, I carried my boots across the kitchen and, leaving Flora there, put them on again in the front hall. I was outside before she got to the door to wave goodbye.

Chapter 10

Dominic Tomaselli (con't.)

. . . and when I got older I joined the
club and raced my birds. . . . I could
still remember when I banded my first
bird, Junior we called him. He was just
a little bigger than the egg he come
out of when me and my old man put that
band on his leg. You got to put the
bands on real early before their feet
get too big. I trained him like I saw
my old man do with his birds. Junior
took to trainin' real good, not like my
boy Leo always arguing with the teachers and me. More like my grandson,
John, a fast learner. Later on I raced
Junior. I still remember Junior's first
young bird race like it was last week.
He come down out of the sky right onto
our loft, the one me and my old man
made. He come from 200 miles away in

just a couple of hours. To me it was
like a miracle seeing that bird fly
in . . .

"Are you always reading student papers?" Betty
asked when she arrived at my house and I answered the
door with Dom's manuscript in my hand. People who
didn't teach English were always amazed at how much
time I spent reading my students' writings. "Give yourself a break, girlfriend," Betty said, handing me her
coat. I grinned. Betty wasn't even inside and she was
already issuing orders.

"It's Dominic Tomaselli's memoir. I'm reviewing it
again," I answered as I hung her coat in the closet.

"Why do you keep poring over that poor dude's
homework like it's got the secrets of the universe en-
coded in it? Do you really think the old man actually
named his enemies and outlined the plots against him?
Bel's reading the victim's last assignment again," she
explained to Illuminada, who arrived at the door before
I could answer Betty. I'd invited them both for Chinese
takeout, so I could fill them in on my meeting with
Flora. By the time they had rid themselves of their
outer garments and alighted on stools around our
gleaming new sink-island, our food had arrived. I felt
a little guilty ordering takeout when Sol and I had
spent our last nickel renovating our kitchen, but even
state-of-the-art equipment required that someone play
chef, and, of late, I often left that role to Sol.

"Well, here goes another five pounds," said Illuminada, eyeing the array of containers I was taking out of
the bag. "You know, *chiquitas,* I gain weight every
time we three look into a death."

"You could eat this whole order yourself, and you'd

still look like a twig," said Betty without rancor. It was
true. Illuminada was small-boned and delicately built.
Betty and I, both blessed with more generous propor-
tions, often teased her about the enviable fact that no
matter what she ate, she never gained an ounce. "Here,
help your skinny self."

As we passed around the containers and dished out
the beef with broccoli, chicken with eggplant, and
steamed shrimp dumplings, I poured the green tea I
had brewed into mugs. "Too cold for beer tonight," I
explained.

"Good call, Bel," said Illuminada. "Now tell me,
chiquita, did the Tomaselli man's daughter name the
name? What've you got?"

"Well, you're right about it being a relative," I answered, pausing to ingest half a dumpling.

"Talk now, eat later, Bel. I'm really curious," said
Betty. "Who does she think dunnit?"

"Flora thinks her Uncle Emilio, her mother's
younger brother, did it," I began, resigning myself to
completing the story before I could get much to eat.
How had I ever gotten by before I had Betty micro-
managing my life? By the time I'd related Flora's sad
speculation, Betty was on her second helping and Illuminada had cleaned her plate and was sipping tea. I resisted connecting her slimness to the fact that, unlike
Betty and me, Illuminada seldom had seconds.

"So, Bel, what do you think?" asked Betty.

"I think I'm going to eat before I tell you what I
think or what else happened while I was there," I said,
digging into the food chilling on my plate.

"While you chow down, let me throw you another
question," Illuminada said, refilling her mug from the
kettle. "Is there anything in the dead man's memoirs

that is at all helpful?" I shook my head and made the thumbs-down gesture with the hand that was not filling my fork. "That's too bad, *chiquita,*" Illuminada said. "Sometimes people do name names or detail grudges in those things. Remember that poor dyslexic girl who kept a journal?" I nodded again.

"Well, this guy wrote mostly about birds, right, Bel?" Betty asked. I nodded. "So unless he was wacked by a bird . . ."

I had wolfed down most of my meal, so I resumed talking. Maybe a quick recap of Leo's deranged assault on his father's lofts would distract me from the second helping that I craved. I sipped my tea and pushed away the apparently bottomless containers of food. "Well, now that you mention it, there is something in Dom's memoirs that might very well be germane. He made several references to his son Leo being a trouble-maker." I hadn't focused on this before, but now that I did, I was annoyed with myself for missing it. I had passed off Dom's references to Leo as the normal in-tergenerational stuff. But now that I had seen Leo in action, I realized that there might be more behind Dom's comments about Leo than the usual father-son conflict. I wondered what else I might be missing, and resolved to continue to reread Dom's memoirs.

When I resumed my story, my voice was more ani-mated than it had been. "Get this. I asked Flora to take me to the roof to see the crime scene and the lofts. When we got up there, we had a little surprise. Flora's brother Leo was running around drunk, and he was hacking his father's coops to bits with an axe. Flora tried to stop him and he threw her to the ground. I did stop him," I said, not without a certain pride in my voice.

"You did what?" Everyone at the table turned as Sol's deep voice entered the conversation. He was home early from a board meeting of the Citizens' Committee to Preserve the Waterfront. We all knew how upset he got if he thought I was jeopardizing my safety. There was an awkward silence. We passed the containers of food to the empty stool Sol stood behind.

"Have a seat," said Illuminada, getting up to give him a hug. "We're just getting to the good part about how your bride takes on an axe-wielding maniac and overpowers him with her red pencil."

"Yeah, and you don't want to hear that on an empty stomach," said Betty, blowing him a kiss, "so here, pol-ish off the rest of this, please."

"Happy to," said Sol, coming around the island to plant a kiss on my forehead before getting himself an empty plate and flatware and sitting down. "And my bride would probably forget this part of the story when she gets around to telling me about it, right, Bel?" Sol's tone was playful, but his eyes were serious.

"Of course not," I said. "I was planning to fill you in on all this later, so now I won't have to repeat myself." When I launched into my narrative I used the tone I used to discuss routine activities like conferencing with a student or folding the laundry. "Flora's younger brother, Leo, was up on the roof chopping down their dad's pigeon lofts. He'd had a few beers. Flora tried to stop him, and he shoved her out of the way. But I'm much bigger than Leo, so I just grabbed his arm and told him to drop the axe, and he did." I finished my story, pleased at how I'd minimized the danger I'd faced and amazed at the difference a verb makes. Leo had thrown his sister to the ground a few feet away. Saying that he shoved her was not exactly lying and was so much less dramatic. I wouldn't display the axe while Sol was around either. There was just no point in worrying him, especially now that time and therapy had minimized most traces of the severe post-traumatic stress he had suffered in the terrible months after 9/11.

"See, I knew there had to be some family members who had it in for him," said Illuminada. As far as I could tell she was making no effort to keep the smugness out of her voice. I was grateful to her, though, because she was shifting the focus of our conversation away from my confrontation with Leo and nudging it in the more productive direction of the motives of Dom's near and dear ones.

"So Bel, you never answered me," said Betty. "What do you think about Flora's story about their Uncle Emilio? Does that sound plausible to you?" Before she paused to let me answer, Betty turned to Sol and said, "Ages ago the dead man loaned his wife's brother Emilio money to pay off a gambling debt. Emilio never repaid it. Then last year he sold his house and Flora thinks he was finally paying up because suddenly her dad had all kinds of money to help with his grandkids' college bills. But she thinks Uncle Emilio got tired of paying and pushed her dad off the roof." Because now his mouth was full of Chinese food, Sol thanked Betty for the backstory with a nod.

"Does he have an alibi? Did they have bad blood between them? Was an autopsy performed?" Illuminada fired these perfectly reasonable questions at me. I shrugged indicating my ignorance.

"Has anyone checked Emilio's bank records to see if the withdrawals match the amounts Flora described?" Betty asked. A good question, but again I shrugged.

"What about Flora's relationship with her uncle? Is there some reason she might want to pin this on him? And what about your buddy with the axe?" Sol's questions were also ones that had to be answered.

"I've told you all I know. Flora's story has a certain plausibility, but I didn't have the time to press her for details if I was going to see the lofts. I can easily talk with her again," I said. "And I can talk to Emilio too." I felt I had to justify visiting the lofts rather than grilling Flora on these issues that were so pertinent to Dom's death. "I'm glad I went up to the roof, though, because not only did I catch Leo acting out, but I also got a look at the houses that back up onto the Tomasellis' yard. There are a lot of windows back there. Somebody just might have seen something."

"Has anyone come forward to the police?" Illuminada asked, clearly skeptical of this line of investigation.

"Not that I know of, but remember, there has been no allegation of murder," I said. "We just might want to ask a few questions on that block."

"It's too cold to go door to door," said Betty. "Let's leave that as a last resort."

"I'll try to find out what I can about Emilio. What's his last name?" As she spoke, Illuminada got out her Palm to record the name she expected me to supply.

Now I was really embarrassed. "You know, I've no idea. I didn't ask." I flashed on Dom's wedding photo. "But you can get it from Dom's obituary. It would be the same as Dom's wife's maiden name."

Illuminada's look of pique changed to one of grudging admiration, and she smiled at me. "Nice recovery. I'll get what I can on both men."

"Would you also get a police report and an autopsy

report if there is one?" I asked. I really appreciated being able to tap into Illuminada's network of obligated city employees, grateful people she'd worked for or with in the past who were only too happy to provide her with all sorts of information on request.

"What do you want me to do?" Betty asked. I regretted that I could not take advantage of this rare opportunity to turn the tables and tell her what to do because I wasn't sure yet. I needed to talk to Flora again.

"I'll let you know after I talk to Flora," I said. Then I had an idea. "But in the meantime maybe your buddy Father Santos will share some insight into the Tomasellis' family dynamics. He's been consoling Leo." Betty's devout Catholicism had become easier for me to understand since I had studied for my adult bat mitzvah and been reunited with my Jewish roots. And it would not be the first time Betty had elicited cooperation from her beloved parish priest.

"Consoling that piece of work sounds like a full-time job, even for Father Santos," said Betty. "I suspect he's counseling him too, and, if so, you know he won't violate that confidential relationship," she reminded us.

"I know, but see what he has to say anyway. He'll find a way to tell us what we need to know," I said. "Just remember, the good padre doesn't want a loose cannon going off in his parish."

"Have you discussed this with Sofia and Sadie?" For the second time that evening Sol's question took me by surprise.

"No. Why?" I answered, trying to keep the impatience out of my voice.

"Well, Sofia knows everything about everybody in

the Italian-American community in Hoboken, and your mother is not exactly a stranger to the psychology of a gambler," said Sol. "And they both knew the victim."

"And they liked him," I said, suddenly recalling that Ma had Xeroxed Dom's obituary and the article about his death. She had wanted me to think about Dom's death. Did she suspect foul play? And Sofia? Sol was absolutely right about her too. What Sofia Dellafemina didn't know about Italian Americans in Hoboken wasn't worth knowing. "Of course, you're right. I'll talk to them," I said. "What was I thinking?"

"Well, you weren't thinking about our wedding," said Sol. Illuminada and Betty looked up.

"*Dios mío,* will you two just get married and get it over with?" Illuminada said, walking towards the coat closet. "Just go to that lovely B & B in Lambertville where Raoul and I stayed for our anniversary and get a justice of the peace to marry you there. And hurry up because at this rate, *amigos,* you are both going to be on Medicare and you won't even need his health insurance." We all laughed at her sly reference to the fact that if Sol and I married, and I retired before I was sixty-five, an increasingly unlikely possibility after the tanking of the stock market, I could get into his health plan.

"She's right that you should hurry up. But you can't elope. I want to be there to throw rice," said Betty. "See you next week. Vic and I are off to Ocean Grove to scrape wallpaper. You should consider joining us some weekend. We'd get done a lot faster with twelve hands instead of four. That's a hint."

"See, Sol," I said, after they had gone. "That's the problem. Betty would be devastated if we eloped. So would Ma. And your mother. And all our kids. It's efficient, but it's unthinkable." I spoke while munching the fortune cookie Illuminada had left uneaten on the table and gathering the empty takeout containers.

"Well, I keep telling you we could get married in the synagogue around the corner and then have a potluck reception here. It wouldn't be fancy, but it would be cheap. And we could include whoever we wanted." Sol looked up from the open dishwasher he was loading.

"I suppose we could. But I can't take that on until the summer, when I'm not teaching. And you know, if we did that, we'd have to supplement what people bring to make sure there's enough. And the whole burden would fall on our local guests because the out-of-towners can't bring food. And where are we going to put all those out-of-towners anyway? We can't sleep everybody here." This list of objections came out as a long whine, the tone I inevitably adopted whenever we discussed our upcoming nuptials.

"I bet our local friends would be willing to take some out-of-towners" said Sol. "We could ask."

"Oh I'm sure they would. Then they'd have to bring all the food *and* put people up too. That's just not fair." The thought of spending our wedding night worrying about whether Sol's granddaughter had finger-painted horses on Betty's walls was less than romantic.

That night I dreamed of Sol and me exchanging vows on the Tomaselli's roof. Our wedding guests threw rice from the windows of the buildings at the back of the house.

Chapter 11

Sam Simon (con't.)

. . . some guys, they never got over
the war, but my life didn't really
start until after the service. That's
when I met my Miriam, that was her
name, but everybody always called her
Minny and she was an eyeful back then.
We was sweet on each other from the
first day, me and Minny, she thought I
was a hero on account of my bad leg
even though I kept telling her I was
running when I got hit by that shrapnel
[*smile*]. Anyway she was working at the
grocery store where I got a job stocking shelves and bagging orders. It was
just a little corner store, no big
deal, her dad owned the place and Minny
used to take the orders over the phone
and like I said I would bag them. Then
I'd deliver them in her dad's car.

I remember we was both there the day
I first met Dino Sorrentino, he was
mayor of Hoboken for three terms in the
seventies. But back then he had a little restaurant, Dino's it was called.
He come into the store all the time to
order for his place. One day when I
brung over his order, he asked me if I
wanted to work for him nights behind
the bar. I was desparate to save up
enough so me and Minny could get married. It took me three years working
two jobs with no time for nothing else,
not even my birds, I sold them all to
Dom and his old man. But anyway me and
Minny finally tied the knot at City
Hall. Dino hosted us for dinner at the
restaurant, and her father gave us the
apartment over the store. Minny and
Dino. Them two changed my life.

"And that's as far as I got for now. Stay tuned."

Sam lowered his manuscript to his desk and looked
around, eager for reactions from his classmates. Sofia
had nodded every time he mentioned a name, indicating her familiarity with the main players in his life. As
Sam read, I resolved to add him to the growing list of
people to talk to about Dom. Sam might know something about Dom's pigeon-racing days and the Hoboken Racing Pigeon Club they'd both belonged to.
"Sam, how long since your Minny die?" Ana's question, posed in her gruff voice, brought me back to the
moment.

"Been eight years. She died while I was locked

up. Minny come to visit me on a Sunday in April and had a stroke the next day. She died within the year." Sam related this sequence in a muted tone, quite different than the one he had used to describe the young Minny.

"Eight years! Tha's a long time. How come you ain't remarried een all that time, a good lookin' guy like you?" Ana's direct question shifted the mood.

Ana's query about the author's life rather than his writing verged on the intrusive, but before I could interrupt, Sam quipped, "Why? You interested in applyin' for the job?" Ana flushed and then grinned. I had to smile myself.

"Maybe Ana is, maybe she isn't, but the fact is you should put more information in your memoir," suggested Hilda. "You skip from Minny to Dino so fast, and you leave out a lot. You don't say what color hair Minny had or her eyes. Same with Dino. You knew him, but lots of people here didn't, like me. What was he like? What did his restaurant look like? What kind of work did you do there? Was it hard to sell your birds? You leave out all the good stuff. How are they going to make a movie out of this if you don't put in the nitty gritty?" Hilda's last line took the sting out of the critique that had preceded it. Not for the first time, I was struck by how this class really taught itself. All I had to do was sit there and listen. Sooner or later someone would offer constructive suggestions, useful editorial advice.

Before I could get too relaxed, though, Sam turned to me, his brow slightly furrowed. "So what do you think, Professor?" Unlike some of my younger students, this generation had come of age when the teacher still had the last word and her opinion mattered.

"I enjoyed hearing about that time in your life, so I agree with Hilda. I'd like to know even more, especially about the people you mention, since they were so important to you. What you have now is a very fine first draft." Sam smiled when he heard this. "Just fill in the missing information when you revise and see how it reads then."

"I'll try, but what if it takes me too long? How am I going to finish telling about my whole life if I put in every little thing? Remember, Professor, I'm eighty-three. I want to finish this before I die." Sam held up his manuscript to emphasize the point he was making.

For a moment I was taken aback by Sam's perfectly reasonable concern. He wasn't the first older author who raced with death to complete a work. "That's a dilemma all authors face, in particular those who are older, but remember that your grandchildren will want to know the details. Why don't you see me after class, and we can arrange to talk more about how to select the most important details to include?" Sam nodded, and I thought the subject was closed.

Then Sofia weighed in, "Look at it this way, Sam, I'm even older than you, right?" Sam had the wit to look shocked at her revelation. Smiling at his reaction, Sofia continued. "So tonight I'm going to make supper, and I invite you over. Should I make a TV dinner in the microwave or should I make eggplant parmigiana with gravy from scratch?"

"Eggplant," Sam answered with a grin and a shrug, seeing where he was being led, but helpless to resist.

"Well, it's the same thing." Sofia leaned back in her chair and surveyed the faces around her for validation of her analogy. When she saw all the other women nodding in unison, she smiled and made a mock curtsy from her chair.

Sam waited until all but Ma and Sofia had left, and then he approached me. "So, Professor, can you make some time to teach this old dog a few new tricks?"

That's how I came to be talking to Sam in my office later that week. Coat in hand, he lumbered into the small space and looked around, taking in the over-flowing bookshelves, piles of portfolios on the floor at my feet, and the view of the area's latest construction project through the grimy window. "Small spread, Professor," he said. I nodded, realizing that his work world had been Hoboken's City Hall, where the size and location of one's office constituted a measure of the occupant's worth.

"True, but we get a lot of work done here," I said, for once feeling defensive about my cubicle. "So have a seat and tell me about Mrs. Simon. She must have been a lovely young woman," I knew that once he had articulated his recollections, it would be easy for him to write them.

He lowered himself into Wendy's chair, his bad leg straight in front of him. He rolled his eyes to the ceiling when he began to speak, as if he might find his wife up there. "She was something to see," he began. "She was a small-boned girl with a waist I could put my hands around." He made a circle with his twisted and liver-spotted hands. "At least I could until our son came along." His face clouded as he shared this connubial tidbit, perhaps regretting the revelation. When he spoke again, his voice was reverent. "That first day Minny wore some kind of dress with a big white collar like a sailor's, you know? It made her hair look redder than fire. To tell the truth, her hair was really orange, and it was long and straight and she had it tied back. She had hazel eyes that always had a twinkle, like she knew somethin' good was going to happen. . . ." The big man sighed.

"She sounds lovely," I said. "I can picture her now. Would you tell me a little about Dino? What did he look like?"

"Dino?" Sam grinned. "They called him 'Weasel' behind his back because he had a long thin nose, and he kind of squinted at you when he talked. Later on he got glasses, but he didn't like wearin' 'em. His hair was always slicked back, and when he started gettin' bald, he kept combin' it over the bald spot the way some guys do." Sam shook his head at the foolishness of these men, and ran his fingers through his own silver locks as if to reassure himself that, though thinning, they were still there. "Dino wasn't good lookin', but he had a big brain and a big smile. That man could get things done. I learned a lot from him. I never did get to use the GI Bill, but workin' for Dino, that was like college for me." Lost in memories, Sam leaned back in Wendy's chair until it emitted a strained squeak. He sat up abruptly. "Sorry, Professor. I don't want to break your chair." His smile was rueful.

"Not to worry," I reassured him. "That chair has held a lot of big guys, and it hasn't given way yet. Tell me, what did you learn as a young man working for Dino?"

"Oh, he knew how to get people out to vote, how to get people to vote how he wanted, how to get the garbage picked up, keep the streets safe, how to make deals, how to get public housin' projects built, how to attract big developers." Sam paused, savoring the recollection of his hero's many talents. "Dino Sorrentino turned Hoboken around, no question about it. And he got me my job as head of ABC, and I had that job for years before . . ." Sam paused. "But that story I'll save for my memoirs," he said with another grin. "My professor in jail told me folks love readin' about how we got there."

"Well, I think your whole story is interesting. It tells a lot about you and about the times you lived in as a GI returning from World War II. And if you write about these people and events the way you just talked about them, your memoir will be a real treasure for those grandkids." Again, his face clouded and it occurred to me that, perhaps, Sam had no grandkids. Annoyed with my tactless assumption, I refrained from asking. Instead I said, "Sam, I have one more suggestion, though. You don't tell much about how you felt when you met Minny or Dino or sold your pigeons. How did you feel? Readers want to know." I was edging up to the topic I was most interested in, but I wanted to do it gingerly. I didn't want word to get out that I questioned the circumstances of Dom's death.

"Like I wrote, Professor, Minny changed my life. And when I met her, I just felt like I had a goal, a direction. I got drafted, and in the army all I wanted to do was stay alive and kill Krauts. After I got home with this," Sam nodded in the direction of his bad leg, I had no real goal, no purpose. But when I met Minny, she became my whole life. I worshiped her. And she worshiped me, thought I could do anythin'. It sounds corny, but she was the first person who ever really loved me." Here Sam's voice broke, and he paused. "You know, Professor, she kept on lovin' me till the day she died. She never blamed me for Dino Jr.'s death and she never believed the bribery charges against me."

"You are so lucky to have enjoyed a love like that," I said, not surprised at Sam's response. After all, memoir writing does require tapping into one's past and that often evokes strong feelings. "Now tell me about Dino," I said, hoping to divert Sam to a less charged topic. "How did you feel when you met him?"

"Well, Professor. You haven't read the first part of my memoir, but my dad left right after I was born, and my mother died when I was ten. I lived with my *bobe,* and she was sick a lot." Sam lowered his head when he uttered the Yiddish word for "grandmother." "So Dino, you could say he was like a dad or an older brother to me. He didn't even care that I was Jewish." Sam shot me a glance indicating that, as a Jew, he expected me to appreciate the value of such an open-minded person. "I felt good about that. I was proud he was my friend. Minny and me, we named our son after him." Another cloud darkened Sam's eyes.

"I bet your son will enjoy having those memoirs of yours," I said, trying to imagine how it would have felt to grow up in the fifties with a hybrid name like Dino Simon. As soon as the words were out of my big mouth, I sensed that I had somehow blundered.

I was sure of it when Sam said, "Our boy died at fourteen when a drunk driver blindsided my car on the Pulaski Skyway. Me and him were on our way home from fishin' with the mayor. He kept a boat at the shore. I wanted to avoid some of the Sunday-night traffic, so I took the Skyway." Sam sighed at the memory of a decision that no doubt haunted him. I shivered, picturing the forbidding stretch of elevated old highway that spans the industrial wasteland between Bayonne and Newark. "I was spared, but the boy, he . . ."

I reached out to pat Sam's arm, muttering, "I'm so sorry, Sam."

Sam coughed and said, "Thanks, Professor. When I said Kaddish for my boy, it was the last time I went into a synagogue." After this sad revelation, he repositioned his leg on the chair, attempted to grin, and added, "You know, the boy never even knew his old man went to jail." Sam shrugged as if to dispel the memories. Then he said, "Anyway, I didn't get that far in my memoir yet. I was tellin' you about the mayor. Like I said before, he helped out with our weddin'. And Dino, he always had a job for me. And later on when young Dino was born, the mayor helped me and Minny buy a really nice house. It's one of the few houses in Hoboken with a garage," Sam said making no effort to hide his pride. In a town where parking was at a premium, a garage was, indeed, a prized commodity.

"Listen, Professor, you'll love this." Sam shot me a conspiratorial look. "It's in the same neighborhood where Dino lived, you know, over on Clinton Street. Mostly Italians lived there back then, so we were the only family with no Christmas decorations. But all our neighbors invited us over for Christmas Eve anyway. And no kids ever egged our house on Halloween either. They just accepted us." Sam held out his hands, palms up, as he described this oasis of anti-Semitism in what most Jews of his generation perceived as an alien and hostile world. "We loved that place. Hell, I'm still livin' in it." Sam paused. Then he turned to me and said, "You really want me to write all that?"

"I sure do. That's like the creamy filling in the Oreo, Sam," I said. "Remember when I read to you from Frank McCourt's memoir? He didn't leave anything out, did he?" The excerpt I'd read from *Angela's Ashes* had been a big hit with all my students.

"No," Sam smiled. "That man really told it like it was."

"So tell me about selling your birds. That must have been hard," I said.

"Not really. I'd only had the birds since I got out of the service. They belonged to a buddy of mine. He never made it back from the war." Sam frowned at the memory of yet another loss. "Me, I was never into pigeons the way Dom was even though I joined the club and all. And like I said, when I got the chance to work nights for Dino, I couldn't take care of 'em. Those damn birds need to be fed and watered and exercised. And you gotta keep the lofts clean." Sam rolled his eyes at the memory. "I didn't know Dom that good, but I knew he took care of his birds, so I sold 'em to Dom for half of what they was worth, just so they'd have a good home, and so I wouldn't have to bother with 'em anymore. Dom, he was the real pigeon lover, not me."

Chapter 12

To: Bbarrett@circle.com
From: Annolin2@earthlink.com
Re: Stress Urinary Incontinence
Date: 02/05/03 14:37:25

Dear Sopping and Suicidal,

I saw your message on the SUI Support Network message board, and want to pass on some advice. Not to worry. Don't give up your yoga class. Just because you couldn't do Kegels the last time you tried, does not mean you are condemned to leaking urine whenever you stand, squat, sneeze, or snicker. You probably weren't doing them right. Kegels are still the answer, but they have a new name. They're called pelvic floor exercises these days, and there's a new way to learn to do them too, a high-tech way. Look for a physical therapist or nurse practitioner who knows how to use a biofeedback monitor to help you discover your pelvic floor muscles. Then when you squeeze the right way, you can actually watch a green spike shoot up on the screen of the monitor. And once you get the hang of it, you can buy an over the counter contraption called Myself and monitor your own squeezes. And here's some more good news. You don't have to practice three hundred repetitions a day like they used to tell us. Just three sessions of ten vigorous repetitions each day will do it! I teach horseback riding for a living, and thanks to biofeedback, I'm back in the saddle!

Sally who's riding high and dry

For years I had been seeking empathy and information from on-line support groups. Betty thought my use of these groups made me an addict. Maybe she was right, but I didn't care. I was hooked. Messages from others facing similar passages had nurtured and guided me as I coped with menopausal symptoms, an aging and ill parent, mothering a pregnant bride-to-be, and being a first-time grandmother. This time I had sought advice after I had erupted in giggles at a faculty meeting, and my amusement triggered another, less pleasant, eruption as well. No way in hell was I going to start wearing sanitary or incontinence pads. And I was a Kegels dropout, having found that doing three hundred repetitions of anything was not compatible with my lifestyle or temperament. So I found Sally's advice intriguing. But I put off following up on it immediately in favor of keeping my appointment with Flora.

Like Sam, she too was coming in for a conference about her work. She looked more cheerful than she had since before Dom's disappearance and death. The cold had reddened her prominent cheeks, her smile seemed less perfunctory, and, most tellingly, her breathing was even. Flora wore a sharp navy-blue fleece ensemble over a white turtleneck and carried a red parka and a red, white, and blue wool scarf designed as a tribute to the flag. No sooner had she sat down, than she explained the reason for her relatively upbeat mood. "Now that I know you're helpin' us get Uncle Emilio, I feel a little better. I got a couple of night's sleep, so I can finally concentrate on my schoolwork. I'm way behind in all my courses, but here." I recognized the sheaf of papers she handed me as the draft of her research paper I'd seen earlier. "I still have this draft we can go over. You said I need help with the citations."

Flora and I spent a good forty-five minutes going over which citations were worthy of inclusion in the text of her paper and which ones should be relegated to the "works cited" page. Unlike those students who thought the more citations they had, the higher their grade, Flora seemed to grasp the concept of selection. Unlike many students, she had not plagiarized from the Internet, but acknowledged all her sources. She was also becoming reasonably competent at paraphrasing, a skill that often eluded novice writers of research papers. When we had finished, she gathered the pages of her draft, stood, and said, "Thanks, Professor B. I'll try to pull this together over the weekend."

She hesitated a minute and then took a telltale deep breath. "I don't want to pressure you, Professor, but I was just wonderin'. Have you got anything on Uncle Emilio yet?"

I did feel slightly pressured by Flora's query, but I was glad she had brought up the subject of the investigation. "No, Flora, not yet. Please, sit down. If you have a minute, I have a few questions I didn't have time to ask you the other day."

"Sure," said Flora sitting again while shoving her paper into her briefcase. "I think I told you everything

I know, though." She inhaled deeply this time, causing me to wonder if indeed there was something Flora had not shared.

"Flora, I'll want to talk to Emilio. I need to find out if he has an alibi for the night your father disappeared." This time Flora's intake of air was sharp and audible. Her eyes widened as if the idea of an alibi was totally new to her. Clearly the woman did not read mysteries or watch crime shows on TV. "And I'd like to find out about his finances, his other debts, his cash flow. I don't even know what kind of work he does. All I really do know is he gambles, and he owed your dad some money. Did he and your dad get along otherwise? Can you tell me anything else about him that might help?"

Flora leaned forward in Wendy's chair, inhaled, and began. "Emilio retired a few years ago. He used to work for Allen's. You know, the window-treatment store? It used to be on First Street?" I nodded, vaguely remembering the shop she mentioned. "It's gone now. Anyway he was their installer. He made steady money, nothing big, but steady. Bought himself a brownstone way back when they were cheap. And he never married, probably because of his face."

"What's wrong with his face?" I asked.

Flora wrinkled her nose and said, "Oh, he's got a nasty birthmark or somethin' on his cheek. It's in the shape of a square patch with little marks like stitches on the sides. People call him Patch, but Mama never let us call him that. So anyway, like I was sayin', he got by fine or he would of been fine if it weren't for his gamblin'." Flora made no effort to mask the scorn in her voice when she uttered this last sentence.

"As for an alibi, I have no clue." She threw up her

hands and shrugged her shoulders. "Frankly, I haven't been able to talk to him or even look at him since Papa—" As she spoke, Flora's voice broke. She closed her eyes and took several deep breaths. "Sorry, Professor. Okay, I'm okay now. Remember I told you my uncle sold his house on Bloomfield Street last year for over $750,000. Leo handled the sale."

"Oh, is Leo a realtor?" I asked, hoping my face didn't betray the astonishment I felt.

"Yes. He took that course at RECC when the little photography shop he had went under. He used to develop pictures. But you know, once they came out with those disposable cameras and then the digital ones and the malls . . . And of course, this bein' Hoboken, his rent on the store kept goin' up and he had less and less business. Finally when it got really bad, I told him to go to real estate school and get a certificate. Father Santos gave him a push too, so Leo went." Flora smiled as if the memory of her role in what I took to be Leo's reversal of fortune pleased her. "He's with Smythe & Higgins. They probably wanted him because he knows the old folks, the ones like Emilio who still have their houses. Emilio's house was Leo's first sale." Flora did not seem to find it odd that her brother, a drunken axe-wielding wild man, should be a player in the high-stakes game of Hoboken real estate, an agent for the most reputable firm in town. "So anyway, after Leo sold Emilio's house for him, Papa asked my uncle to start payin' him back. I figure Emilio made a payment, and that's where Papa got the money to give John and Mary."

"I see," I said, nodding. "That makes sense. But tell me, did Emilio and your father get along? Were they close?"

Flora shook her head and inhaled. "To tell you the truth, Professor, Uncle Emilio and Papa, they sort of tolerated each other while my mother lived. Emilio was younger than my mother, and she helped raise him. Emilio came to our house for dinner on Sundays and sometimes during the week. Papa got him into the club 'cause he thought the birds would distract Emilio from gamblin', but Emilio never really took to it like Papa did. In fact, he used to bet on the birds." Flora's pursed lips indicated her disapproval. "But after my mother died, we saw less of him even though at first I kept invitin' him over—out of respect for her, you know?" Here Flora sighed, a lengthy exhalation that seemed to leave her literally deflated, as if dredging up even these rather mundane details of familial history had drained her of both air and energy.

I resisted my pangs of sympathy and persisted with two more questions, hoping to catch her off guard. "Was it like that with you and Leo? Did you help raise him?"

Flora brightened unexpectedly, almost managing a grin. "You could say that, I guess. You probably think I didn't do such a good job, right? That was some performance he put on the other day," she said, shaking her head. "He felt really bad afterwards." She sounded as if we were discussing the antics of a wayward teen rather than the destructive rampage of a drunken adult male brandishing a lethal weapon.

"Well, I do wonder about him. He's a bit younger than you, right?" Flora nodded. "And how did Leo and your dad get along?" I asked, determined to elicit some kind of useful information about Leo.

"Well, Professor, you probably figured out by now that I was a daddy's girl." Flora lowered her eyes modestly. "Leo was my mother's pet. Not that Papa didn't try. He tried to get Leo involved with the pigeons. But Leo didn't want anything to do with the birds. He liked soccer. When Leo started high school, things got worse between them. Leo's real smart, but he didn't study like I did. He was always in trouble. Papa wanted him to go to college, but Leo wouldn't even talk about it. Another thing was Papa didn't approve of any of Leo's friends, guys or girls. And Leo got into fights. But it was all normal teenage stuff, nothin' big." Flora shrugged, dismissing the father-son conflict that, perhaps, had scarred Leo's psyche and earned repeated mention in Dom's memoirs. "Once Leo grew up and got married and started workin', him and Papa got on a lot better. They weren't close like me and Papa, but they didn't fight no more. And after Leo's wife left him, me and Papa invited him and my nephew to live with us."

I made a mental note of the fact that Leo had an ex-wife. My next question, based on an assumption, was designed to trap Flora. "Did his wife leave him because of his drinking?" I recalled only too well the man's beery breath. Flora exhaled again and closed her eyes. I waited for her to continue.

"Oops, sorry. Should I come back in a few minutes?" Damn. It was Wendy. I was supposed to schedule conferences with my students only when Wendy was teaching or at home, and she did the same. The system usually worked, but my meeting with Flora had gone into overtime.

Flora catapulted out of Wendy's chair saying, "No, I'm sorry. I'm on my way. I didn't mean to take up so much of your time, Professor B." Trying not to collide with Wendy, Flora backed awkwardly out of our office holding her parka and briefcase in her arms. "I have another class, and I'm late already. Thanks again, Professor B."

"Bel, I keep telling you. You have to limit the length of your conferences. Our students are so needy that you could spend the rest of your days talking them through their life crises." Wendy lowered her books onto her desk. "So what was that woman's problem? Is she out of work? Is one of her kids in trouble? Is her mother sick? Or maybe her boyfriend's getting nasty?" Wendy's litany of the woes that sometimes prevented our students from succeeding academically was not exaggerated.

"None of the above. Not exactly." I answered absently, certain that Flora had fled the office to avoid my inquiry into Leo's drinking. "She's the daughter of the old man in my memoir-writing course, the one who died, remember? I told you about him. She thinks he was murdered. I said I'd—"

"Let me guess," Wendy said. "You're going to try to help figure out who killed him." She swiveled in her chair to face me. "Bel Barrett, you are impossible. You have no business meddling in these murders all the time. Although I have to admit, you seem to have a flair for it." She paused, perhaps recalling how my sleuthing had saved her precious urban kayaking club grant a few years ago. "But that's not the point. You've already got yourself an extra course to teach, and you're on I don't know how many committees this semester."

Wendy stopped mid swivel and looked me in the eye. "But that's not the point either, Bel. The point is you and Sol have a wedding to plan, remember?" Wendy resumed rotating until I held out the jar of

M&M's. She grabbed a big handful and began to divide them into piles by color. Since the stock market's plunge had decimated her IRA and indefinitely postponed her retirement, Wendy had tripled her usually modest intake of M&M's.

"We're working on it," I said, wondering if I wasn't, in fact, using Dom Tomaselli's death to avoid thinking about the wedding.

"Well? Have you set the date? I want to get it in my calendar. We don't want to miss it. The kids say that for you and Sol, they'll fly in." Wendy was getting out her Palm as she spoke.

Picturing a guest list that included not only all our friends, but all their kids too, I despaired anew. I loved Wendy's kids, but ours had been a prolific generation and, to make matters worse, lots of our friends' kids, like ours, were partnered by now. "No, no date yet. No place either," I mumbled apologetically, anticipating her next question.

Wendy snapped her Palm shut. "Well, maybe that's just as well because I got a great idea for a venue. I was working on this year's urban kayaking grant, and I went over to the Nature Center at the Meadowlands to talk with the resident naturalist. Bel, they hold weddings there! You could have your wedding indoors or out depending on the season. Either way, you'd have a view of the Manhattan skyline, and I know how you love that lineup of buildings. And you'd have those gorgeous grasslands in the foreground too. You could have lots of people. There's plenty of parking. What do you think?"

"It's an interesting idea. I'll talk to Sol about it." I tried to imagine getting married in the shadow of a landfill the size of a small mountain, which was also part of the view from the Nature Center and which natives had affectionately dubbed Mount Garbaggio. But, in fact, the Meadowlands were lovely, and the idea might appeal to Sol, because, like Wendy, he was green to the core.

"I'm sure you could get your rabbi to perform the ceremony there and then you'd just need a caterer. What do you think of Kathy's Kitchen? They only use organic produce and free-range chickens." As if to stress her environmentalist credentials, Wendy popped only green M&M's into her mouth.

"I'll talk to Sol. It's an interesting idea. I appreciate your thinking of it. Let me know if you get any other brainstorms," I said. But I didn't mean it. I didn't want to think about that endless guest list, bank-breaking caterers, or calendars. Instead I was imagining all those M&M's she had carefully sorted mingling in Wendy's stomach, the greens, the reds, the browns, the yellows, and even the new blues.

"Well, you better think fast. I'm sure you have to reserve way in advance," said Wendy.

"Right. I'll e-mail Sol now," I said, booting up my computer and logging on. "Otherwise I just might forget."

Chapter 13

To: Bbarrett@circle.com
From: LDugan@juno.com
Re: Stress incontinence
Date: 02/12/03 06:03:15

Dear Sopping and Suicidal in Hoboken,

I was in your soggy shoes for a long time. According to my doctor, my pelvic floor muscles began to sag after I had the twins. I didn't start leaking urine though until years later when I hit menopause. Estrogen depletion was the straw that broke my pelvic floor muscles. My uterus slumped and my bladder shifted, so whenever I coughed, or lifted a bag of groceries, or even got out of the car, I'd leak. I'm a mother of four and a high school principal, so I don't have time for leaking. I also didn't have time for Kegels. I barely have time to eat or sleep. But I didn't want to support the booming incontinence-pad industry for the rest of my life either.

I needed a quick fix. So my doctor suggested "sling surgery," a technique that's only six years old with a success rate between 75 and 91 percent. After sneezing on stage at a school assembly with predictably embarrassing results, I figured I had nothing to lose and opted for the procedure. Unlike the incontinence surgery of the past, it seemed simple enough. The doctor inserted a strip of synthetic mesh tape through a small incision in my vagina and looped it under my urethra. Well, let me tell you, that tape is my new best friend! It supports all those sagging, slumping organs of mine. I feel like a new woman. Try it. It worked for me. Good luck!

Laverne, who's born again

Thoughts of sling surgery preoccupied me so that I didn't e-mail Sol about Wendy's wedding-site suggestion. And I didn't mention it to him right away at dinner because we were meeting Sarah Wolf at La Isla. Sarah is managing editor of the *Jersey City Herald*, a position she was promoted to after she broke the story I gave her revealing who really killed RECC's first woman president. Sarah had been very helpful during my struggle to figure that out. So it only made sense that, in return, she got the scoop that led to her promotion. And, perhaps a little bored within the confines of her new position, my adventure-loving friend had continued to offer support with subsequent cases, providing access to the paper's archives as well as cover and company on some of my investigative sorties. I was glad of this not only because she was an intrepid companion, but also because, since we'd long ago given up the aerobics class where we met, it was good to have an excuse to get together.

Sarah entered, red-faced and breathless from the cold. When she pulled off her multicolored wool cap, her graying shag crackled with electricity. "I've just taken the afternoon off to stuff envelopes with flyers about the upcoming antiwar rally in DC," she said, exasperation sharpening her voice. "Who ever thought we'd have to be doing antiwar stuff again? At our age?" She shook her head and added her coat to the pile on the banquette opposite Sol and me in one of the too-small booths in the storefront restaurant. I didn't want to get into a heavy discussion of the coming war because the very thought of our invading Iraq triggered all Sol's post-9/11 fears of further terrorist attacks here, not to mention his own not-so-inner dove.

I needn't have worried. Before we could answer, Sarah whipped out a recent photo of her grandchild Hannah, now a lanky five-year-old. From behind a PEACE NOT WAR placard, the child grinned her grandmother's ready-for-anything grin. "Isn't she something? Would you look at that smile?"

"I am," said Sol, staring pointedly across the table at Sarah. He continued in his deep, rich voice. "It's the siren smile of a true vixen, and it's yours, Sarah." Sarah blushed, while I admired my love's way with words and women. He was a charmer all right. Meanwhile, no slouch in the proud grandparent role himself, Sol took out his wallet and handed Sarah a photo of his own granddaughter, an elfin figure mugging for the camera in her mother's lap.

"Oh, Sol, Maya's so grown-up looking," Sarah said. "And is that Alexis or a babysitter?"

"That's Alexis. I'm the babysitter usually, and nobody can accuse me of looking like a teenager." His rumbling chuckle made it clear that Sol was not complaining about his role as ad hoc child-care provider even though, when summoned, he often dropped everything and drove two hours to take care of Maya in upstate New York.

"Sol's the reason Alexis still looks like a kid," I said. "She and Xhi hardly ever have to worry about not being able to get to work. And they've never left Maya with a stranger. He's the best grandfather in the world," I added, lest Sarah think I harbored resentment over Sol's frequent absences. Actually, I was jealous because he saw much more of Maya than I did of my faraway Abbie J. And I did think Alexis took advantage of him just a little.

Not to be outdone in the show-and-tell games grandparents play, I took out an entire small album Rebecca had sent filled with photos of the indisputably adorable Abbie J. "I mean is this kid precious, or what?" I said without a trace of modesty.

Sarah flipped through the photos, oohing and aahing over Abbie J on the swings, Abbie J on the slide, Abbie J at a birthday party, her face smeared with chocolate cake. "I see she's grandma's girl. She's a walking ad for denim and a developing chocoholic. And she's got that look. See?" Sarah held up a photo of Abbie J running, her brow creased, her eyes narrowed, and her hair an orange blur behind her. "That's the look you used to get in aerobics. You weren't going to quit until you'd done the count even if it killed you." Sarah paused. "I'm so glad we still have these old-fashioned photos. You can't easily whip out your laptop and subject your friends to a digital slide show in a restaurant."

"You're right," Sol said. "Although Bel's portfolio comes pretty close," he joked. "Sarah, there's a bottle of wine in my coat pocket. Would you grab it, please? I picked it up next door while I was waiting." La Isla doesn't have a liquor license, but it's owned by the man who owns the large liquor store two doors away, so it doesn't need one. "We should raise a glass to all these kids," he added.

"Here. Here," said Sarah pulling a bottle of Chilean merlot from the pile of outer wear like a magician extracting a rose from behind someone's unadorned ear. An alert waitress materialized with a corkscrew, wineglasses, and menus. In a moment she had the wine open and poured. Sarah lifted her glass. "May they live happy, healthy, and useful lives in a peaceful world." Sadly Sarah's toast struck me as the pipe dream of the perennial peacenik she was, given the fact that American forces were at that very moment mobilizing to strike in Iraq. As if to acknowledge the futility of her wish, Sarah shrugged and said, "We can dream, right?"

"Damn right," Sol and I echoed in unscripted unison, clinking glasses all around and then raising them to our lips.

"Well, like we used to say in the bad old days, 'Make love not war.' That's one reason I was so pleased when you e-mailed me that you two are actually getting married. A wedding is the perfect antidote to war. *L'chayim*," Sarah said, "to life." Once again we raised our glasses. "So, have you set a date?" She glanced across the table, first at Sol, then at me.

"I'd drag her off to City Hall right now, if the place were still open," said Sol, glancing at his watch. "But Bel's hung up on the guest list."

"Why? Aside from me, who do you really need there?" Sarah asked with a smile. "Seriously, you know, Bel, there is a place where you could get married and have as many people as you want and not have to worry about parking or crowding."

"Wendy suggested the Nature Center at the Meadowlands," I said, noticing Sol's eyes suddenly glow green the way they did whenever he thought about the few swaths of undeveloped land left in our crowded corner of the world.

"Interesting," Sarah said slowly. I could tell she was considering it. "But I like my idea better." She smiled smugly, wanting to be cajoled into sharing her brainstorm.

Sol obliged. "So tell us. Where?"

"The restored railroad terminal at Liberty State Park," she announced with the air of someone trumpeting a royal birth.

"Where RECC holds graduation?" I sputtered, picturing Sol and me in our mortarboards and other academic regalia exchanging vows to the strains of "Pomp and Circumstance." "Where Altagracia Garcia was killed?" My mind was now flashing to the scene of that long-ago murder, a gala fundraising event at that very train station at Liberty State Park.

"Think about that skyline view. It's so close you could touch it. And if it rains, you could just move everything into the terminal." Sarah snapped her fingers. "It's perfect."

Misunderstanding Sarah's gesture, our waitress hurried over, looking frazzled. "I'm sorry. We're very busy tonight. Are you ready to order?" She stood with her pad poised.

"I'm always ready to order," I said, hoping to change the subject.

But as soon as we had each listed our choices, and the waitress hurried to the counter to call them in, Sol picked up where we had left off. "No, Liberty State Park is too grim now."

"You mean because of the murder?" said Sarah. "Would that bother you, Bel?"

"I'm not sure. But I think it's the post-9/11 view that would sadden Sol, right, love?" I reached over to squeeze his arm. I knew I was on target when he put his hand over mine and held it there. I didn't usually speak for Sol, but I knew that the sight of the spires of lower Manhattan with gaps where the Twin Towers used to be was always going to be painful for Sol to contemplate.

"Right," said Sol, "but what about Wendy's idea? The Nature Center out in the Meadowlands? It's close by, it's interesting . . ."

"It's smelly," I added with an unmistakably dismissive thumbs-down gesture. In spite of decades of cleanup and the presence of malls, hotels, and upscale condos, on occasional balmy days the Meadowlands were still redolent of the pig farms and landfill that had been part of the area's history for too long. Now in my mind's eye, Sol and I stood before our thousands of assembled guests, all of us wearing gas masks. "Besides, that was the scene of two murders," I added just in case my first argument met with resistance.

By the time the waitress brought our *sopa de pollo,* a rich chicken broth made satisfyingly substantial by chunks of chewy yucca, I needed all the comfort the classic brew could provide. I was relieved when, for a few minutes, we abandoned our conversation in favor of slurping. Energized by the soup and the respite from wedding planning, I mused on whether or not Sarah could be useful in untangling the snarled strands of the Tomaselli family's fiscal and filial affairs. At first I didn't see how. But suddenly, while blowing on my soup, I realized how my old friend could help. When we resumed talking, I focused the conversation in a new direction.

"Sarah, do you remember reading an obit about an old man, a World War II vet, who froze to death in Hoboken a few weeks ago?" I asked.

"No. But, you know, I don't remember much these days," Sarah said, lightening her self-deprecating remark with her trademark grin. "He's too old to have been a student of yours, so who was he to you? Why do you ask?"

"Well, actually, he was a student of mine in a continuing ed course on memoir writing that I'm teaching this semester at the Senior Center." I paused, giving Sarah a moment to connect the dots.

"Damn, Bel, you *would* take on an extra course. Like you don't have enough to do. No wonder I haven't seen you since God knows when. No wonder she doesn't have time to get this wedding together," Sarah added, simultaneously demoting me to the third person and turning to Sol for affirmation of her view of me as a hopeless workaholic.

"I hardly see her anymore either," said Sol. "When she's not teaching, she's poking her nose into other people's business." Sol's tone was jocular, not hostile. I could tell he knew where I was trying to lead the conversation and was trying to assist.

"Aha! I get it." exclaimed Sarah. "Of course, I should have known. You think this old man was killed, you're hot on the trail of the bad guy . . ." Sarah made a big show of mopping imaginary sweat off her brow with her napkin before continuing. "And you want me to tag along and help."

"Whew, I thought you'd never ask," I said, pleased once again that even though, like most of our peers,

Sarah couldn't remember much, she could still put two and two together when she wanted to.

"So what do you want me to do?" So great was her curiosity that it lent Sarah's inquiry the intensity of a demand. She could barely wait until the waitress had set down our plates. The extreme winter cold had made comfort-food junkies of us all, so Sol had ordered *arroz con pollo,* a steaming fricassee of chicken and rice. Sarah had chosen *boliche asado,* Cuban pot roast, and I was sticking with my favorite, *pollo asado,* or plain old roast chicken. "Jeez, how am I going to finish this after all that soup?" Sarah said, staring at her plate, barely visible beneath slices of meat and gravy. A huge bowl of rice also challenged our appetites.

"That's why they invented the doggy bag," Sol replied, digging into his food.

"Don't whine. Just eat," I teased, helping myself to some rice.

"Okay. So tell me about this dead veteran. You think he was killed?" By the time I had filled Sarah in on the details of Dom's life and the circumstances of his death, we had foresworn dessert, and asked for the check. "Okay. I'm game. It sounds easy and," Sarah spoke with a nod to Sol, "very safe. Besides, I've always wondered how those birds find their way home."

Chapter 14

Dominic Tomaselli (con't.)

Racing pigeons ain't like racing a
horse. A horse got a rider, a jockey to
steer it and push it and tell it where
to go. A horse, he can see the race-
track. So can the rider. So can the
spectators. But a bird got no path to
follow, nobody else to steer him, he's
out there on his own in thin air. Hes
got to figure out what way to go. The
Kentucky derby is about a mile and a
half but pigeons race hundreds of
miles, the fastest horse clocked ran
about 43 mph but the fastest pigeon
made 92 mph. And you, you never see
your own birds when their flying, You
don't see them start because you or
someone from your club trucks them to
the starting point usually miles away,
And you don't see them the whole time

111

their in the air. You only see them at
the end when they come in. When a horse
gets to the finish line, his race is
over, everybody sees him run thru that
tape. But the end of a pigeon race is
not really the end. Once in a while, a
bird gets to right over the home loft
and he don't want to come down just
yet, So you gotta send up a chico.
That's a bird trained especially to
lead another bird home. Kinda like a
sheep dog. And even then its not over,
you got to take the band off the bird,
stick it in the capsule, and get it
into the clock or it don't count.

The longer I pored over Dom's memoir, the more
certain I was that the clue to his death lay in his passionate lifelong involvement with pigeons and pigeon
racing. And that's what I hoped to explore with Sarah.
But several days would pass before we could imple-
ment the plan I'd outlined to her at La Isla. In the
meantime, I had promised to drive Ma and Sofia to the
dentist after my last class on a frigid afternoon. They
had made back-to-back appointments with the hygienist for routine cleanings. Sofia's daughter and I had
agreed that occasional stints as chauffeur were far
preferable to worrying about Ma and Sofia driving, so
a few years ago we had persuaded them to surrender
their car keys and sell their vintage vehicles.

As I helped them into their coats, my mind was on
Betty's admonition to talk to Dom's family members.
Even though my hunch led me to think Dom's death
would not be explained by his relatives, I would pump

Sofia for information about them in case my hunch proved wrong. This would not be the first time I had picked Sofia's brain in the dentist's waiting room. It eased her pretreatment anxiety to regale me with tidbits about people she knew, and she trusted me not to betray her confidences. Ours was a good deal all the way around. Experience told me there would be plenty of time to grill her on Dom Tomaselli, his brother-in-law Emilio, the high-stakes player, and Dom's really volatile son, Leo. I would also have a chance to see if Ma had any insight into Emilio, the gambling man.

One at a time, Sofia and then Ma, held on to my arm as we picked our way down the steps and into the car. I prayed we wouldn't slip on the icy pavement. Although Ma and Sofia were a generation ahead of me, all three of us suffered from osteoporosis and had integrated weekly doses of Fosamax into our lifestyle. I sighed with relief when we made it to the car without incident. The ride was short, and, mercifully, the small parking area in front of the dentist's office had been plowed and salted. The Goddess of Parking was with me! There was one remaining space. I edged the car into it and escorted my charges into the waiting room, again, one at a time.

It was only after I had hung up our coats and we were settled in adjacent chairs, that I said, "So Sofia, is it true that Dom's son, Leo, you know, the realtor, is up for an award from the K of C?" I had fabricated this scenario to jolt Sofia into revealing everything she knew about Leo without reflecting on why I wanted to know, and it worked. I didn't want to tell Ma or Sofia that I was looking into the possibility that Dom's death had been anything other than an accident. The fewer people who knew what I was up to, the better.

"Are you kidding? Who told you that? That kid's been trouble since the day he was born." I suppressed a smile at the thought of the forty-something Leo being referred to as a kid. "His mother, Renata, she spoiled him rotten. Do you know, she carried him everywhere until he was nearly four?" Sofia rolled her eyes at this example of maternal excess. "And right from the start he always liked the girls. And they liked him. Even my Marie had a little crush on him once upon a time." Now I had to smother a giggle at the thought of Sofias's uptight and matronly daughter in the same room with Leo Tomaselli let alone having once had the hots for him. Who knew?

"Renata always said how the boy drove Dom crazy. The kid didn't want anything to do with the birds. But even worse, he got a scholarship to St. Peter's and then he got himself expelled. I don't remember what for," Sofia added before I could ask. I hoped I could remember to check that out. Sofia continued, clearly on a roll. "But Renata always made excuses for him. Broke his father's heart when he wouldn't go to college. I swear that kid never held a job until he was married and started working at something or other in New York. Then he ran that ratty little photo-developing shop downtown for years. Then all of a sudden he's like a hotshot real estate agent." Sofia sniffed and searched her bag for a Kleenex. I pulled a clean one out of my pocket for her so she wouldn't get distracted, but she seemed to have wound down because just then she turned the tables and asked me a question. "So did someone in the K of C tell you that he's getting an award?" Sofia's brow furrowed. Undoubtedly she was distressed at having run out of information on Leo and, even worse, at not being privy to the latest rumors about him.

"I thought I overheard someone talking about it at Dom's wake," I said, purposely vague.

"Dom would have liked for the boy to get an award. He told me that Leo really grew up after he got married," said Ma quietly. "Remember Dom didn't have to invite Leo and his son to live with him and Flora after Leo's wife left, but he did."

Before I had even absorbed the surprising fact that Ma seemed to know a lot about Dom, the white-coated hygienist appeared and summoned her into the treatment room. "Well, Dom was good to those grandchildren of his, and Flora always adored her brother. They wouldn't want Leo's boy growing up without a woman in the house," remarked Sofia to Ma's back. Sofia and Ma often quibbled, and each was partial to having the last word.

"Why did Leo's wife leave him?" I asked, again hoping to elicit a juicy tidbit from Sofia before she became too curious about my interest in the Tomaselli family.

"What I heard at the time was she was going to college, and she ran off with a professor," Sofia said with a shrug. I took a moment to marvel anew at how so many of my colleagues, especially the men, had time to seduce students. In fact, their legendary lechery had become a literary and cinematic cliché. Even if I wanted to follow suit, I had always had too many courses, conferences, papers, and committee meetings to allow time for even the most efficient of dalliances. While I was silently registering this inequity, Sofia was saying, "But that marriage wouldn't have lasted. I could see that from the start. Claudia was beautiful, like Renata, Leo's mother. You should have seen her. And artistic too. Very modern, not the type to stay home and raise kids." In a rare moment of tact, Sofia paused, clearly editing her next line so as to avoid insulting me by casting aspersions on all working mothers. What she finally said was, "Sooner or later she would have gone."

"Did she just abandon their child?" I asked, feeling a stirring of sympathy as Leo the Terrible began to morph into Leo the Lovelorn in my overly empathetic mind.

"Well, you tell me. She just never came home from class one day is what I heard. Years later I think she showed up to see the boy." Sofia frowned as she passed on this sad speculation.

"At least there was a strong extended family there, what with Dom and Flora and Emilio," I said, now hoping to glean something useful about Uncle Emilio, whom Flora was so eager to accuse of her father's murder.

"Emilio? Oh, you mean Patch?" said Sofia. "Everybody calls him that because he has a mark on his cheek that looks just like a patch somebody sewed on. Anyway, Dom was like a rock for his kids and grandkids and even for poor Patch. Up until just the last year or so, the man really was a rock," said Sofia with a sigh. I held my tongue, hoping she would say something about Emilio. When Sofia spoke next, she rubbed two magenta-tipped fingers against her thumb. The lurid gleam of her nail polish lent drama to even this familiar gesture. "Everybody knew that Patch DeFranco owed Dom money since forever, but Dom was always decent to Patch out of respect for Renata, or maybe just because he was decent. Who knows?"

"What was that debt all about?" I prodded.

"Well, it's no secret either that Patch gambles,"

Sofia said. "Not for fun like your mother and me," she added hastily. Sofia and Ma tended to be a little defensive about their own predilection for the one-armed bandits and blackjack tables at Atlantic City. "But for real. And he's not very good at it, I guess." She paused a moment, obviously allowing me to contrast Emilio's ineptitude with the not inconsiderable talent she and Ma displayed. "Or maybe he was just out of his league, I don't know. But I heard from a friend of Renata's that he owed to some nasty people." Sofia grimaced. "Renata was worried sick. That's why Dom lent Patch the money."

"What was Renata like?" I asked, curious about a woman who would carry a four-year-old up stairs and talk her hard-working husband into giving away their grandchildren's education fund to enable her brother's gambling.

"I wonder what's keeping your mother" Sofia said with a start. Straightening in her chair, she looked in the direction of the treatment room.

"Oh, you know how she has to have her gum line scraped by hand rather than by machine. She hates the noise the machine makes in her head," I reassured Sofia. "It always takes a little longer that way."

"I hope that's it. I just don't want her to have to go through another root canal," said Sofia. In spite of their bickering, the two women were extremely fond of one another. After Sofia had passed Ma a roll of toilet paper under the partition in the ladies room of the Senior Center, the two widows connected and quickly discovered they shared not only sorrows but also pleasure in the gaming tables. It wasn't long before Sofia invited Ma to move into her home. Ma, then living with Sol and me, had leapt at the chance to reestablish her independence. Their unorthodox housing arrangement was a gamble for both women, and it paid off. It proved to be an affordable alternative to hiring live-in companions or moving to an assisted-living facility, or living with family. Better yet, though neither would admit it, their relationship had become an affectionate and caring sisterhood.

"You were telling me about Renata Tomaselli," I said, hoping Sofia would not notice the slight urgency in my voice. I really did want her to tell me about Renata before Ma came back and interrupted or changed the subject.

Sofia leaned back in her chair again, apparently reassured by my explanation. To my relief, she resumed our conversation. "Like I told your mother, Renata was perfect for Dom." It interested me that Sofia and Ma had been discussing Dom's family. I wondered if they too were suspicious of his death. "She was a pretty woman. Quiet, but nice enough. She was very proud of Dom's war record. And as long as he didn't interfere with the way she ran the house and raised the kids, she gave him free rein to spend as much time as he wanted with those birds. It always seemed like a trade-off to me. Dom would be late for dinner when he was waiting for a bird to come in or he'd miss one of the boy's soccer games if the pigeons got sick or if he was registering birds for a race at the club. I remember she used to say, 'Listen, he could be out drinking or gambling or with other women. At least I always know where he is.' " Sofia paused. "My husband would have liked a wife like that," she said with a sigh. I swallowed another smile, inspired by the thought of anyone daring to arrive late to Sofia's table.

"And remember, Dom put up with Patch too," Sofia

added, giving me a look that said tolerating errant in-laws should be above and beyond the call of spousal duty. I recalled that Sofia was unfailingly pleasant to her whiny sister-in-law, who made an annual weeklong pilgrimage to Hoboken to visit the graves of her brother and her parents. "Ah, here she is. You were in there so long, I thought you were getting all your teeth pulled," she said. As Ma emerged from the treatment room, Sofia's smile was at odds with her sarcasm.

"That's what I feel like," Ma said, rubbing her jaw. "Go ahead. It's your turn. She's waiting." Ma gestured in the direction of the smiling hygienist. Sofia stood and followed the woman obediently. Ma took Sofia's seat next to me and immediately began to replace her lipstick with the unerring exactitude of long practice.

Trying to sound as if I were just making conversation, I said, "Ma, did you know Dom's brother-in-law Emilio was a gambler? He lost big to some really sinister people. Apparently Dom lent him the money to repay the loan and may have actually saved his life. Isn't that amazing? Dom used some kind of insurance from a car accident that he'd been saving for his kids' education." I paused as Ma capped her lipstick and rubbed her now-vermilion lips together in a gesture I recalled watching as a child. She pulled out a compact, opened it, and checked the results of her efforts in the mirror. Satisfied, she put the lipstick and compact back in her purse and clicked it shut.

"Dom was such a good soul," said Ma. "Like your father." I started. This was the highest compliment Ma could pay any man and not one she bestowed lightly. She usually reserved it for her grandson.

At her mention of my father, my eyes had filled, so I was caught off guard when she said, "As for that brother-in-law, well, according to Dom, he was a real sad sack, a born sucker. And like they always say, if you're in a card game and you don't know who the sucker is, you're it."

Ma's cryptic cameo of Emilio was interesting, but it paled beside my realization that Ma and Dom had apparently been close enough to discuss family members and share confidences. Had Ma and Dom been—I flinched inwardly even as I grudgingly allowed this concept access to my brain—involved? I felt a sudden belated kinship with my kids who were astonished when, after my divorce, I began dating occasionally. But Ma was not forty-something. She was eighty-something. Could my bereaved Jewish mother, a former court stenographer with a penchant for poker possibly have been involved with an Italian-Catholic widower who cleaned schools for a living and was passionate about pigeons? Again I saw Dom's serious gray eyes, recalled his sweet disposition. I realized also that this unlikely romance, if that's what it had been, had blossomed beneath my nose in the memoir class when I'd divided the group into pairs of writing partners. Dom and Ma had been partners a couple of times.

Often in my classes writing partners became friends or, occasionally, more than that. But Ma? Before I could banish the possibility of Ma being romantically involved with anyone, I heard Sofia's words echoing in my head. When I had asked her about Dom's wife, she had said, "Like I was telling your mother," or something close to that. They hadn't been questioning the cause of Dom's death. Rather Ma must have asked Sofia about Dom's wife. Why would she do that? Because she was interested in him. After all, hadn't I grilled Sol's son-in-law, Xhi, about Sol's ex-wife at the first opportunity? A new love interest is usually curious about the woman who preceded her.

The possibility of some kind of bond between Ma and Dom raised new questions. What else had Dom confided in Ma about his relatives that might be helpful? Did Ma and Sofia, in fact, harbor any notions that Dom's death was not an accident? Did they know that Flora had asked me to look into it? Should I tell them of my involvement? I was so preoccupied with these questions that it wasn't until I was face-to-face with Emilio "Patch" DeFranco that I confirmed the accuracy of Dom's unflattering description of him. But that was later. First I needed to see what Illuminada had managed to learn about Emilio and Leo.

 **Chapter 15**

To: Bbarrett@circle.com
From: pwrichards@lineone.co.uk
Re: Soggy and Suicidal in Hoboken
Date: 02/19/03 07:59:23

Dear S & S,

In my Kegels clinic at National Health, my Kegels coach
advocates using a visualization tool along with biofeedback to help one contract the right muscles, you know,
down there. It's quite simple really. What she says we
should do while we're Kegeling is pretend we're meeting
the queen. After all, one wouldn't want to pass gas when
meeting the queen, so one sort of holds one's tush. This
has worked jolly well for me. I'm quite certain you can devise an American equivalent. Cheerio!

Priscilla

While considering sending Priscilla a tape of *The
Vagina Monologues,* I did try to imagine an American

version of her visualization tool. Was there an active American political leader inspirational enough to motivate me to "hold my tush"? The idea was, unfortunately, laughable, too laughable, and so, ironically, Priscilla's well-intentioned suggestion became part of the problem rather than the solution. But because it amused me so much, I shared it with Illuminada and Betty when we got together that evening at Betty's condo.

"Don't make me laugh like that again, Bel," Betty said as she emerged from the bathroom wiping her eyes with a Kleenex. "You're not the only one whose bladder is competing with her tear ducts."

This was news to me. I'd not realized that Betty shared my predicament. It was hard to imagine her having a body part that she couldn't control. Besides, she was five years younger than I was. "You have SUI?" I said. "You never mentioned it."

I must have sounded reproachful because Illuminada chimed in, "Well, *chiquita*, don't take it personally. Not all of us are comfortable broadcasting our elimination problems."

"I couldn't have put it better myself," Betty said. "But now you know my sordid little secret. And, girlfriend, if one of those dripping dames you channel online comes up with an answer, let me know because, in case you haven't noticed, I'm wearing a path to the powder room lately."

"I'll forward you the ideas I've gotten so far," I said. "What does your doctor say?"

"I work for a living, so I don't have time to go rushing off to the doctor for every little thing," Betty said. I remembered that neither she nor Illuminada had had a mammography until I dragged them to the Englewood Imaging Center a few years ago.

"What does yours say?" she asked. My doctor-phobic friends saw no contradiction in exploiting my tendency to seek medical attention for every hangnail. They always asked me for a second opinion, second-hand that is, about their own maladies.

"Oops. I've not mentioned it to her in years," I said. "It wasn't so bad once I started taking estrogen. But now that I've parted from my patch, it's a real nui-sance. I actually bought some sanitary napkins." The fact that Illuminada was not reminding us of the time made me wonder if, maybe, she too suffered from SUI. But Illuminada had experienced an easy, hot flash–free menopause and she was Betty's age. Could she possi-bly have a flawed pelvic floor? Then I remembered her bout with breast cancer. Even Illuminada was not to-tally immune to the scourges of midlife. Maybe she was a closeted SUI sufferer.

"The incontinence pads are much better," Betty said. "They're worth the extra money."

"Well, *chiquitas,* this is very interesting, but are we going to sit here all night doing commercials for dia-pers, or are you going to listen to what I've found out about Emilio DeFranco and Leo Tomaselli?" Illumi-nada's tone was not quite as strident as usual, confirm-ing my suspicion that our conversation had not been totally devoid of interest to her.

"I'm all ears," I said, settling into the welcoming cor-ner of Betty's leather sofa and curling my stocking feet beneath me. "Especially since, to be honest, I didn't get anything too new or exciting from Sofia and Ma. We're still looking at a gambling bachelor brother-in-law and a charming bad-boy son. So what did you get?"

Illuminada was curled in the big easy chair opposite the sofa and spoke from notes on a printout that she held in her lap. She was getting used to trifocals, so she lowered her head when she referred to the sheet of data. Her black hair bisected by a silver stripe curtained her eyes, but her slightly accented words were clearly audible. "Emilio DeFranco has had a few parking tickets, and he was arrested for passing a bad check. But the charges were dropped when it became clear that he had no idea the check was no good. Someone had given it to him to pay a debt." I nodded, remembering that, according to Ma, Dom had considered Emilio a sucker. Dom was right. Not only did Emilio lose big to the wrong guys, but even when he won, he couldn't collect.

"Anything else? Any gambling related problems? Were you able to get access to his financial records?"

"Would I still be in business if I couldn't check people's finances?" Illuminada asked with exaggerated huffiness. "He has about $750,000 in the bank. Most of it's been there since last March. He put it in CDs. I wish I had his finances." She sighed, no doubt recalling the loss she and Raoul had taken when the stock market tanked.

"Didn't he sell his house? That must be where he got that big chunk of change." Betty was good at answering her own questions. "Damn. I sure wish I'd put my 401K in CDs." In the wake of the market's imitation of the Titanic, the much maligned CD had certainly made a comeback.

"Even now I think CDs are an odd investment for an inveterate gambler. And it seems odder still that a gambler who's a loser still has the money he acquired almost a year ago," I said, once again thinking aloud. "And that's it?" I addressed this question to Illuminada. "Nothing about his gambling?"

"No, just his work history," she said with a glance at the paper in front of her. "And it's very ho-hum. He worked as an installer for Allen's Draperies and Blinds until he retired right around the time the store went out of business. And that, *chiquitas,* really is it. I'm sorry, Bel." I was sorry too, but not surprised.

"Well, if most of the money from the sale of the house is still in the bank, it's unlikely that he paid Dom," I mused. "Unless maybe he has some other source of income that isn't traceable. Flora will be disappointed to have her theory shot down, but it doesn't look as if her Uncle Emilio had any reason to push his elderly brother-in-law off the roof to his death. But I'll still talk with him. I have to try to find out what, if anything, about him didn't make it into his rather innocuous paper trail."

"Was there anything more interesting on Leo?" I asked, rearranging myself on the sofa.

"Not really," said Illuminada. "He was expelled from St. Paul's Preparatory School for breaking the nose of a kid he thought made a pass at his girl of the moment. So he graduated from Hoboken High a couple of years late. He played soccer. He was picked up once with a bunch of other young people who were brawling in the street after the bars closed and was released with a warning and a fine. At twenty-one he married Claudia Alston of Morristown, New Jersey. They rented an apartment in Jersey City. He worked for a photographer in New York, where she modeled for a little over a year, and then he got a job at a film-developing shop in Hoboken. When his boss retired, Leo was able to buy the business although not the building it was in. It was called Second Street Photo and was on the corner of Washington and Second, where the Johnny Rockets is now." Illuminada looked up to see if we were still with her.

"I kind of remember that place," I said. Hoboken businesses came and went like germs in a day-care center. It was impossible to keep track of them all.

"He finally gave up the store, and two years ago he enrolled in a certificate program in real estate at RECC. Since he finished, he's been licensed and works with Smythe & Higgins."

"What about his wife?" asked Betty, beating me to the question.

"They had a kid, John Dominic, in 1985. He filed for no-fault divorce and sole custody in 1986 and moved back in with his father after that. He has a pile of unpaid parking tickets. I didn't follow up on the ex-wife. Do you want me to?"

"Not yet." I was quiet for a minute, digesting all the data Illuminada had unearthed about Leo and wishing it included something even slightly sinister. Fistfights fueled by adolescent jealousy and drunken rowdiness were common and regrettable but not predictable precursors to patricide. And naming his son after his father was hardly the act of a man who would later push said father off the roof.

"Well, don't even bother asking what I learned," said Betty in the voice of a pouting diva. "I mean what could I possibly learn about Leo Tomaselli from his spiritual advisor that would interest either of you?" Betty's eyes glowed with pleasure. She always enjoyed making us beg for information.

I obliged. "Okay, okay, Betty. Please tell us. Please," I said in the voice of a whiny child. Illuminada responded to this ritual by sticking her finger down her throat and pointing to her watch.

"Damn!" Betty grabbed her head with both hands. Before Illuminada and I could react with alarm, she said, "I made us some popcorn and hot cider and then you all got me going so I forgot to bring it in. It's probably cold by now. Damn! Damn! Damn!" Illuminada's eyes lit up. Popcorn was one of the few foods that tempted her to overindulge. She could turn her back on an open bag of M&M's, but she would sell her mother for a bag of popcorn, the more buttery the better.

"Relax, *chiquita*, better late than never!" Illuminada called to Betty. *"Dios mío,* remember the time I forgot to serve the salad until after we'd finished the flan?" Illuminada chuckled as she spoke. Clearly the prospect of popcorn worked on her like a mood enhancer. But I had to chuckle too. We all had stories of serving dinners that were missing whole courses because of our increasingly unreliable short-term memories.

"It was good when you did serve it, though, a nice palate cleanser," I said. "I told you about the time when I forgot to serve the cranberry sauce at Thanksgiving and nobody missed it, remember? Then Sol's mom mentioned it in her thank-you note. Leave it to her. That woman is something else."

"She's a piece of work, all right, but I liked her the one time I met her. It'll be good to see her again at your wedding," said Illuminada.

Before I could contemplate the role Sol's eccentric mother might play in our as yet unscheduled and unplanned wedding, Betty re-entered. She carried a bowl, big enough to swim in, brimming with fragrant popcorn in one hand and a pitcher of steaming mulled cider in the other. "I nuked everything," she announced, lowering the goodies to the coffee table. When she returned this time, she brought mugs, napkins, and individual bowls. She poured cider while we helped ourselves to popcorn.

But fulfilling her role as hostess did not prevent Betty, always a formidable, if forgetful, multitasker, from telling us what she had found out about Leo Tomaselli. "Actually, Father Santos didn't tell me anything that wasn't public information. He met Leo years ago when he christened John, Leo's son. The boy's mother wasn't Catholic, so there was some sort of to-do, but nonetheless Father Santos christened the baby. Then when Father needed a soccer coach for a church youth-league team, he asked Leo to do it. Leo coached at St. Paul's for years. I asked if that was because John played on the church team, and Father Santos said John played off and on, but the boy is really not an athlete. He spends a lot of time on his schoolwork. Apparently Leo coached because he likes kids and he likes soccer." When Betty stopped talking, she raised the mug of cider to her lips and sipped it. Then, smiling sweetly, she said, "So that's not exactly the profile of a stone killer, is it?"

"Damn, Betty, after that buildup, I thought you'd really learned something useful. Father Santos didn't say anything about Leo's drinking or his divorce or his relationship with his father?" I made no effort to hide the fact that I was disappointed although, again, not too surprised.

"If he knew anything about any of that stuff, he wouldn't be able to share it," said Betty. "He did say that the loss of Dom was a blow to all the survivors, especially Leo, but we knew that. Father Santos seems to have taken Leo under his wing a long time ago. Maybe that's really why Leo coached." Betty didn't even sound defensive about the fact that the data she had supplied about Leo made the man seem an increasingly unlikely candidate for patricide.

"*Dios mío,* you don't think there was anything between them like, you know . . . ?" Illuminada raised the question I had briefly entertained and then dismissed.

"No, I don't. I told you, Father Santos does not sexually abuse his parishioners," said Betty, looking exasperated. In the climate of distrust spawned by the recent revelations of widespread child sexual abuse by Catholic clergy, she was used to defending her beloved priest.

"Maybe Leo just appreciated the interest Father Santos took in him because Dom had been so preoccupied with his pigeons," I said, recalling Sofia's description of Dom's priorities. "I assume Sofia didn't tell me any of this because Father Santos's parish is in Jersey City and her network is not as reliable there." Again I was thinking aloud. "I'm just going to have to go talk to Leo and Emilio myself and see what I can get out of them."

"Okay, *chiquita,* but easier said than done if you don't want them to catch on that you suspect them of murdering Dom," said Illuminada. It always amazed me how that woman, a modern female Demosthenes and a non-native speaker at that, could enunciate perfectly clearly around a mouthful of popcorn. "You need a plan."

I have to admit I was pleased by how surprised both my friends looked when I announced, "I have a plan. In fact, I have two plans."

Betty put her empty mug on the coffee table and stood, "Well, girlfriend, wait until I get back, and then tell." She took off to the bathroom. When she returned in a few minutes, she said simply, "Okay, now go ahead."

Illuminada just pointed at her watch and refilled her bowl.

"Okay. My first plan is simple. I'll join the happy hordes of home buyers apparently unaffected by the stock market's dive. There are lots of them eager to cash in on the new low-interest rates by buying one of Hoboken's highly prized and even more highly priced row houses."

"God bless them, big spenders all," intoned Betty.

"I'll use Leo Tomaselli as a realtor." I sat back and made no effort to mask my smile of satisfaction.

"But Leo has met you. He has to know you already live here," said Illuminada, sounding annoyed that I'd overlooked such an obvious problem.

I was ready for her and leaned forward to speak. "Right, but if Leo or anybody else who already knows me asks why I, who already have a Hoboken home, am looking at another one, I'll tell them I'm scouting for my daughter who's moving East." I sank back into my corner of the sofa and waited for a reaction. Illuminada and Betty both smiled. That Rebecca, Keith, and Abbie J would some day leave Seattle and move back to New Jersey where they belonged was, in fact, a long-cherished and totally unfounded fantasy of mine. That they, who had no home to sell, could afford to buy one in Hoboken, where, since the seventies, real estate had continued to appreciate beyond all imagining, was equally farfetched. But although Betty and Illuminada were privy to this, Leo Tomaselli wasn't, so my plan was solid, and they knew it.

"It works, *chiquita,*" said Illuminada with a grin. "Just remember, things have changed since the last time you looked for a house. Today Rebecca would pick out properties she sees on-line and ask you to preview them for her." Illuminada was right, of course.

I looked at Betty to see what constructive suggestions she might have. "You go, girl," was all she said. "Just hope your realtor doesn't figure out what you're really up to when you two are alone in an empty house. Maybe Sol should go with you." And then, as if she couldn't pass up the chance to bug me, she turned to Illuminada and asked, "Wouldn't you think that a woman who could come up with a foolproof plan for an undercover investigation of two murder suspects could pull together a simple wedding?"

Illuminada yawned and said, "It's really late. Let's not go there tonight. Plan B?" She looked at me expectantly.

"Emilio is one of two or three surviving members of the Hoboken Racing Pigeon Club. Sarah Woolf and I are doing a feature story on the club for the paper. She'll do the photos and I'll do the interview. She'll actually publish it. She's setting it up for next week." I was pleased with the simplicity of this familiar arrangement. "There's no cover to blow, so I can use my own name."

Illuminada stood. "Sounds good, *chiquita*. It's worked before." She walked toward the bedroom, where Betty had stashed our coats. "Let's go if you want that ride." We had come in Illuminada's car, so I followed her into the bedroom.

When we stood at the door bundled into our bulky coats, Betty said, "Vic and I are going down the shore to strip paint again this coming weekend. If you two and Sol and Raoul would come down in a few weeks when we start steaming off wallpaper, I promise all the popcorn and M&M's you can eat and two terrific restaurant meals on us. We figure we could get the whole first floor done in one weekend if we all do it.

Randy's going to come down and help too. So why don't you let us know which weekend would work for the four of you? Or would you rather I just e-mail you some dates and you can get back to me? I'll do that. Good night." Betty, having at last organized the work party she wanted, stood in the doorway waving.

As Illuminada and I walked to opposite sides of the car, she said, "I don't remember saying yes, do you?" She sighed. "But I guess we're going to a painting party."

"Looks that way," I replied. We both knew better than to argue with Betty when her mind was made up. "Somehow a visit to the shore in late winter is less than appealing, and I get sore muscles when I even think about lifting a roller, but I guess they really need help, so we'll go and do our bit. Betty and Vic always come through for us."

"That's for sure. Anyway, if we help paint now, we can freeload without guilt this summer," said Illuminada as she backed the car out of Betty's driveway. "I could get into July and August weekends down the shore, couldn't you?"

"I guess so," I answered half-heartedly. At that moment the summer pleasures of surf and sand seemed remote. My mind was occupied with drafting the script I would use when I called Leo Tomaselli.

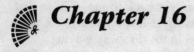

Chapter 16

To: Bbarrett@circle.com
From: Rebecca@uwash.edu
Re: your wedding
Date: 02/19/03 19:45:17

Mom,

Please give us as much of a heads-up as you can before your wedding. Keith and I both have to arrange to get the time off. He'll have to get a friend who manages another complex to pinch-hit for him, and I'll have to give them a lot of notice at both the restaurant and the clinic. If there's anything I can do from here, let me know. If you send me the invitations, I can address and stuff the envelopes and then stamp and mail them. And, Ma, please don't even think about getting married in that gray tent with the fringed sleeves that you wear to everything. I don't want to fly three thousand miles to see my mom looking like the big spender at a New Age toga sale. Get something new and sexy

and e-mail me a photo before you take the tags off.
Gotta rush.

Love,
Rebecca

This was a pretty stern message from the daughter
who, not too many years ago, had announced her own
impending wedding and her pregnancy in one unfor-
gettable e-mail. But Rebecca was right. Sol and I
would have to settle on a date soon if we expected our
kids to be in attendance when we exchanged vows. For
a brief moment I felt galvanized. We could set a date
before we made up a guest list! But even as I pictured
us doing that, my latent inner wedding planner reminded me that the size of the guest list would determine the venue, and, in turn, the availability of the
venue would determine the date. There was no getting
around it, Sol and I had to sit down and compile a
guest list. We had both written doctoral dissertations
and countless academic papers, so surely we could
write down the names of the people we wanted at our
wedding. I resolved to speak to him about it as soon as
he got back from his latest babysitting junket.

Having once again put off taking action, I glanced
anew at Rebecca's message. The thought of shopping
for a wedding dress was almost as paralyzing as the
thought of committing to a guest list. I liked my gray
knit dress. I liked it when I bought it in 1992, and I still
liked it. In '92 the dress had flowed around my body in
soft silver folds that contrasted with my dark hair.
More recently it hugged what I tried to think of as my
curves and complemented my mostly gray frizz.

But maybe my fashion-savvy daughter was right,

and I should get something new. If only Rebecca lived
nearby, we could go shopping together, and that would
be fun. The image of us cloistered in a dressing room
deciding on skirt lengths and colors stayed with me so
that by the time I phoned Leo Tomaselli, I had practically convinced myself that my cover story was real
and that my daughter was coming back to Hoboken to
live. I had already proved that I was a match for Leo
Tomaselli, who would, after all, be trying to sell me a
house, not hurt me. I made an appointment for the next
afternoon, using Rebecca's husband's last name. A
quick on-line search had brought up two row houses
that met Keith and Rebecca's imaginary criteria, and I
asked to see them. Leo offered to pick me up and show
me both properties.

I was ready when he phoned from his cell to say that
he was double-parked outside. I bundled up in my red
coat and hurried to meet him. When I had made my
way to the passenger side of the car, I saw that Leo was
on the phone. He reached over and opened the door,
but he didn't really look at me, so I had a few moments
to reassess him. I barely recognized the man. Away
from Flora's maternal aura, he looked older, more like
the forty-something he was. At Dom's funeral and on
the roof he had been stubble-faced and disheveled, but
today he was clean shaven, and his slicked-back dark
hair looked newly trimmed. I was close enough to see
the few strands of silver that already highlighted that
carefully coifed hair and the lines around his mouth
and eyes. A pale blue shirt collar and the knot of a
cranberry-print tie were visible at the open neck of his
gray parka.

After a moment or two Leo pocketed his phone and
turned in my direction, presumably to offer a greeting.

But when he recognized me, his eyebrows contracted, and a crimson flush crept up from beneath his collar. His outstretched hand froze over the gearshift between us. Talking as fast as I could, I grabbed that suspended hand, shook it, and settled myself into the passenger seat. "Listen, Leo. Forget about the other day. You were upset, and, believe me, I understand. I lost my own dad not too long ago." I lowered my eyes, and swiped at them with the back of my gloved fingers. "Rebecca Roche is my daughter, and she and her husband want to move back East with my grandbaby." Again I lowered my eyes and swiped at them. "Her husband Keith's got a great job offer in Manhattan, so if they can find a place . . ."

I let the sentence dangle. Leo gripped the wheel with both gloved hands, but made no move to drive. He took a deep breath, and, for a moment, I wondered if he reacted to stress the way his sister did, in which case I would probably have to do respiratory therapy. When he swiveled to face me, I saw that the gray eyes boring into mine were his father's. When he finally spoke, Leo's words were neither unpredictable nor interrupted by anxiety-fueled inhalations, but his hands still clutched the steering wheel. "You're Flo's prof, and you taught my old man too. It was decent of you to come to see Flo at the house. I'm sorry about the scene I made." He faced the steering wheel and shook his head at the memory, as if by doing so he could dislodge it from his head. "Flo's right. I shouldn't drink." Leo faced me again and managed a tentative but winning smile. "I appreciate your giving me another chance. I'll try to help you find your daughter and son-in-law a house."

As we pulled away from the snow-piled curbside, I

had to admire Leo's straightforward manner and his attempt to salvage his professionalism. "I suppose everybody tells you this, but you have your dad's eyes. I was very fond of him. His classmates and I miss him." Leo nodded, squinting in the glare of the sun reflecting off the snow that lined the street. "Everyone enjoyed his memoir, too. We all learned a lot about pigeons," I said.

"I bet you did," Leo said. "My old man was all about pigeons." After we had driven just a few blocks, Leo executed a classic Hoboken parking option. He pulled the car into a spot in front of a fire hydrant that he seemed to view as a vertical welcome sign, red against the snow piled around it. Then he flipped on the hazard lights. "Come on, Professor. This first place is around the corner on Sixth Street. Right here's as close as I can park. Let's take a look." Before I had even picked up my purse, Leo was out of the car and around to my side holding open the door. "And while we're walking through, you can tell me a little about what the young people want. Like how many kids do they have? Do they need a yard? A home office? Do they work out? You know, the stuff that will help me to know what else to show you in case you don't like what you see today."

The narrow two-story house was apparently empty, but Leo opened it with a key he carried and followed me in silence as I walked from the living room to a genuinely vintage eat-in kitchen, the only two rooms on what is known in Hoboken as the parlor floor. "No bathroom down here?" I asked, knowing the answer.

"No. But you could probably put in a small one off the kitchen," he shrugged. "There's a pantry that might work. See." He held open the door to a closet with floor-to-ceiling shelves. "She must have done a lot of canning," he said. "Nice little yard, though. How many kids they got?"

"One so far," I said, picturing Abbie J in this house just a few blocks from mine. I followed Leo over to the kitchen window, where he stood looking out at the snow-covered patch of yard. "In warm weather they had a garden here," he said. "Vegetables and flowers."

"I know. I saw it on the website," I said. "It was lovely. My daughter's a physical therapist and my son-in-law is in insurance," I offered. "Neither one of them works at home." There was no point in telling Leo that Keith was really an on-site property manager, somewhere between a super and a concierge, whose benefit package usually included an apartment in the fancy complexes he managed. Meanwhile I became aware that playing the part of the potential buyer was interfering with my ability to size up a murder suspect. I needed to get Leo to talk about himself and his father. "You know, I hate thinking of the way your dad died, out there in the cold without anybody knowing where he was."

"I do too," said Leo, suddenly making a fist and banging it against the wall next to the window where we stood. "Believe me, Professor, I do too. But you know, it's funny, me and my sister were afraid something like that would happen. He used to wander around on that roof talking to those damn birds at all hours. And a couple of times he wandered off into the neighborhood and disappeared for a half a day." Leo turned to face me. "He was a little better when he started taking that course of yours. He took his meds, so he'd feel good enough to write. It helped him a lot." Leo sounded more polished than Flora, but then she had been at home until recently and he had been running a business.

"That must have been a big relief to you and Flora," I said, hoping his expansiveness would continue.

"Yeah and our kids too, the both of them. My boy, John, was very attached to the old man and Flo's Mary, she was too. And my sister," Leo added, rolling his eyes. "Flo was making herself crazy, Professor. She probably didn't let on to you, but when the old man started to lose it, her hair started falling out in big clumps. Finally she had to go on meds herself just to cope with him not taking his meds. Can you beat that?" Leo rubbed his forehead as if Flora's visceral connection to their father confounded him.

"It must have made you angry to see her so upset," I said. I had no idea if this was true, but it was bound to provoke a reaction, perhaps in the form of a revelation.

"Nah. I know where Flo's coming from. I was like that when our mother got sick." For the first time, Leo's face clouded and he blinked. "I was my mother's favorite, but Flo was always daddy's girl." Leo shrugged. "My mother never spoiled her like she spoiled me." He blinked again. "And my dad . . . well, he didn't hit me or nothing like that, but Flo was, like they say, the apple of his eye right from the start. When she was a kid, she helped with the birds. I wasn't interested in those damn birds.

"C'mon," he said brusquely, as if he suddenly remembered why we were there. I followed Leo up the single flight of stairs to what was the bedroom floor. There were two small bedrooms, a bathroom with antiquated fixtures that would not be featured in a Restoration Hardware display anytime soon, and a hall closet. "This's it?" I asked, disappointment dripping from every short word. "It looked so much bigger in the pictures on-line, and I don't really know how to imagine square footage." I sighed. It was getting easier and easier to see Abbie J occupying one of those tiny rooms and harder and harder to see Leo as a murderer. Even the memory of him silhouetted against the late afternoon sky as he threw his sister to the ground was fading in the glow cast by the possibility of grand-mothering up close.

"We should talk money," Leo said, sounding re-lieved to be discussing business. "What's their range?" Leo was ushering me ahead of him and down the stairs as he spoke.

"The kids are prepared to go as high as $700,000." Leo didn't blink at this low figure. Everybody knew that larger three-story homes in Hoboken often sold for a lot more than that. "My husband and I will help with the down payment. I think we need to be looking at slightly bigger homes in that range. The other one they wanted me to look at is bigger, isn't it?"

"Yes. That one's three stories. Let's take a ride up there. And I have another one I'd like to show you that I just got the listing for. It's not even on-line yet." Leo turned and flashed a smile of encouragement, and I re-called Sofia's mention of him as having once been a charmer.

"It's hard for me to have family so far away. It must have been great for you and your son to grow up under the same roof with his grandfather and an aunt and a cousin," I said once we had resettled in the car.

"It would have been better for him to grow up with his mother around," Leo answered, his hands tighten-ing on the steering wheel.

This was more than I'd hoped for. I didn't even have

to contrive to raise the subject of his marriage. "I assume you're divorced. I am too. It was hard on my kids, but they're okay now. Did your ex live nearby when your son was growing up?"

Leo shrugged. "I lost track of the bitch about ten years ago, when she stopped sending him Christmas cards." Leo made no effort to hide his bitterness. "For a while she lived in Brooklyn, but she didn't see much of John. She never wanted a baby, and I wouldn't let her get rid of him. She didn't want any part of us after he was born." Leo ran his fingers slowly through his hair as if to massage away a painful memory.

"Did she have a career that a baby would have interfered with?" I asked.

"Nah. She was in school, art school. I met her in a bar. I was on the rebound."

Leo's short sentences indicated his distaste for the topic, but I persisted. "Oh?"

Leo's attempt at a laugh came out as a self-deprecating snort. "Yeah, Professor, I was on the rebound from my mother." I didn't react, hoping he would go on. "After she died, I spent a lot of time in bars. And Claudia, she looked a lot like my mother did in the photos we have of her when she was young. So I married her."

A small pickup truck was parked at the hydrant he had been headed for, so Leo began to cruise the block looking for a legitimate space. We made several circles before he spotted someone pulling out a few doors down from the FOR SALE sign that, I assumed, marked our destination. "This place is being sold because the guy just up and left," said Leo, neatly making the transition from his personal story to the business we ostensibly had between us. "The couple only bought it a few years ago.

They fixed up part of it, and now they're splitting. No kids, though," he added as if to reassure me.

This house was an imposing three-story brownstone on a lovely tree-lined block of Bloomfield Street. Rebecca would love it. Again Leo let us in, and we stood in the foyer while I got my bearings. Leo took a phone call, so I began to wander through the rooms on the parlor floor. "Does the fireplace work?" I asked when he joined me in front of the imposing mantel of blush-colored marble. "I can't recall what it said in the on-line ad."

"No. They hadn't gotten around to having it restored yet. But that's not hard. Goes for a couple of thou," he said beginning to circle the empty room. "Great exposure. Lots of natural light here. And lots of original detail. Look at that plasterwork on the ceiling," he said pointing overhead at the wreath of molded flowers twining around the periphery of the room. "This is a classy property. You know, Professor, it's a great investment too." We were staring out the window of the kitchen into a spacious yard with a big tree in front of a wooden fence that followed the property line. "You say there's a basement apartment here?" I asked. "The kids could use the income from that to pay for this."

"Well, it's not exactly an apartment yet, but it just needs a kitchen," Leo replied. I winced, having recently endured a kitchen renovation from which Sol and I were still recovering, both psychically and financially. "There's already a full bath down there and a big room. You could easily make a really marketable studio out of it," said Leo. "Want to see it?"

"Sure, but let's look at the upstairs first." We quickly toured the two large bedrooms with the bath off the connecting hall on the second floor and went up to the

next floor. The large airy room at the top of the stairs
had a pitched roof and small windows high up on the
walls. "Used to be the servants' quarters," Leo said. I
hardly heard him, so busy was I envisioning the room
as Abbie J's playroom, a home for her countless toys
in primary colors, her books, her crayons and paints,
her CDs and her Playdoh. Just as I pictured her latest
finger paintings hanging by clothespins from wires
strung along the walls, Leo's voice interrupted,
"Wouldn't this make a great study?"

"I guess so. It would also be an interesting artist's
studio. Didn't you say your ex-wife was an artist?" I
asked, hoping this demi-sequitur would prompt Leo to
reveal more about himself.

"Yeah, I did," he said. "The bitch was an artist. But
listen, Professor, what's with all the interest in my ex?
Are you buying a house or auditioning me for Jerry
Springer?" I felt a tightening in my gut. Leo's voice
was suddenly menacing and his words bounced off the
angled walls and echoed in the empty room. Leo the
obliging broker had reverted to Leo the psychotic axe-
wielding abuser without the axe. Why hadn't I waited
until Sol was around to come with me? Leo reached
into his pocket. Did he have a gun? I froze. He stood
between me and the stairs. How had I let that happen?
I could feel sweat beading my scalp.

Just as I shifted my weight and braced to dodge a
bullet or make a dash around him for the stairs, I heard
a woman's voice. "You'll just love the top floor. It used
to be the maids' room, but it would make a terrific
home office or studio or even a nursery . . ." There
were booted footsteps on the stairs. Another realtor
was showing the house. I probably owed my life to
multiple listing.

I glanced at my watch and then at Leo and said, "I'm sorry. I didn't mean to offend you. It's gotten late, and I have another appointment. I'll walk home from here. You can show me the basement apartment another time. Thank you." I pushed past the three people making their way up the stairs, leaving Leo to descend on his own.

Chapter 17

Dominic Tomaselli (con't.)

Like I said before when I enlisted in
WW II I was in the Pigeon Service of
the US Army Signal Corps in Ft. Monmouth, NJ, I brought a lot of my best
birds with me and donated them to the
army and trained pigeons there until I
went overseas. Well it was vets from
that same unit coming home from WWI
that started our club. Way back then
they didn't even have a building but
that didn't stop them. Sometime in the
1930s, now I forget what year, the members put one up themselves, they used
donated wood and brick and the skills
they had. It don't look like much, especially now with them big buildings
all around it but we used to have over
a hundred members and when it came time
to register for a big race we had to

hire cops to stand by the door to keep
things orderly. . . .

Eager to see the interior of Dom's pigeon club, I was
glad I'd arranged to go there with Sarah, especially
after Leo's outburst. When I told Sol about that, he responded as I'd predicted he would. Initially he was
angry that I hadn't waited for him to accompany me.
"What the hell is the matter with you, Bel? Do you
have a death wish? The minute I turn my back you're
doing a bad imitation of a postmenopausal Lone
Ranger. Do I have to follow you around like Tonto to
keep you from getting into situations you can't get out
of?" was how he put it.

It was hard not to giggle at the image of us as portly
midlife Jewish versions of the masked cowboy hero
and his trusty sidekick, but I managed. "Sol, I did get
out of that situation," I reminded him. "And I told you
I don't know if Leo really had a gun. I might have exaggerated the whole thing. You know I tend to do that.
He's probably just another divorced dad with a mega
chip on his shoulder. He's mad at his ex-wife, he's mad
at his poor dead father . . . and now, he's mad at me," I
said. "He'll have to get a grip if he's going to make it
as a realtor. No one wants to deal with an agent who
goes ballistic."

"Sounds like he's an alcoholic who's off the sauce.
They have very short fuses," said Sol. I was relieved
that he was now speculating on what made Leo tick
rather than chastising me. "All their impulse control is
focused on not drinking. They don't have any will
power or discretion left to keep them from giving in to
the urge to rant or fight."

I resolved to review the long list of alcoholics we

knew who no longer drank to see if they conformed to
Sol's interesting theory, but first I wanted to get back
to my rereading of Dom's journal. While I was envisioning the pigeon fanciers orchestrating a kind of
urban barn-raising to build their club, Sol sat hunched
over the Sunday *New York Times* staring at photos of
young American soldiers, many younger than Mark,
trekking towards Baghdad, vulnerable. Frowning, Sol
looked up from the paper. "Sarah's right," he announced. "We should be making love, not war. Let's
make a list of guests. Come on."

"In a few minutes," I said. I didn't want to discour-
age his attempt to ward off the fears those photos inspired in him, but I really needed to finish reading. "I
just got to the part about the races and I want to finish
it."

"Jesus, Bel, how many times have you read that
damn thing?" Sol's question was purely rhetorical, so
he didn't wait for an answer. "Refresh my memory,
would you? Wasn't checking out this Tomaselli guy's
murder supposed to be a walk in the park, a no-
brainer?" Sol's sarcastic question, although articulated
in deep and measured tones, resonated with his growing resentment. "Bel, the real no-brainer is our guest
list. If you'd spare fifteen minutes to go over it with
me, we'd have it done. See?" He reached over and ex-
tracted a piece of paper and a pen from a drawer behind him. "I've already started it. You can add names.
Here." To my amazement, he handed me the sheet of
paper, which had a column of names on it.

I put Dom's journal aside, reached for the paper, and
glanced at the names. At once I noted glaring omis-
sions. "What about Wendy's kids? And Sandi's boy?
And Sofia's family?" I could hear my own voice, shrill

against the Oscar Peterson CD that provided the background music for our Sunday morning.

I was just getting warmed up when Sol slid over to my end of the sofa. He tossed Dom's memoir to the floor, took the pen and paper from my hand, very deliberately placed the paper on the coffee table in front of him, leaned forward, and began to append the names I had reeled off to those already listed. Without looking up, he said, "In fact, you don't have to write a single word. I'll just add those people myself. What's Sandi's boy's name?"

"Joel," I said, dumbfounded by the fact that we were actually, at long last, Making Up the Guest List. "And what about Xhi's parents? They're Maya's other grandparents. You can't leave them out." My voice sounded less shrill. Sol kept on writing. "Let me see that list again, please," I asked, hoping to atone for my mini-scream fest. Sol handed it to me. I scrutinized it carefully this time. "It's a little short on neighbors. Besides the Illysarios and Felice Aquino and, of course, Luci, I'd like to have Joey P and Tony. And you don't have Delphine here, either."

"That's why we're doing this together," Sol said, looking up from the paper, which now had the beginnings of a second column of names on it. "In fact, love, that's why we're getting married. I'm useless without you." He grinned and began to hum the tune to some obscure old love song that only he knew. His gentle humor and gravelly voice reminded me yet again why I was marrying him.

After I had made several more additions to the list, I said, "I can't think of anyone else. We've got our families, our friends and neighbors, our colleagues. I really think that's it." I grabbed the paper and stared at it.

Then I counted the names. "Okay, so we're still way under a hundred people. It's more than we can afford to feed properly, but fewer than I'd feared."

"Well, now we can just live with this list for a day or two and see if we remember anybody we've left out. Let me scan it and make a few copies." Sol had recently invested in a printer with scanning and copying capability and welcomed any excuse to use it. We now had multiple copies of grocery lists, phone messages, and receipts. In a few minutes he held up several copies of our newly minted guest list. Seeing them, I felt a wave of relief. Now I was free to concentrate on navigating my way through the web the Tomasellis had woven, the web that had trapped Dom. I turned back to his memoir. Rereading it seemed the best way to prepare to meet Emilio DeFranco and the rest of the surviving Hoboken Racing Pigeon Club members the following day.

That morning it was still bone chillingly cold, and fresh snow blanketed the ground. There was not enough to inspire President Woodman to cancel classes, but just enough to force Sol and me to begin our morning with a brisk shoveling session. I rescheduled my memoir-writing class for Wednesday morning so my older students wouldn't have to brave the snow. Even so, by the time I finished teaching my other classes and returned to Hoboken to meet Sarah, I was tired. We connected at the PATH station and commandeered a taxi to take us to the Hoboken Racing Pigeon Club. It would have been possible to walk, but Sarah carried a video camera and other equipment, so we opted for the cab.

"I just can't get over how the west side of this town has changed," Sarah remarked as we passed block after block of condominiums. Some were in renovated schools, and one was in a former fire station. But most of this luxury housing was new construction built after the razing of abandoned warehouses, mills, or boarded up homes and stores. "These condos are really fancy too. Look at that ad," she directed, pointing at a billboard on the wall of a building still under construction. "It's going to have a gym with a lap pool and a landscaped courtyard, and underground parking. Frank Sinatra wouldn't know the place if he came back now," she said.

"Not much chance a that, lady. He didn't come back when he was livin', so he sure ain't gonna show up now," said our cab driver, guffawing at his own humor. Sarah and I smiled at the old man's joke. I was glad we had not said anything about the real motive for our visit to the pigeon club.

"You girls goin' there for the birds or the music?" he asked. In the back seat, Sarah and I exchanged a look that marveled at how, after feminists had waged thirty years of struggle, this chatty Hoboken cabbie could still refer to us as girls. We let it go.

"We're with the *Jersey City Herald*. I'm writing an article about the Hoboken Racing Pigeon Club, and my friend is taking photos," I answered. "What music?"

"I take bands over there sometimes. Parta the club's a recording studio now," he explained as he pulled up in front of a nondescript gray two-story building in the middle of a lot. It was dwarfed by the taller buildings in the surrounding area. The words HOBOKEN RACING PIGEON CLUB were legible over the door. I handed the driver our fare and a generous tip, in spite of his semantic slip. "Thanks, girls. Need help with that?" he asked Sarah who was hauling her equipment out of the front seat, where she had stowed it.

"No thanks," said Sarah sweetly as she flipped the heavy bag over her shoulder with what looked like an effortless motion. Through clenched teeth, she muttered, "Damn. I'll be at the chiropractor's before the week is out after that maneuver." I could tell from her grin, though, that she wasn't sorry if, having failed to impress the old man with her advanced years, she tried to dazzle him with her strength. I took a camera case from her, and we made our way to the door.

Once we crossed the threshold we left the world of condos and the light rail and were transported back to the Hoboken of an earlier era. The small bar with an American flag on the wall behind it filled most of the room. The club looked like a cross between one of the Italian men's clubs that had once been the nucleus of several Hoboken neighborhoods and a very small VFW hall. A closer look revealed that the true focal point of the room was neither the bar nor the flag. It was an oversize blowup of a black-and-white photo elaborately framed and hanging over the door. The subject of this behemoth picture was what appeared to be a truck giving birth to a flock of birds. The truck was parked in a field, its side flaps open and angled upwards, lending the vehicle the appearance of a great winged creature run aground to birth the birds swarming out from beneath the flaps and filling the sky. On the back of the truck was the portrait of a large pigeon in profile with the words HOBOKEN RACING PIGEON CLUB clearly emblazoned in an arc above it.

"Are you goils from the *Jersey City Herald*?" asked a man who rose from a stool at the bar and greeted us in the accent of old, blue collar, pregentrified Hobo-

ken. In those days, men were men and women of all
ages were "goils." Even today, in this world, we were
"goils." Sarah and I didn't even bother to exchange
glances this time. The speaker's posture was stooped,
and his white hair reduced to a thin fringe circling his
bald pate. When he turned towards Sarah, I saw the
quadrant of brown skin that seemed to be stitched onto
his left cheek that had earned him his nickname. I
quickly averted my eyes. If he had seen me stare, he
gave no sign. The gnarled hand he extended signaled
welcome. We all shook hands and exchanged names.
"Patch DeFranco here," he said softly. He certainly did
not look like a killer, but neither had the last murderer
I had exposed, so I reserved judgment.

After a flurry of introductions, Emilio took our coats
and draped them over some chairs on the side of the
room. Sarah was beginning to set up her equipment
when two other elderly men entered, hugging themselves against the cold and stamping the snow off their
boots. One was bandy-legged and wore knee-high
boots and a pea jacket that had seen better days. On his
head was a navy blue wool cap pulled down over his
ears. His unusually pronounced wrinkles hung in folds
above his eyes and around his mouth, almost obscuring
those features. He looked familiar and I wondered if,
perhaps, I had seen him at Dom's wake.

"This here is Tommy Lucca and that's John Derdowski," said Emilio, pointing first to the man in the
pea jacket and then to his companion. "Richie, our
president, he's in a home." Emilo lowered his head for
a moment. "But Tommy here, he was president a few
years ago, right, Tommy?" Tommy nodded. "Ya know,
me, I ain't raced no boids in years and never won
nothin' when I did. But we useta play a lotta cards."

Perhaps it was nostalgia for bygone card games or regret over the races he never won that tinged Emilio's voice with sadness. But his demeanor brightened slightly when he glanced at the small man who was finally peeling off his jacket. "Tommy's a winner like Dom only now he's got arthritis bad like me." Emilio held up his knobby and swollen hand and stared at it as if he found it hard to believe it was his. "But Tommy, he can tell ya about racin' and about this club. His old man was a charter member, right, Tommy?" Tommy smiled shyly and pulled off his cap. I hoped he would prove more talkative when I began to interview him, and I also hoped I would still get to talk with Emilio.

"And this here's John. He's been around longer than God, but he don't race no more on accounta his ticker." Emilio covered his own chest with his hand as he spoke. "But John, he useta have some fine racers, right John?" When John acknowledged this introduction with a smile, it raised only one side of his mouth, as if he'd suffered a stroke. John was taller than his friends and thin with sun-spotted skin and bright blue eyes. He wore a hooded olive green army jacket not unlike one I'd bought in an army-navy store in the seventies and worn until one of the kids appropriated it. "We're all of us vets," Emilio added as an afterthought.

I nodded my appreciation of this information and jumped on it as my opening. "Dom was a vet too. And I'm planning to focus this story on Dom, to make it a kind of tribute to him and to the club," I explained. "By the way, I want you to know that I really appreciate your coming out on such a cold day."

"We ain't got nothin' better ta do," said Tommy. Perhaps fearing that this had not sounded sufficiently altruistic, he added, "And we wanna do right by Dom and da club." John and Emilio smiled agreeably.

"Well, I appreciate your cooperation," I said. "Now before we get started, tell me, do you mind if I tape the interview?" I took out my tape recorder and held it up. When no one protested, I said, "Good. That makes my job so much easier. Thanks." Tommy led the way to a card table off to the side of the room, and we seated ourselves around it. Sarah was moving about the room on her own, photographing whatever she thought we could use in the article. I knew that she was also keeping an eye out for anything at all that might shed light on Dom's death.

I wanted the men to relax and warm up a little in the hope of encouraging them to speak freely and, perhaps, let out something useful. "Before we talk about Dom, though, I need a little background. I don't know anything about pigeon racing. Please tell me, what's that picture all about?" I said, gazing up at the photo of the truck.

Tommy was the first to reply. "Dat's da club truck, da truck we usta have," he said. Then, perhaps realizing that this was obvious from the sign on the rear of the vehicle, he flushed and added, quickly, "Back den tings was different. We could afford ta have our own truck ta take boids ta da release point. Dat's how many members we had, how many boids we sent ta races. Dis club was big back den." Tommy sat straighter in his chair when he recalled the club's former glory.

John added, "Yeah. We had to have cops to do crowd control on the night of a race. That's how many people we had here. It was something else. Of course, that was way before we had to let the music people in. This room was a lot bigger before we put up that partition."

He pointed to a wall on one side of the room. "We own the building outright, but we have a pretty high heat bill." John's voice was matter-of-fact, his accent almost nonexistent.

"I bet," I said, wanting to acknowledge John's contribution, but trying to direct the conversation in what I thought might be a more productive direction. "How far did you drive the birds before letting them go?" I asked, nodding at the picture.

"Hundreds a miles," Tommy said. "In da service guys carried pigeons behind enemy lines, and dey flew back across da Channel ta der home lofts. Dey got like a piece of iron or sompin' in der heads dat tells 'em right where ta go." His voice was soft and reverential.

"Don't they mind being caged up?" I asked, pointing to the photo where I could see the small compartments from which the pigeons emerged.

"Nah. Dose boids were bred ta race. Dey got used ta da trip. In da army GIs useta carry dem into battle in pouches on der chests and da boids got useta dat too. Like I said, dey're bred from racers ta race, dey're trained to race, just like horses. Look ad 'em." Tommy pointed at the walls where framed color portraits of pigeons ringed the room.

Until I met Dom Tomaselli, almost everything I knew about pigeons I had learned one day years ago when I made the mistake of standing under a popular roost at a bus stop. The rest of my pigeon lore I had picked up in yoga classes, where I enjoyed coercing my reluctant hip joints into the pigeon pose. Of course I had noted the pigeons in the rooftop scene in *On the Waterfront,* but then I'd had eyes only for the young and studly Brando. "They don't look much different from regular city pigeons to me," I said.

This time, Emilio spoke first. "Come on, would ya bet yer week's wages on a street rat? That's what we call a pigeon like you see on the street." I nodded to show that I understood. "After the truck took off wit the boids, we used ta sit around this club and have a few and bet real money on them doves 'cause we knew they was blue-blooded racers."

"Yeah, Patch's right. And people pay big bucks for those birds, even today. I once read a newspaper article about a Belgian racing pigeon that sold to a Japanese man for $144,000." John shook his head at the enormity of this transaction. I flinched to hear Emilio's cruel nickname used to his face, but he seemed unperturbed.

"Dat was Playboy in ninety-one. He won da Barcelona race. Dat bird flew 620 miles," said Tommy. "A boid like that sure ain't no street rat, Professor." When he shook his head, wattles beneath his chin swayed back and forth. It occurred to me that, bandy-legged and wattle-necked, Tommy had, perhaps, begun to resemble the birds he so admired. "Look at da thigh muscles on Caesar here and his chest girt. He got real power in dem muscles." I followed Tommy's finger as he pointed at one of the portraits. "Caesar come from a long line a racers."

"He is pretty impressive. And 620 miles. Wow. That's a long way," I said. "Do any of the birds not make it home?"

"Sure," said Tommy. "Hawks get 'em sometimes. And hunters. And we don't race 'em in winter, but dey still got tail winds and summer storms that come up sudden. And now dey got all dese wires and pollution and tall buildin's. You know, in some towns dey got zonin' rules now against pigeons like dey was some

kinda vermin?" More than a trace of bitterness animated Tommy's voice as he recounted this injustice.
"We don't got lofts here at da club no more because of
so many wires and tall buildin's here, da boids can't
make it back." Again he shook his head, setting in motion the folds of his neck.

"Aw, let's face it, Tommy, we don't have lofts here
anymore because most of our members are dead like
Arnie and Luis, and Toro, and now Dom. Or they're
sick or too damn old like poor Richie," said John,
whose eyes darkened as he noted these grim demo-
graphics. "Sam still belongs, but he stopped racing
years ago. He just kept up his membership so he could
come down here on election nights and campaign for
Dino." John smiled, pleased to recall that although
humble now, his club had once been a center of power.
He shook his head as if to exorcise the past. "No, who
you got here today is pretty much what's left of the
club. Even Dom, he stopped racing years ago. It was
his blood pressure wasn't it?"

"John, I'm glad you mentioned Dom," I said without waiting for anyone to reply. The time seemed right
to focus the conversation on my real interest. "Maybe
each of you would share a memory of Dom, and I
could use that." Then I quickly turned my request into
an assumption, when I added, "Who wants to start?"
This was a ploy I'd fine-tuned in the classroom and
which usually proved transferable to other situations.

"I got one ting I'll always remember about Dom,"
said Tommy, apparently emboldened by his last outburst. "Da boids need a lotta attention. Ya gotta give
'em da right food and grit and enough water and make
sure dey got clean water to bade in and ya gotta train
'em and clean out da lofts." He looked ruefully at his

boots when he said this. "Dey gotta get vitamins and medicine when dey get sick. Ya gotta keep 'em separate, da mated pairs and da singles." I nodded, wondering what this lecture had to do with Dom. "So one time I had a problem wid my gall bladder." Tommy gripped his gut as he recalled the offending organ. "It come up real sudden." He winced at the memory. "And Dom, he took care a my boids for six weeks until I got outta da hospital and back on my feet. And I had about eighty boids back den, and he did too. So he took care a all my boids and exercised 'em and alla his too and went ta woik every day. I'll never forget what he done." Tommy said, his tiny eyes glistening like small gems embedded in wrinkles.

"Wow, he sure sounds like a great guy," I said, trying to mask my disappointment. "What about you, Emilio? What's one of your favorite memories of Dom?"

"Excuse me, but could I tell you mine, 'cause I can't stay much longer. I've got a doctor's appointment, and my daughter's picking me up in a few minutes," said John, looking at his watch.

"Sure, John, go ahead." I hoped that I would not run out of tape before it was Emilio's turn.

"One fall night we were registering birds for a big race. There must have been a hundred guys here from all over the county with carriers full of birds, so that means there were probably over a thousand birds, maybe fifteen hundred. Dom was behind the table, and he had to take information from each racer. You know, the guy's name, the band numbers of all the birds, the name of the loft, all that stuff. You'd have thought he was registering the damn birds to vote." John smiled, pleased at his joke.

"So anyway after he wrote down all that information

by hand, 'cause remember, we didn't have computers back then, he had to check to see if the bird's leg bands matched and put a rubber band on each one. Then he put the bird in one a them little crates, either one marked COCKS or one marked HENS. I remember each crate had room for only twenty-five birds, so he had to keep track of that too. Then Dom had to knock off the clock for every one of the racers. That was so it would be set to record when the birds came in and the owner couldn't cheat.

"This night, the guy who took registration fees showed up late, so Dom was doing that for a while too. With all these people and birds and a time limit for loading the birds in the truck, Dom handled each one of those pigeons like it was his own newborn child and never raised his voice. I'll always remember how hard Dom worked that night and how he never messed up or got mad." John sat back so that his weight was on only the back two legs of his chair and looked to the others for confirmation of his view of Dom.

"Yeah. Dom was like a machine sometimes. He never missed a number or dropped a boid or nothin'," Emilio said. "Right, Tommy?"

"Yeah. And anudder ting about Dom, I remember." Then, frowning, Tommy turned to me and asked, "Is it okay if we got two memories a Dom?"

I nodded, annoyed with myself for initially imposing any limits on the men's reminiscing. "The more memories, the better," I said. "I need all the help I can get with this article."

"Well, one time I was at his loft returnin' some feed he lent me or sompin', and he was just bringin' in his boids from a trainin' flight. All but one was back, a dove. The sky was empty. But Dom spotted dat dove. I

swear she musta been five miles away, but he saw 'er."
Shaking his head at his dead friend's uncanny pigeon-
spotting ability, Tommy stood and made his way towards an unmarked door behind the bar. " 'Scuse me.
Gotta see a man about a horse."

John looked at his watch and hurriedly put on his
army-navy jacket and waved goodbye. I shivered as
the open door let in a blast of cold air. Emilio and I
were more or less alone. "Thanks for your patience,
Emilio. So tell me, what do you remember about
Dom?" I listened for the reassuring whir of the tape
and was relieved when I heard it.

"Ya probably don't know it, but Dom was married to
my sister, so I got a slightly different take on him." I
nodded. I was disappointed when Emilio did not follow up that promising opener with a revelation of a
family feud or secret. Instead he shook his head and
said, "Dom's the one who got me into this club way
back when, but ya know, after my sister died, we, ya
know, we kinda went our ways."

"That happens," I said, trying to decide if I should
attempt to focus his ramblings or just let him go on and
hope that sooner or later he'd reward my patience with
a nugget of useful information. I avoided looking at the
mark on his face, instead directing my attention to his
eyes. "Like Tommy said, Dom put in time with the
boids. Maybe he should've been home, you know, with
his family a little more." Emilio leaned towards me and
lowered his already soft voice. "It was me who took
my sister to the hospital when Dom's boy, Leo, was
born. And I'm the one took Leo to the emergency room
when his arm got broke at a soccer game. So I got a
different take on the Boidman of Hoboken." A scowl
creased his brow.

Then, apparently regretting his remarks, Emilio said, "But that stuff I jus' told you, about the family, it's off the record, right?" Again I nodded, not wanting him to stop airing the Tomasellis' dirty laundry. "But even if I got a lot of bones to pick with my brother-in-law, one thing I gotta say for Dom. He never let nobody tell him what to do. Even at the end there when he was kinda wacko, he was still the only one of us who wouldn't sign. And no matter what Tommy there or John or me or even the lawyer said, he still wouldn't sign. And I gotta hand it to him for standin' by what he thought was right." Emilio looked up at me to see if this enigmatic offering would satisfy my reporter's need for an angle.

"Wouldn't sign what?" I asked, trying not to let my voice betray the excitement I felt. Finally I was onto something.

"Oh yeah, I shoulda said. Some big outfit wants to buy this clubhouse." Emilio looked around the modest room, and the birds on the wall stared back. "The members own it. But we don't use it no more really. So I signed. John signed. Even Tommy signed, and Sam Simon, and the guys in the nursing homes, their families signed, but not Dom. He refused to sign unless we stood by the club's deed or whatever." Emilio rubbed his bald pate as he recalled his brother-in-law's principled refusal.

"What does the deed say about the sale of the building?" I asked, wondering if, in the years before Hoboken real estate prices had skyrocketed, the group's founders had placed limitations on who could sell or buy this humble structure.

"Our lawyer, he says the deed says the building can't be sold while it's still in use except to anudda pigeon club. But there ain't never gonna be anudda Hoboken Racing Pigeon Club," Emilio said, his diction emphatic as if to stress the gravity of this pronouncement. "You hoid what John said. But Dom, he said we gotta make the club into a museum or give the money from the sale to the Bergen County Racing Pigeon Loft." When Emilio jerked his head north in the direction of Bergen County, his birthmark caught the sunlight. "And he wouldn't change his mind even though he coulda used the money for his grandkids schoolin'. My sister woulda had a bone to pick wid him turnin' down a hundred and fifty thou." Emilio made no effort to disguise the scorn in his voice now.

"So now that Dom's dead, this building can be sold?" I asked, knowing the answer, but wanting to hear him say it. "Yeah. My nephew, Leo, he's in real estate, ya know." Emilio's shoulders again straightened with pride, this time in his nephew's accomplishments. "He sold my house, and he's selling Dom's." I managed to keep my mouth from gaping open as I tried to digest this bombshell. When he spoke again, Emilio's eyes gleamed. I knew that gleam. I'd seen it in Ma's eyes when she peered over a fan of high cards and smiled at her hapless opponent. "Yeah, Leo says the club house sale's a done deal, and I'm in for a piece of it."

Chapter 18

To: Bbarrett@circle.com
Re: Personal
From: Florag@juno.com
Date: 02/26/03 23:45:24

Professor,

I need to talk to you at your earliest convenience. But I looked on the conference sign-up sheet on your office door and all the slots are taken. I'd like to talk to you for a minute after class tomorrow to see if there is some other time you are available.

Flora

The slightly formal tone of Flora's e-mail was at odds with her usual friendly style. I was not surprised. After my run-in with Leo, I'd been expecting to hear from her. Leo must have gone home and given her his version of that encounter. Flora would have understood at once that I suspected Leo and gotten upset. Well, I was upset too, and I had a few things to say to her. In my reply I suggested that we get together at the RIP for a cup of tea after her class.

But before her Cultures and Values class met, I had to run into a video store and rent the John Sayles film *Lone Star* to show as part of our examination of factors influencing Mexican Americans. From there I rushed across town to the Senior Center to meet with my memoir writers, whose class I had rescheduled from Monday. I arrived at the center breathless and harried. "Take eet easy, Professor. Here, seet down," said Ana, group mother hen. She had followed her own advice and ensconced herself in her chair.

"Here, Professor, I got you a cup of tea. I didn't know if you took sugar, so it's on the side," Ellen said, handing me a steaming Styrofoam cup and several packets of sugar. "Here, use my stirrer." Her simple gesture touched me. Students in continuing education courses didn't get graded, so Ellen could have no motive other than kindness.

Before I could get too smarmy, Sam, who had limped in while Ellen was handing me the tea, said, "Ellen O'Malley, you're too old to be teacher's pet," and we all laughed, including Ellen. It was her turn to read, and she had made copies of her manuscript. "It's not as long as it looks," she said apologetically, as she handed round the thick packets of paper, each one carefully secured with an oversize paper clip. When Sofia, who sat on my right in the circle we now routinely formed, handed me mine, I leafed through it. I felt as if I held a piece of the past in my hand. Every line of Ellen's neat printing was followed by the skipped line once mandated by school teachers now long dead. The left hand margin bore the faint imprints of the holes through which the rings passed in the retro three-ring looseleaf notebook she carried. Remembering the smudged and sloppily written pieces of torn paper I'd inflicted on my grade-school teachers, I realized that Sam's good-humored greeting probably held a kernel of truth. Ellen had undoubtedly been a teacher's pet before she'd become a teacher herself.

"I'm starting with right before Sheila's nephew brought her to my house," said Ellen by way of reprise. "That's where I left off."

Ellen's account of a reunion with her friend from County Donegal during the latter's visit to America for a grandchild's wedding had riveted the group. Before she began to read, she removed the paper clip and placed it carefully on the desk in front of her.

"It was eleven o'clock, and I was as nervous as a child before first communion. On the phone Sheila had sounded the same as ever. At first I thought her voice had gotten a little lower, but later I realized that I had forgotten to put my hearing aid in when I picked up the receiver." Ellen's classmates responded to this with empathetic nods and smiles. "I figured she must still have her wits about her to have found me in the phone book after all these years." Again her classmates smiled, no doubt pleased that another peer had escaped the dreaded demon of dementia.

Encouraged, Ellen continued. "I wondered what Sheila looks like at eighty-seven. Is she humpbacked like me? How has her life gone since her Jim died? And what will she make of me now? I've no husband, not even a dead one, and no kids."

Ellen's humorous but deprecating description of her single and childless status provoked rueful glances among her listeners. By the time she finished her account, there were few dry eyes in her audience. Even though her classmates were moved by her tale, they had one or two suggestions to help her improve the telling of it. Once again, I had little to add to their sensible critique, and we all left appreciating anew the drama inherent in all of our stories.

I had promised to have a quick lunch with Ma and Sofia, so I drove them home and let them force some of their to-die-for leftovers on me. Who could resist homemade chicken soup and chicken pot pie on a cold winter day? As I contemplated this orgy of comfort food, Ma said, "So we figure you're looking into Dom's death, right?"

"Right," I said, too taken aback to deny it. "How did you figure that out?"

"Your mother always thought there was something fishy about Dom falling off his own roof. She also figured you'd think so too and wouldn't be able to resist poking your yenta nose in," said Sofia, looking pleased that after a few years of living with Ma, she could throw an occasional Yiddishism into her conversation. "And then when you were grilling me at the dentist again just like you did when poor Louie Palumbo was killed, we knew."

"After all, we weren't born yesterday." Ma accompanied this statement of the obvious with a familiar look that said, "You should feel guilty about not confiding in me. I'm your mother."

This look never failed to appeal to my inner adolescent, so I was about to respond reflexively with something sharp and defensive when Sofia, always eager to keep the peace between Ma and me, trilled in falsetto, "Better Bel grilling than the dentist drilling." To

Sofia's credit, Ma and I quickly united to thumb our noses at her bad rhyme and worse voice.

"Well, you're both right. I am looking into Dom's death because his daughter also doesn't believe it was an accident and she asked me to. But I don't have any real answers yet, so any information you come across is welcome. I just don't want you two saying anything to anybody or doing anything to put yourselves at risk," I said, giving them my own version of The Look. This was a glare that clearly said, "If you cross me on this, find yourself another ride to the dentist." I modulated the impact of my stern stare with a compliment. "This soup is so good. I swear, Ma, Mark must have inherited his talent in the kitchen from you."

"Well, he certainly didn't get it from you," she retorted. As a self-professed takeout queen, I was only too happy to cede her that round. I pushed my empty soup bowl away and began to blow on the steaming portion of pot pie Sofia had just served me.

"So what did you two *overhear* on the bus to the casino that might have bearing on Dom's death?" I asked. I fought the impulse to burn my tongue by attacking the pot pie before it had cooled just a little. Then I gave in and took a bite.

"Well, we happened to be sitting behind two members of Gamblers Anonymous," Ma began.

I nearly choked on a mouthful of still very hot chicken and peas. "What the hell are members of Gamblers Anonymous doing on the bus to the casinos?"

Ma rolled her eyes. Clearly she was distressed that, in spite of all her preaching and her excellent example, she had raised a daughter who at fifty-something still talked with her mouth full. With tightened lips, Ma handed me a napkin before answering. "I assume they are former members or lapsed members or something like that. How many times have you eaten a bag of M&M's after a Weight Watchers meeting?" I ignored this dig. "That's not the point, Bel."

"The point is that they were talking about a man named Emilio who was a success story from their local chapter. The man has apparently given up gambling now for over a year." Sofia looked pleased to be the one who offered up this tidbit.

"Did they give a last name?" I asked, recalling only after I'd asked the question that members of 12-step groups don't often use last names. So I was not surprised when both Sofia and Ma shook their heads.

"But if it is Dom's brother-in-law, that means something," I said. "I should be able to get Illuminada to find out if it is." I was thinking out loud, and I stopped myself. Sofia was at the stove boiling water for tea. While she was just out of easy earshot, I said, "Ma, you and Dom were pretty close. Did he say anything at all about old feuds? Did he talk about enemies? Family squabbles?"

"Dom had only two topics, his grandkids and pigeons." Ma sure didn't sound as if she and Dom had been romantically involved, one of the speculations my query had been designed to corroborate or disprove. "He was a sweet, sweet man, but he didn't say much about his kids, except he was glad Leo had settled down, and he was glad they were all together. But he was always bragging about his grandkids, and he doted on them. A lot of us do that. You know," she said. "A lot of us feel that being a grandparent is a second chance."

Sofia returned to the table with a pot of tea. She had

overheard enough of our conversation to say, "It really is a second chance for me. With my grandkids I get to be the way I always wanted to be with my own kids, but," she shrugged, "back then I didn't have the time or the knowledge." She paused with the teapot in her hand. "You know, the psychology." A tremor began in Sofia's chin, threatening her steely composure, not to mention the teapot.

"Well, you two did a terrific job with your kids anyway, if I do say so myself," I said, hoping to lighten the mood. Ma grinned at me; Sofia managed a smile and poured the tea. For a few moments we three sipped in silence, each lost in her own thoughts.

My thoughts were awhirl with the efforts to synthesize the different and seemingly conflicting snippets of information I'd taken in since Sarah and I had visited the Hoboken Racing Pigeon Club. The ability to find patterns connecting apparently unrelated matters had come to me as I got older. I thought of it as Mother Nature's way of compensating me for the loss of youthful beauty and bladder control. But in order to recognize patterns, I needed time to think, to ponder the deceptively random items and see how they meshed.

Later that day I tried to concentrate on what I had learned so far about Dom's death while my class watched *Lone Star,* which I'd already screened. But I couldn't really focus my thoughts. I was aware that Flora had entered class uncharacteristically late, returned my greeting with a perfunctory nod, and appeared to be using an inhaler from time to time during the movie. Although she usually relished taking part in class discussions, Flora did not participate in the conversation that followed the film.

After class the two of us walked in silence to the

RIP diner. Once seated, we ordered and then, taking a whiff from her inhaler, Flora let loose. "Professor, I told you. It's Emilio who pushed Papa off the roof. So why're you talkin' to my brother? I told you he's upset now. You saw yourself how upset he is. He come home the other day and said you were lookin' for a house for your daughter and askin' him all kinds of personal questions. Right away I knew you weren't buyin' a house. You think Leo's a suspect." The way Flora's voice rose when she uttered her brother's name made it sound as if suspecting him of murder was tantamount to accusing Jimmy Carter of being a warmonger. I didn't argue, but waited to hear her out.

"I mean he said he lost it and went off on you, but I don't blame him. That's none a your business." Flora interrupted her tirade to accept the coffee the waitress handed her. "I'm thinkin' a just forgettin' about it," said Flora. "I can't take much more a this. I can't concentrate on my schoolwork or nothin' anymore. I gotta use this damn thing in the daytime now." Near tears, Flora held up the yellow inhaler.

"Flora, I'm sorry you're upset. But I am looking into your father's death as you asked me to. And the deeper I look, the less convinced I am that your uncle is the only viable suspect." Flora opened her mouth to argue, but before she could speak, I continued. "Please hear me out, Flora. Your safety may depend on it." At this Flora took a drag on her inhaler and stared at me with the doomed look of a child awaiting punishment.

"Flora, did you know that your brother is planning to sell your father's house? The house you live in?" Disbelief and shock washed over Flora's face, widening her eyes, flaring her nostrils, and quickening her already labored breathing. The hand that held her coffee cup trembled, and she lowered the cup.

"I suspected you didn't know. Well, I heard that from your Uncle Emilio when I interviewed some of the members of the Hoboken Racing Pigeon Club for a newspaper article. Emilio didn't want it on the record, but he made no effort to hide the fact that he didn't think very much of your dad for neglecting his wife and son in favor of his pigeons. And one more thing, Flora, Emilio made no mention of owing your dad money." Flora's face reddened, but she did not reach for her inhaler.

"But he does . . ." she said.

"Flora, please just listen. I'm almost done. Emilio told me your dad was the only member of the Hoboken Racing Pigeon Club who refused to sell the clubhouse building to a developer who wanted to buy it." Again Flora's face registered surprise. She listened attentively to my explanation. "They want to raze it and build a condo there. But your father wanted to turn the clubhouse into a museum or sell it and give the money to the Pigeon Club of Bergen County. Flora, there were probably a lot of people who were mad at him for standing between them and $150,000. That would be each person's share of the sale price."

When she finally spoke, Flora's voice was breathy, the whisper of a ghost. I had to lean forward to catch her words. She was still processing the first part of our conversation. "Professor, what you said about Leo . . . about sellin' the house. . . . The house is in both our names. Leo can't sell it unless I agree." Flora was anything but stupid. I watched her as, again resorting to the inhaler, she came to terms with the fact that her beloved younger brother whom she had nurtured and made a home for was planning to sell that very home out from beneath them all. I admired her courage. Sickly and bereaved though she might be, she faced the question with the unthinkable answer: What would Leo do if she didn't cooperate?

"That's true. We just don't want Leo to lose his temper over your refusal." Now that I had said it aloud, Flora flinched. I steadied her trembling arm with my hand and said, "The thing is, Flora, that from the point of view of someone on the outside of your family looking in, Leo seems to have had a lot more reasons for wanting your dad dead than Emilio did." Flora nodded, tears filling her eyes. "In fact, Flora, again from the point of view of an outsider, Leo's a loose cannon. He could go off anytime."

Chapter 19

To: Bbarrett@circle.com
From: Staceyps2much@hotmail.com
Re: Join the crowd
Date: 02/27/03 16:32:14

Dear Soggy and Suicidal,

Stop wallowing in self-pity, darlin'. Do you think you're the
only gal in the world who ever peed on herself at a meeting? When the posies on the altar made me sneeze, I wet
my pants at my boy's wedding right up there in the front
row of the church. And stop blaming it on your kids just because you had vaginal deliveries. Your young'uns may give
you heartburn or migraines or agita, but not Stress Urinary
Incontinence. I had my three bouncing boys with
C-sections, and I still got SUI. Hell, honey, even a few men
get it, and last I heard they don't give birth at all.

But we're not alone! There are about 13 million of us out
there peeing out of turn. The gurus who keep track of our
numbers can't decide if 1 out of every 3 gals over 18 or 1
out of every 4 is blessed with SUI, but either way, that's a

lot, including Debbie Reynolds. I saw her on TV the other night pushing some drugs that are supposed to help.

But listen up. Before you become a Kegels quitter and take drugs or have an operation, ask your doctor to zap your pelvic floor muscles with a little electrical stimulation to toughen them up enough to do kegels. It worked for me! Now I tell my bladder what to do instead of the other way around.

                                                              Stacey

Applying electric shock therapy to my pelvic floor muscles sounded so extreme to me that every other muscle in my body contracted in spasms of empathy when I tried to picture it. Nevertheless I included Stacey's message along with others I had saved and copied them all for Betty and Illuminada. I handed each of them a folder when we got together next at Illuminada's house. Without acknowledging my offering, Illuminada took it and shoved it into the drawer near her phone.

"Thanks," said Betty with a yawn as she took the folder and wedged it into her briefcase.

"You've got those circles under your eyes again," I said, "and you're actually yawning in my face, so what's going on? The accreditation getting to you?"

Betty yawned again. "Yeah. It's just a couple of weeks away now, and Woodman is freaking out." She held her hands to her head. "But I put in a whole day on it yesterday while he was at a colloquium in Trenton. I think I've got it pretty much covered." Illuminada and I looked at each other in tacit acknowledgment of our friend's exceptional organizational ability. If Betty thought she had something covered, you better believe it was.

"But, *chiquita*, all work and no play is not good for you. It's not bad enough you push yourself all week, but then on the weekends you go down the shore and slave away on that damn pleasure palace of yours. This is not a healthy lifestyle," said Illuminada.

"Look who's talking," I muttered. This time Betty and I exchanged looks. Illuminada's penchant for overwork was well known. We had seated ourselves around the Guttierrez's chrome and Formica kitchen table in their meticulously reconceived fifties kitchen. Illuminada's husband Raoul liked nothing better than haunting flea markets and dumpsters in search of the detritus of other people's lives that he could restore and reuse.

"Well, if you two want to erase these circles and stop me from yawning, put your muscles where your mouths are and come down and give us a hand. How about the weekend of March twenty-first to twenty-third? That's when we're stripping the paint off the paneling and steaming away three layers of old wallpaper. I was going to e-mail you about it." Betty gazed imploringly from one of us to the other.

"Okay, okay. But e-mail me anyway to remind me to talk to Sol and look in my book," I said.

Illuminada nodded. "*Si, chiquita.* E-mail me the date. I'll talk to Raoul. He actually enjoys dirty back-breaking labor." Betty grinned. Getting what she wanted never failed to revive her. She had stopped yawning and was eyeing the pot Illuminada had placed on a trivet on the table. "So, *chiquita,* are we here to volunteer for Vic and Betty's Habitat as Investment project, or did you come because you can't resist Mamacita's *rabo encendido*? Or is it because, just maybe, Bel has solved the mystery of who killed that poor old man and wants to tell us?" As she spoke, Illuminada ladled out steaming portions of the oxtail stew her mother had made.

Ignoring her question, I said, "Tell your mother this is delicious. Thank her for me."

"You haven't even tasted it yet," said Illuminada. She took the pot back to the stove, replaced the lid, and rejoined us.

"It smells wonderful. And it's perfect for tonight. Girl, you are so lucky to have that woman living upstairs. She just whips up this stuff and brings it down here. You don't even have to rub a bottle or say abracadabra or anything," said Betty holding a forkful of stew up to cool. "Hell, you don't even have to dial and order."

"No, I just have to try not to shoot her when she gets on my nerves," said Illuminada. "But she's been pretty good this week." Illuminada looked around for a piece of wood to knock and rapped on the door of a cabinet behind her. "Mmmm, this really is good." Having acknowledged her mother's culinary prowess, she looked expectantly at me.

"Well, I've got more questions than answers. Why don't I play this tape of my interview with Emilio DeFranco and the other pigeon club members while we eat?" I suggested. "Then I'll tell you about my latest run-in with Leo Tomaselli and some interesting things I learned from Ma and Sofia." Betty and Illuminada nodded their assent, so I placed the recorder in the center of the table, turned up the volume, and pushed PLAY. When we emptied our bowls a few minutes before the tape ended, Illuminada brought the pot of stew back and walked around the table, serving Betty and me each a second helping.

"So Leo's selling the family home. Does his sister know that?" asked Illuminada when the tape ended.

"She does now," I said. "I sat down with her and told her I thought Leo was much more likely to have pushed her father off the roof than her Uncle Emilio was."

"Well, they both had motives," said Betty. "Leo must have felt neglected by his father. Hey, who likes being rejected in favor of pigeons?" She shook her head at the very idea of such poor parenting. "And then this Emilio character wasn't happy with the way Dom treated his sister, Dom's wife, or the boy."

"And then there's the debt. I didn't hear Emilio mention that." I was always amazed at how Illuminada remembered all the ins and outs of cases.

"No, he didn't," I said. "Flora insists he still owes it. And meanwhile, Ma and Sofia heard that in the last year a man named Emilio has become a poster person for the local Gamblers Anonymous. Go figure. But let me tell you what happened when I tried to get Leo to show me a house." I recapped the story of my rendezvous with Leo including its unpleasant denouement.

"You shouldn't have gone alone," said Betty helping herself to the greens from the salad bowl that Illuminada had brought to the table. "I thought Sol was going with you."

"He had to go upstate to babysit again," I said. "I didn't know how long he'd be gone, and I just didn't feel like waiting." I looked to Illuminada for validation of my impatience and met her icy stare.

"*Chiquita,* you do not go into deserted houses with murder suspects, especially when you are unarmed and have no backup." She circled her index finger beside her head to illustrate her opinion of my sanity. "But what's done is done," she said with a sigh. "Just don't do it again."

"Yeah or you won't live to see your wedding day," said Betty. "If there's still going to be a wedding."

"There is. Sol and I actually put together the guest list last weekend." I was glad to have some progress to report. "Now all we have to do is rob a bank to feed all these people. I just wish we could afford to turn the whole thing over to one of those wedding planners who would check out venues, prices, caterers and all that stuff and then put it together for us, so it would be a zipless wedding." Betty and Illuminada raised their eyebrows in unison, indicating that they had not read *Fear of Flying,* the book whose female narrator had expressed a desire for a "zipless" sexual experience, one free of logistical or emotional complications. "I'd just like a completely hassle-free wedding, that's all," I explained. "But Sol and I will figure something out. Yes, there will definitely be a wedding."

"In my lifetime, *chiquita*?" Illuminada asked. I threw my crumpled napkin at her. "Okay, back to business," she said. "I have a court appearance in the morning, and I need to review the evidence I'm presenting before I go to sleep."

"Right. Here's what we know so far." I sat up a little straighter to summarize. "Leo Tomaselli is a wild card who may or may not be a problem drinker. He resents his dad for neglecting him and his mom and favoring his sister and the birds. Leo married a woman who also rejected him. He raised their son. He's got a short fuse. He ran a small not very successful film-developing business for years, and is now a newly minted realtor. He coaches soccer. He may be planning to sell the family home." I paused for breath. Betty had taken out her Palm Pilot and was typing as I talked.

"Then we've got Emilio DeFranco, brother-in-law of the deceased. Emilio installed curtains for a living. He has arthritis, which may be why he retired. He allegedly owed Dom a lot of money that he borrowed to pay a gambling debt. Rumor also has it that he is now a reformed gambler. He sold his home a year ago and put the money in CDs. He resented the deceased for neglecting his family and, probably, because he owed him money." I stopped speaking for a moment. Then I added, "And last but not least, they've also got a deal to sell the clubhouse that Emilio was party to, and Leo knew about it but Dom had put the kibosh on. Emilio and Dom each stood to make $150,000 if the sale went through."

We were all quiet when I finished. Betty broke the silence. "You know, maybe Leo also stood to earn something on that deal. Maybe he's the broker. And, of course, without Dom, each member will get a little more money from the sale of the building."

Illuminada nodded and, speaking slowly, said, "Maybe Emilio hasn't quit gambling at all. Maybe he's just raised the stakes." When Betty motioned for her to continue, she said, "Well, *chiquitas,* not many gamblers are highly motivated to quit, but here's this lifelong player who suddenly sells his house, puts the money in CDs, and joins GA." She snapped her fingers and added, "Yes. It fits. See, he's got arthritis, so he can't work and maybe he can't even hold a deck of cards anymore." I nodded recalling the swollen joints of Emilio's hands. "Then he hears about the clubhouse deal and wants more than just his share of the selling price. He wants a piece of it, wants to invest. That's the newest chance he's taking, the one he's saving his money for. That's why he wouldn't pay back Dom. He probably told Dom he'd make good on his debt after the sale of the clubhouse." Illuminada's eyes gleamed as she contemplated the coherent scenario she had created out of the pieces of Emilio's life.

"Maybe Emilio told Dom he'd pay him back right away if Dom signed the contract agreeing to sell the clubhouse for profit," said Betty just before she excused herself and headed for the bathroom. "Wait 'til I get back," she called over her shoulder. Illuminada finished the last leaves of salad in the bowl and cleared the table. She put something into the microwave and by the time Betty returned, the familiar aroma of buttered popcorn made the kitchen smell like the lobby of a movie theater.

"So what do you think, Bel?" Betty asked after we had relocated to the Gutierrez's comfortable living room, each with a bowl of hot popcorn.

"I'm not sure. You know, I just can't see Emilio as a killer even though I agree with everything you've both said. I can imagine him trying to get Dom to sign by withholding payment and all that. I agree that he may see investing in the development project that's going to happen on the site of the clubhouse as his latest gamble. Maybe he even joined GA to help him hold on to his money so he'd have it when that happened." I opened my hands, palms up, and shrugged before I summarized. "But I just don't see him pushing his brother-in-law off the roof. I've got to find out if he has an alibi for that night."

"That reminds me," said Illuminada. She reached behind her and handed me a folder. "I almost forgot to give you this. It's the autopsy report."

I took the folder and said, "So what's the cause of death?"

"It's inconclusive." Illuminada frowned with annoyance. "The victim sustained a head injury, but it's unclear as to whether it was the result of his fall or whether it occurred just before that and was made worse when he landed and sustained further abrasions to his head." Illuminada sighed. "In other words it doesn't really tell us much. So we're back to square one. What about how Dom neglected Emilio's sister and Leo? That alone might have motivated Emilio to kill him."

"But you heard Emilio. He told me, a total stranger, a reporter yet, how he felt about Dom. I think it made him sad. I don't think it turned him into a killer," I said, remembering Emilio's fringe of white hair and soft-spoken manner. I hoped he had an alibi.

"So you think it was Leo?" asked Betty, her Palm suspended over her bowl.

"I'm not sure. I agree he's got lots of motives and a very bad temper. But he's also a single dad who coaches soccer, a guy who raised a son who got accepted to Princeton. I know that in itself doesn't mean anything, but . . . Look, Leo's best friends are his former parish priest and his sister." Betty raised her eyebrows. "Okay, that could be kinky, but the bottom line is I'm just not sure about him." I dug into my popcorn as if I might find the certainty we all sought at the bottom of the bowl.

"Well, I am. And I don't think his sister is safe alone in the house with him," said Illuminada.

"Leo's boy John still lives with them. He's a senior in high school. But I did persuade Flora to get someone else to stay upstairs with her. She promised me she'd invite a friend over. I didn't want her to take any chances. I've been wrong before, and I wouldn't want anything to happen to her."

"So what's our next move?" asked Illuminada, stretching her legs and putting her empty bowl on the coffee table.

"Would you find out whatever there is to know about the development project that's going to go up on the site of the clubhouse?"

"The honcho behind that has as good a motive as any of the man's relatives," said Betty. "Big-money builders don't take kindly to old guys who block their projects."

Her comment was so astute that I instantly forgave her for interrupting me. "Any information on the developer would be most welcome," I added, blowing a kiss to Betty. Illuminada nodded as she made a couple of quick notes in her Palm.

"And I guess you should check into John Derdowski and Tommy Lucca and maybe even some of the other members of the pigeon club. After all, they might have wanted to get Dom out of the way too. And they might have had access to his roof." I didn't feel too guilty giving Illuminada all this work because I knew she would delegate the background checking to a computer savvy staff member who would do most of it online in a matter of minutes. I was the one yawning now. "I'll ask Flora to bring me all of Dom's papers, whatever she has. I want to see if she knows where Leo was at the time their father was up on the roof. And I want to see the lofts again."

"Isn't there anything I can do?" asked Betty. "I don't have a lot of time, but . . ."

"Well, if I have to talk to the folks whose windows

look out on the Tomaselli's yard, I probably shouldn't go alone."

Betty nodded. "Okay. I'm game. But this whole thing is not exactly the no-brainer you thought it was going to be, is it?"

"No, it sure isn't. But going door to door shouldn't take that long, especially with two of us doing it. And a witness would be so useful." I spoke in the wistful tone of an incurable optimist, one used to championing students whom others had given up on. My words met with total silence.

Finally Illuminada said, "Dream on, *chiquita.*"

Chapter 20

Ana Luisa Guzman (con't.)

I allways remember that day in 1979
when we move out of public housing to a
beatiful apartment with the rent control, we move to a four family house on
Madison between 4ᵗʰ and 5ᵗʰ st., We have
three bedrooms! One is for my daughter
another one for her boys and one for
me. Before that Rosa allways to sleep
on the sofa in the liveing room and the
boys they have their own room and I
have mine. It was the first time in her
25 years on this earth that my Rosa
have her own room. Back then I have a
job sewing, so I keep a little money
out and buy her lilac colored curtains
and a mashing cover for her bed, I put
them up before she come home from work,
My Rosa cry when she see.

But after we live in their a few

months in the middle of the nite, I
smell smoke, I ran into Rosa's room,
smoke is everywhere. I shake her, wake
her up and we wake up the boys, smoke
and fire was coming up the stairs, we
have to go out the fire excape in our
nite cloths. Fire was coming out from
the windows and from the roof. Like I
say I will never forget that nite but
thanks God we all made it out exep for
the old guy on the top floor, Gustavo,
he live all by hisself . . ."

Ana read slowly until she got to the part about the
fire. Then her accent became even more pronounced
and her words tumbled out faster and faster, reminding
us of our own fears of fire and recreating the sense of
urgency she had felt as she and her family fled the
burning building. I saw Ma nodding. No doubt Ana's
story reminded her of her own fire-haunted tenement
childhood. Sam too nodded and shook his head, no
doubt recalling this violent period in Hoboken's history. Along with the group's appreciation came questions and suggestions, all tactfully phrased. Ana noted
them carefully in the margins of her draft. When the
class was over, the room was still abuzz with conversation inspired by Ana's reading, but I didn't have time
to stay. I had scheduled a visit to Flora's home, where
I hoped to collect whatever papers of her father's she
had been able to find as well as to take another look at
the lofts. I really wanted to determine which houses
across the yard afforded a view of the Tomaselli's roof.
I assumed Leo would be out selling houses. I had no
desire to inflame his temper with another run-in, but I

hoped to establish whether he had an alibi for that night.

Flora greeted me at the door and ushered me in. "I want to apologize for being so angry last time. You know, about Leo. I know you're tryin' a help. It's just that I couldn't take for anything to happen to Leo now that Papa's gone." Tears welled in Flora's eyes.

I patted her arm and said, "Not to worry. I understand how upsetting all this has been. And I hope you're right about your brother. How has he been acting lately? Has he said anything about selling this house?"

Flora shook her head. "No. He drove John down to see Princeton today." Flora's face brightened at the thought of her nephew's exalted college plans. "John's never even seen the campus. Leo took the whole day off, and John skipped school. The Fathers don't mind as long as he makes up his work. Them two wanted me to come, but I have classes later on. I missed enough school already." Flora's voice was animated, her eyes clear. "I told them to stop by Newark on the way home and take my Mary out for supper."

I was relieved that Leo was not only out, but out of town. "That will be a nice treat for her," I said. Then, hating to remind her that Leo was still a prime suspect, I asked, "Flora, do you know where Leo was on the night your dad died?"

Flora looked away. "He coaches on Monday nights. He come home around ten and went to bed, I guess. Maybe John remembers. You want me to ask him?" I nodded, knowing that whatever alibi Leo had for the hours the family slept was going to be flimsy with only his son and his sister to corroborate it. "But like I told you, Professor, I never heard Papa go up, and I never heard Leo neither. And Leo would have had to go right past that door." She pointed at the kitchen door leading to the back stairwell.

"Well, it wouldn't hurt to see what John says anyway," I replied with a resigned sigh. "So Flora, may I take one more quick look at the lofts?"

"Sure. Let's go up there before you take off your coat. See? I finally got a runner on the floor now. You don't have to take off your boots this time." Flora pointed down to where a swath of rough brown paper crossed her immaculate kitchen floor. She was putting on her own boots as she spoke.

We climbed the stairs to the roof, where someone had shoveled away a lot of the snow. "Leo's afraid too much snow up here will make the roof leak, so he shoveled some off after that last storm." I nodded, realizing that Sol and I should probably do the same thing. The flat roof that was so ideal for pigeon raising, container gardening, and sunbathing, becomes a menace when overloaded with heavy wet snow. I noticed that all the debris from Leo's hatchet job on Dom's coops was gone, and two wooden and wire cage-like structures remained. "So here's the last of Papa's lofts, Professor," said Flora. "This was the one he used for breedin'. Sometimes he had ten or twenty birds nestin' in here. You know both the males and the females sit on the nest. Of course, the female spends more time at it, but still, the male takes a turn. Some people race their female birds while they're still nestin' 'cause that makes 'em fly home faster, but not Papa. He waited 'til they was ready to mate. He thought that was better for the birds." Flora paused, lost in a memory.

"You know a lot about the birds. Did you ever race

any yourself?" I asked her as I made my way over to the edge of the roof.

"Nah," Flora said. "When I was a kid I helped Papa. I liked workin' with him. I liked listenin' to him tell his stories about the war and the birds. Then when I got older, I had too much homework and housework. And I was, you know, goin' out and all that teenage stuff." Flora joined me at the low wall and crossed herself as we both stared down at the garden below.

"Flora, do you ever see neighbors at these back windows?" I asked.

"We had a peeper in the neighborhood when I was small. He used to come outta the back door of that house there and hide in the bushes. Papa spotted him down there one night and called the cops and that's how they finally got him." Flora smiled at the memory of her dad's contribution to this rare triumph of justice over prurience. "But I never saw nobody else at any windows."

"Well, I sure wish somebody over there saw what happened here the night your dad died." I gestured at the rows of windows across the yard.

"If I hear anything in the neighborhood, I'll let you know," said Flora. "But nobody said nothin' to me yet. You ready to take a look at Papa's scrapbook now?" She hugged herself and I could see that she was cold. I too shivered against the raw wind. I nodded and we retreated into the house. I was ready for a cup of hot tea, but Flora produced a bowl of thick lentil soup and a loaf of Marie's brick-oven bread instead. "I'm still tryin' to make up for how bad I was last week at the RIP," she said with a smile. "I figured you needed lunch before you go back to the college."

Still shivering after I took off my coat and boots, I

was grateful for the hot soup and still warm bread. We ate in silence for a few minutes. When Flora finished her soup, she pushed her bowl aside and wiped the table carefully before pulling over a large maroon leather scrapbook bulging with tattered yellowed newspaper clippings and old black-and-white photos. "I started this for Papa when I was just a kid. I pasted in all the articles about him that were in the paper. I shoulda kept it up better, but once I got older, I didn't make time. Papa loved this book. We used to look through it together sometimes," Flora said, sounding a little weepy.

"See, Professor. There's Papa with Hoboken Harry, one of his best racers." The dark-haired man in the picture had posed with a pigeon perched on his upheld wrist. The man and bird were facing one another, their profiles to the camera. "And here he is with one of Hoboken Harry's squabs. See?" Flora pointed at a photo of the same young man. The tiny head of a baby bird poked out of his cupped hands. "And here, this one's way out of order, but it's Papa in his uniform when he got his medal." Flora's voice rang with pride. And there indeed was a very young Dom looking every inch the soldier with several decorations gleaming from his chest. "Yeah, me and Papa, we useta love lookin' through this book." Kids are always curious about their parents' early lives, so Flora's interest in photos and newspaper clippings focused on her dad did not surprise me. But I did wonder if either of Flora's parents had ever made a scrapbook for Flora.

When I left her house that afternoon, I was carrying a large plastic shopping bag containing Dom's scrapbook and copies of all the papers that he had kept in a small metal safe in his closet. "Papa wasn't much for banks," Flora had explained.

I decided to drive slowly around the corner. I wanted to see the fronts of the houses Betty and I would have to visit. There were, I figured, at least four row houses with windows in back that offered a view of the Tomasellis' roof. From the car I couldn't tell if any of the houses were still single family or if they had all become multiple dwellings for condo owners. I called Betty and left word that I wanted to make those visits as soon as possible. I knew her plate was already pretty full, and I felt a little guilty to be adding to her workload. But she got back to me before I had gone two blocks, and we made plans to meet the next night.

Then I called Ma. "What is it, Sybil?" asked Ma, the minute she heard my voice. "Are you all right?" This greeting of hers was basically unchanged since I'd left for college. It reminded me of my mother's constant anxiety about my wellbeing when out of her orbit as well as of her often-voiced conviction that I only phoned when something was wrong and I needed help. I smiled, realizing that this time something was indeed wrong and, in fact, I did need her help.

"I'm fine, Ma. But I need your help. Could you and Sofia find out when Gamblers Anonymous meets and go a couple of times?" I asked.

"I told you, Sybil. Our visits to the casino do not make us problem gamblers," said Ma, her voice resigned to repeating this reassurance. "Why are you calling me in the middle of our Scrabble session? I was just about to take Sofia for all she's worth with a *q* word on a triple-score square. We've been all through this before."

"I know that, Ma. Actually, I'm not worried about

your gambling," I said, crossing my fingers because every once in a while I did worry about it. "I want you and Sofia to chat up Emilio DeFranco and see if he has an alibi for the night Dom died."

I waited while Ma communicated this to Sofia. "Bel needs us to go undercover to a GA meeting. Isn't that a hoot? She wants to know if Emilio D has an alibi for when Dom was killed." I couldn't hear Sofia's response, but in a moment Ma said, "Sure, we'll find out when and where they meet and go."

"Just let me know when and where, Ma, and I'll pick you up and drop you off, okay?" I said, rushing the words to get them in before she hung up to call Gamblers Anonymous. Her enthusiasm for this task left no doubt that Ma missed the excitement of the courtroom, where she had recorded criminal trials for years—and I came by my taste for sleuthing legitimately. I could have done this bit of undercover work myself, but Emilio knew me now and, besides, maybe a few sessions of GA would be good for the Odd Couple.

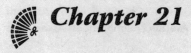 **Chapter 21**

To: Bbarrett@circle.com, Sol @ juno.com
From: Cillysario@hotmail.com
Re: Wedding bells
Date: 03/04/03 17:22:46

Bel, we missed you at the neighborhood ass'n meeting last night. Sol told us that him and you are finally making it legal. Congratulations! He said you hadn't set a date yet, so after the meeting some of us went out for a few beers like always and me and Ilona and Joey P came up with an idea. Its a little unusual, but they told me to ask you anyway. Why don't you wait until Fall and tie the knot at the Block Party? We figure you waited this long, another few months wouldn't matter. And your rabbi's right around the corner, she wouldn't mind coming over. There's already food and music, we'd just order a little more and you two could make a contribution for what your friends and family eat. (We would waive our admission charge when they showed their invitation) And of course, all your devoted neighbors would be there to arrange everything and celebrate at your side. What do

you think? Get back to me so I can put it on the agenda
for a vote at the next meeting.

Charlie Illysario, President
Park Avenue Neighborhood Association

Before I could dwell on the wacky but not unap-
pealing prospect of our wedding guests having their
hands stamped and their faces painted while they
chowed down on sausages and peppers at the annual
Park Avenue Neighborhood Association block party, I
got a call from Illuminada. Her voice was low. "*Chiquita,* the developer we were discussing yesterday? Remember?" When I assured her I did, she went on.
"Well, he's a client of mine," Illuminada paused,
choosing her words, "a good client of mine." She lingered over the word *good* just long enough for me to
register exactly what she meant. "We do background
checks for his organization all the time. And we also
do a lot of pilfering-prevention work for him too. You
know, at their construction sites. His name's Jonah
Bechstein. Raoul and I have been to his kid's bar mitzvah and to the family's holiday parties at their home in
Short Hills. He knows me. I suggest you devise a pre-
text for talking with him, but count me out."

"Well, if you're so buddy-buddy with this guy, do
you think he's capable of killing an old man to speed
up a project?" I asked.

When she answered, Illuminada assumed the tone
she might use when explaining something to a men-
tally challenged child. "It doesn't matter what I think.
I've got a conflict of interest here. If he goes to jail, and
his organization goes belly-up, I lose a lot of work."
Before I could reply, she added, "And if he doesn't go

to jail, he's not going to take kindly to knowing that I suspected him of murder. You can talk with him and size him up yourself, Bel. Just do it in a public place this time."

"Can you at least find out if he has an alibi?" I asked, annoyed at both her tone and what, just then, I saw as her skewed priorities.

"I'd rather you try first, *chiquita*. If he seems like a viable suspect and you can't find out any other way, then I'll try," said Illuminada. *"Caio."*

"Illuminada's right, of course," said Sol that night over dinner. I had been whining about my friend's annoying decision to recuse herself from this part of the investigation. "It is a classic case of conflict of interest. So, my love, how are you going to get to meet with this guy, to check him out?"

"I have a couple of ideas," I said, holding my plate out.

Sol looked at me expectantly as he placed a chicken leg and half of a baked sweet potato on my plate. "More salad?" he asked. When I shook my head, he repeated his query. "So, tell me what you've got in mind."

"Well, one idea is to pass myself off as a zoning officer looking for a little under-the-table money to vote in favor of a variance on a parking or square-footage regulation that might obstruct his project," I said, for once grateful for Hoboken's long tradition of granting questionable variances to developers. "He'd have to cater to a zoning officer."

"I'm sure he already has. In fact, he probably knows them and everyone in their offices. And he probably paved the way for this project before he even made an offer on the clubhouse," Sol said. I tried not to resent the disappointment in his voice. He had clearly expected better of me.

"I know. But I've just started to think about it," I said. Defensiveness lent my words a whiny sound. "Have you got any ideas?" Sol often came up with excellent strategies for solving problems that flummoxed me.

"There was a huge spread about him in last week's paper. He's got quite an ego. Sees himself as heir to the legacy of Dino Sorrentino, the mayor who 'opened the doors to development' in Hoboken in the seventies." Sol snarled as he repeated the clichéd phrase that described the beginnings of Hoboken's gentrification. "Bechstein's the one who converted that abandoned mousetrap factory into a mix of luxury condos and affordable housing. He's got a huge project going up on the waterfront right now." Sol frowned at this evidence of the failure of years of his own effort to limit waterfront development in Hoboken.

Flashing him a sympathetic look, I said, "Damn. That shoots my other idea." Now there was disappointment in my own voice. "And damn my lousy memory. Would you believe I actually saw that article? Sam Simon brought it into my memoir-writing class to show me the part about Dino Sorrentino." Sol looked blank. "Sam's the ex-con who used to work for Sorrentino. Sorrentino was one of Sam's idols, and Sam wanted to show me that he's still influential today. Damn."

"What, you thought you would go with Sarah and interview Bechstein?" Sol asked, pushing his empty plate aside and turning his attention to his wine.

"Yes. I figured he would have an ego and agree to an interview, but if he's just been profiled . . ." I hesitated.

Then it came to me. "I know. I'll invite him to speak to one of my classes. In Cultures and Values we often have speakers." Sol looked dubious. Anticipating his reality check, I continued. "No, he'll come. In fact, to ensure that he accepts, I'll make it a debate between him and his old nemesis. I'll invite Marlene too. And the press. Maybe even our local cable station will feature it." Now Sol grinned. No developer aspiring to break ground anywhere in Hoboken would let Marlene Proletariat, president of the Citizens' Committee to Preserve the Waterfront and rabble rouser par excellence, speak without rebuttal.

Sol smiled and raised his glass in a toast. "Good work, woman. He'll buy into that for sure. He'll have to."

"And so will my students. It'll be a perfect illustration of how our culture and our values interact and conflict. We can even visit the sites of some of the big condo cubes that have gone up recently. I love it!" I exclaimed, nearly spilling my wine.

"What I really like about it is that you're not meeting with this hotshot murder suspect in some deserted spot all by yourself," Sol said. "You'll be on your turf with lots of company."

"Speaking of home turf and lots of company, wasn't Charlie's suggestion that we get married at the block party a hoot?" I asked, getting up to clear the table. "Rabbi Ornstein-Klein may not be orthodox, but she'd still draw the line at those sausage-and-pepper heroes. And the ceremony would have to be after sundown cause the party's always on Saturday."

Sol looked up from loading the dishwasher, another frown creasing his brow. "You're right, of course, but I thought it was an interesting idea, and damn nice of them to want to do it. I wouldn't mind having Gene 'D' Singing Plumber play at our wedding though, would you?" Sol began to hum "My Guitar, A Six Pack, and You," one of Gene's band's signature songs. He lumbered over to where I stood at the fridge and grabbed me around the waist. By the time the fridge door slammed shut, we were dancing around the kitchen to the slightly off-key music of our two voices belting out the lyrics of Gene's song.

The next night was a lot less fun. Betty and I left RECC together at about 5:30 and drove to Hoboken. She was on her cell phone for the whole ride reassuring President Woodman, who was home with the flu, that the schedules she'd prepared for the impending accreditation visit would, indeed, be printed on time. We stopped at my house just long enough to use the bathroom and drop off my book bag and Betty's briefcase. Then we walked west across town among the throngs of young people making their way home from their offices in New York.

The sidewalks were still narrow pathways between waist-high piles of shoveled snow, so we had to walk single file for much of the way. Because we'd not yet had the chance to talk about how we were going to approach the occupants of the apartments, I quickly shared a plan I'd devised when I'd awakened sweating the night before. One of the advantages of being off my estrogen patch and once again visited by night sweats was the opportunity to do some serious uninterrupted thinking. "Let's tell them we're part of a citizens' crime watch. Here, pin this on my coat." I handed Betty a big white button saying CITIZENS' CRIME WATCH that I'd taken from a drawer of buttons I'd hoarded.

They dated all the way back to my anti-Vietnam War days. I had another one for her.

We took off our gloves and pinned the buttons to each other's coats. I talked while I worked the pin into the heavy fabric of Betty's parka. "We tell them there was a burglary across the way on the night of Dom's death. Access was from the roof. Then we ask if anybody saw anything. We give them a number to call if they or anyone else in their household did see something. Got it?" By the time I finished these instructions and we had put our buttons on, our temporarily ungloved hands were numb, and we were hugging ourselves and stamping our feet. Betty nodded and grunted something under her breath.

The first house had four names and four doorbells. Betty rammed the top doorbell belonging to "Marshall" with her finger. We heard a young female voice say, "Jeannette, is that you? Wait, I'll buzz you in." Betty and I looked at each other, shocked by the intercom which, I'm embarrassed to say, hadn't figured in my low-tech plan at all. But we were equally shocked by the fact that Ms. Marshall had buzzed us in without even waiting for Jeanette to respond. I was willing to bet that our eager-beaver hostess hadn't lived in an apartment or a city before. Betty and I exchanged a thumbs-up at our good luck and trudged up the four flights of stairs.

The woman standing at the top of the stairwell was about twenty-two. She was still dressed in the charcoal gray pantsuit she had worn to work, and her cheeks still bloomed crimson from the cold. As soon as she saw us, she retreated towards the open door of her apartment. Moving quickly and babbling about getting out of the cold, I stepped behind her and stood on the threshold before she could close the door in our unfamiliar faces. "Who are you? I was expecting a friend," she sputtered, her eyes wide as she trailed me into her apartment. Betty followed. Ms. Marshall eyed our pins.

Betty delivered our spiel in such a genial voice that I could see our reluctant hostess relaxing as she took in two cold but harmless-looking midlife mamas concerned about local crime. She walked over to the TV on which lines of soldiers marched and turned down the volume. I had counted on the fact that like many of the yuppies who lived in Hoboken, she had no idea what went on in the mile-square city where she slept each night. I was willing to bet that she still voted in her suburban hometown. I was right. Her selective ignorance worked to our advantage when I flashed the copy of a newspaper article detailing the alleged burglary Betty had mentioned. Ms. Marshall did not suspect that the article described a breaking-and-entering that took place last year, and that I'd purposely smudged the address.

"So were you home on Monday, January twentieth? Can you check your datebook and see? And if so, did you happen to notice any unusual activity on that roof?" I walked over to the window and stared out over the top of the cream-colored café curtains to the Tomasellis' roof and pointed.

"Gee, I'm sorry. Even if I was home, I never look out the window." She glanced at the TV. "That's my little window on the world." Just then the buzzer sounded. "That's probably Jeanette. She's bringing up dinner. You're going to have to excuse me now." She buzzed Jeanette in. Clearly our audience was over.

But as we headed for the door, Betty turned to Ms.

Marshall and reprimanded her. "You know, girl, you didn't give us a chance to identify ourselves on your intercom. And I didn't hear you checking out your friend just now. You keep on letting strangers in here, and one of these days, you're going to have visitors you don't want."

Ms. Marshall looked contrite. "You're right. I'll be more careful. And for sure I'll let you know if I hear of anything." She held up the paper Betty had given her with the phone number on it, and stepped once more to the door.

As we walked downstairs, we ran into Jeanette, almost hidden behind a bag of Chinese food. We stood still on the landing while she passed us. Then, taking advantage of the fact that we were actually in the building, we knocked on the doors of the other three apartments. No one answered on the third or second floors, so we slipped a Xeroxed leaflet with our mission and my phone number on it under each door. A male voice responded to our knock on the door of the first-floor apartment.

"Omigod, Miz Ramsey! Omigod. Wait a minute. Lemme straighten up a little. What're you doin' here? I mean it's totally cool to see you. Is everything all right? Is Randy there?" Words spilled out of the dark-skinnned young man wearing navy sweats. His round face had registered surprise, pleasure, embarrassment, and concern in rapid succession. He peered over Betty's shoulder as if expecting to find her son Randy behind her in the hallway.

"Well hello, Howard," said Betty, looking a little surprised herself. "Bel, Howard Tuttle. Howard's an old friend of Randy's. Howard, my friend, Bel Barrett. Then with a mischievous gleam in the eye that had taken in the pants and jacket on the floor and the extensive collection of empty takeout containers and newspapers on the coffee table, Betty added, "Randy and Howard have the same decorator." Poor Howard had begun clearing the sofa of old mail, presumably so he could offer us a seat. "Howard, be still a minute," Betty ordered. He froze. Betty went over to him and enveloped him in a bear hug.

"Now listen here, Howard. Don't go cleaning up on my account or Bel's either. We've both seen worse at home, and we can't stay." To say that Howard looked relieved to hear this would be to understate his reaction. "But before we explain what we're doing here, tell me, how's your dad?"

"He's cool, Miz Ramsey. I was just reading an e-mail from him," replied Howard, nodding in the direction of the computer across the room. "I'm going to have dinner with him tomorrow night, in fact. I'll tell him you asked. But seriously, what are you doing here?" Now it was his turn to eye our pins.

Betty gave him the same spiel she'd given the young woman upstairs. While she spoke, I walked over to Howard's window and peered through the wrought-iron bars common to many first-floor apartments for yet another view of the Tomasellis' roof.

"Geez, I wish I could help. I don't know if I was home, but even if I was here, I was probably on-line." He nodded in the direction of his PC. "I don't know if Randy told you, but I've been out of work since November. I was downsized, so when I'm here, I'm pretty focused on Monster.com. I had an interview today, though," he said, his face brightening. "Anyway, I'm sorry. I wish I could help," Howard repeated.

"Well, you can actually. When the two tenants above

you get home, would you ask them if they saw anything? We left them these," said Betty, handing
Howard the Xeroxed sheet with my number.

"You bet, Miz Ramsey," Howard replied, taking the
paper. "Hey, do you want me to call you a cab? It's
nasty out there." He pulled a cell phone out of the
pocket of his sweats.

"No thanks, Howard, we have three other buildings
to visit tonight," Betty said. "Good luck with your job
search." She blew him a kiss, and we were on our way.

"I wonder if the units in that building are condos or
rental apartments," I mused as Betty and I trudged up
the stairs to the next building.

"I remember Randy telling me Howard had bought a
condo in Hoboken a year or so ago," said Betty. "He was
a broker and right before the market dived, he got a big
bonus at the holidays. That's what he did with it. It
looked like a nice enough unit. But he paid top dollar."

We had no time to speculate on how the changes on
Wall Street might affect the value of Howard's investment. As soon as I rang the doorbell of the top apartment occupied by someone named Thaxton, we heard
a female voice through the intercom asking, "Who is
it?"

Betty started to give her spiel and the voice said,
"Go away or I'll call the cops."

Without discussion, we pushed some of our leaflets
through the door and left that building. "Bummer," I
said. "Look, there are lights on in the other three units
in that building too. Damn. Let's say we've got a package or a pizza or something at the next place." Betty
nodded, and in a few minutes we found ourselves in
the apartment of a modishly stubbled and tousled
young man named Acevedo on the top floor of the

third building on our list explaining to him and three equally stubbled and tousled friends why, in fact, we had no package.

"You're worse than telemarketers," began the one who, presumably, had let us in. "You actually come barging into my home . . ."

Betty cut him off, saying in her most imperious tone. "We'd rather be home, son, believe me. Listen up and we'll be out of here in a minute." And she rattled off an accelerated version of her spiel. While she talked, I checked out the view of the Tomasellis' roof. This building was directly opposite Flora's home. From the window I could see one of Dom's two remaining lofts, its slatted sides silhouetted against the full moon.

"Right, we'll call you, lady. Bye now," he said. I looked back and saw him crush the paper I'd handed him even before he had closed the door to his apartment. And so it went. We got into a few more apartments, but no one had seen anything. We ended the evening over thin-crusted pizzas at Grimaldi's on the way home. "When I first moved here in the early seventies people used to sit at their windows and keep an eye on kids and neighborhood goings-on. I guess they don't do that anymore," I said, stating the obvious.

"Right, girlfriend," said Betty. "But we had to make sure. Besides, maybe somebody who wasn't home will call with a lead."

"Right, and if you believe that, I have a bridge . . ."

Chapter 22

Hilda Fairclough (con't.)

When Leland carried me over the threshold of 22 Forest Road, Morristown, New
Jersey, he made me close my eyes. I'd
never seen the inside of the two-
hundred-year-old abandoned farmhouse
that he'd bought after we'd both admired it from the car on a Sunday afternoon drive not long before our
wedding. Once an inn, the house was
close to the road. It was gray clap-
board with shutters hanging from the
windows at all angles. There was an old
barn out back and a kitchen garden long
ago run to weeds. When I opened my eyes
that day, I fell in love with every
weathered board and rusted nail in the
place. We spent our honeymoon repairing
the roof and clearing out the garden.
We lived there for over 65 years . . .

When I thought about Hilda's account of her unorthodox honeymoon, I couldn't help but think about Sol's and my wedding. But I was still too busy teaching, reading student papers, and setting up the debate between Jonah Bechstein and Marlene Proletariat to do much more than think about it. To compensate for our lack of initiative, Sol and I had made a WEDDING TO-DO list, so at least we could be clear about what tasks we were not doing. It was Sol's contention that getting a marriage license was a task we could accomplish easily and quickly and then cross off our list. A list crosser-offer from way back, I agreed.

The Registrar's Office was housed in the same building as the Senior Center, so Sol met me there after the memoir-writing class in which Hilda had shared her recollections of her beloved home in Morristown. I'd asked Ma and Sofia to act as the two witnesses we needed, in exchange for a ride home. They were happy to comply, providing they could treat us to a celebratory lunch. This worked for me because I was eager to hear what they had learned about Emilio DeFranco from their attendance at two meetings of Gamblers Anonymous.

The process of obtaining the license really was relatively simple yet too bureaucratic to be personally meaningful or romantic. We stood at the counter, declared our intentions, and then Sol wrote a check. We pushed the check and our birth certificates and passports under the glass partition. In a few minutes the registrar had typed up the license, and we all signed it. We might have been having our car registration renewed, it was that matter-of-fact. After presenting us with our copy of the signed red-sealed document, the registrar handed me a plastic bag and, in a solemn voice, said, "And here's a little wedding present for you. Something to get you started right. Much happiness to both of you."

Surprised and relieved to hear at least some recognition of the fact that officially registering our intent to marry had been a significant act for us, I thanked him profusely and we left. It wasn't until we got outside and I opened the plastic bag that I guffawed so hard I nearly wet my pants. The City of Hoboken had blessed our union by presenting me, the antidomestic goddess bride, with samples of bathroom cleanser, laundry detergent, and furniture polish.

Because I was laughing dangerously hard, we took refuge in Zafra's, a nearby storefront restaurant featuring South American food. Once I emerged from the tiny ladies room, we ordered. I was glad Ma and Sofia were with us to turn the rather ho-hum event into a mini-celebration. With great fanfare, I produced the WEDDING TO-DO list from my book bag, and Sol crossed off "License."

"Wasn't Hilda's reading something?" asked Ma, in between spoonfuls of flavorful, hot chicken soup. "Imagine having your home where you lived for sixty-five years become a hotel." We had all ordered the soup, a Carribean specialty chock full of cumin-spiked vegetables and chicken that proved just perfect for a cold day in New Jersey.

"Remember, she said it was originally an inn," I countered. Then, turning to Sol, I explained, "Their classmate sold her Morristown manse, and the new owner turned it into a B & B."

"Yes, and they invited her back for a weekend. The house is all different now. The room where she gave birth to her first two babies is called The Bower. It has

Victorian floral prints all over the walls and drapes, and the furniture is all white wicker. Hilda hates it," said Sofia. "I don't blame her."

"Well, she took all her real antiques with her, didn't she?" asked Ma. "She said she sold the house empty." She gave me a look as I picked up my soup bowl to drink the last drops of broth. I put the bowl down.

"Yes," said Sofia, not to be deterred. "In her living room the new owners serve wine and cheese, and they've put a gazebo where her vegetable garden used to be." Sofia sounded indignant, no doubt because she had once boasted a legendary vegetable garden and still grew tomatoes from seed in containers every summer.

"One of her children's rooms is now called Love Nest, and it's wall-to-wall hearts, including the bed and the bathtub," said Ma with a chuckle. "She said the kid used to have model airplanes all over and once kept a pet iguana in the tub. The room she used as a guest room is now the Sahara Suite. You know, a desert fantasy filled with pillows and silk hangings and a tented bed. Very Lawrence of Arabia."

"Well, Sofia, your empty nest is sort of a B & B & S." Sol loved teasing the Odd Couple.

"What's that?" asked Sofia, looking up from her soup bowl.

"Bed, breakfast and supper," Sol answered with a grin. "You've got Sadie here as your permanent paying houseguest."

"I suppose that's true," Sofia said. "But it's different because she's not a stranger. And the house is still the same as it always was."

"Amen," said Ma.

"And I'm still living there," added Sofia, as if daring any of us to challenge her.

"Amen," we all intoned again.

"Well, I thought Hilda's piece was fascinating. I hope that soon she feels better about having sold that big old place and moved to a condo here near her kids," I said. Then, rather abruptly, I redirected our conversation. "And speaking of selling houses and condos, I'm curious about what you two wormed out of Emilio De-Franco at GA. Tell me everything." We were sharing three appetizers and an entrée, so when our waiter brought our fresh corn *tamal,* Brazilian kale sautéed in garlic, fried bananas, and shrimp in red sauce, Sol and I apportioned this abundance of exotic comfort food onto four plates.

"Well, it was just me," said Ma. "Sofia couldn't go."

"Why not?" Sol and I chorused, concerned at the idea of Ma braving the winter cold and slippery walks, not to mention facing a possible murder suspect on her own. When they hadn't called Sol or me for a ride, I'd assumed Sofia's daughter had driven them.

"We were all set to go together when I remembered that Patch installed my drapes. You know the opaque mauve ones in my bedroom and the translucent dark green ones in the parlor?" Sofia's voice was tinged with regret. "It was years ago, but we couldn't take the chance he'd remember me." She patted her hair with her hand, as if to reassure herself that she was, indeed, a memorable-looking woman. "Besides he and I have a lot of mutual friends, and they all know I'm not a compulsive gambler." She contemplated her plate. "Sadie, after that soup, I'm never going to be able to finish all this."

"Me either, but it's going to be great for dinner tonight," said Ma. "We'll just nuke it. Anyway . . ." I could tell that having organized their next meal, Ma was impatient to tell her tale. "Anyway, I took a cab to Jersey City." When Sol and I looked up together, she said, "That's where they meet. There is no GA in Hoboken. So anyway, I took a cab to St. Paul's Church and went into the basement, and there were five people, three women and two men, sitting around a table. I recognized Emilio right away because of his, you know, that birthmark." Ma fingered her own cheek as she spoke. "I pretended I was shy and ill at ease. The other man, Pete, talked about how, after not gambling for almost five months, he got drunk and placed a bet with a bookie. He wanted to win enough to replace what he lost in the market." Ma, who had already done that, shook her head. "A younger woman named Honey went on about using some of her welfare check to buy lottery tickets each week so she could send her kid to private school. And another woman, I think her name was Estrella, talked about how she didn't let herself get suckered into betting on something or other in her office." This was too much information as far as I was concerned, but I didn't want to hurry Ma since she was clearly enjoying recounting her exploit.

When she continued, her eyes flashed and her voice was unusually animated. "Emilio said something about how he had tried to quit gambling for years before he joined GA and about how they shouldn't get discouraged. He spoke softly, so I had to listen up. He talked about how other GA members had helped him to resist temptation. He said he went to church more now and volunteers at the homeless shelter in Hoboken. He gave out his phone number and said if anybody wanted to call him for support, he was available. Here's his number." Ma handed me a card with a phone number on it.

"Did you get to talk?" I asked, eager to know how she had presented herself.

"Of course. I let them persuade me to tell my story," said Ma.

"And what was your story?" asked Sol, also curious.

"Oh, you'll just love this," said Sofia, clearly amused by what she already knew of Ma's cover.

"I said I had a landlady who was a compulsive gambler who always wanted me to go to Atlantic City with her. When I went, I too gambled and lost more than I could afford. But I felt I couldn't refuse to accompany her, and I kept hoping I'd win my money back." Ma's eyes were aglow with mischief and she turned to Sofia. "Well, since you couldn't go with me, I thought I'd get you involved somehow."

"But that's not the best part," said Sofia. "Guess how she got back to Hoboken. Just guess." Sofia's vicarious pleasure in Ma's undercover adventure was becoming more apparent with each revelation.

Sol and I looked at each other, knowing the answer. "Well, Sadie, since the acorn doesn't fall very far from the tree, and since you are your daughter's mother, I figure you asked this murder suspect to drive you back," said Sol with a resigned sigh.

"Even if he isn't a murderer, I can't see him driving. He's very arthritic," I added.

"Well, we were the only two there from Hoboken, so we shared a cab," said Ma. "And that's when I found out about his alibi." She paused, milking the moment.

I was losing patience, and, taking my cue from Illuminada, glanced at my watch. "Ma, I have another class to teach in Jersey City at two-twenty. Does he have an alibi?"

Ma continued, picking up the pace but still not get-

ting to the point. "So while we waited we were talking
about our arthritis, you know, what we take, who our
doctors are, you know, the usual." Sofia nodded. I
began to seethe, realizing, not for the first time, where
my own propensity for extended narrative came from.
I signaled our server for the check. "He was telling me
how his nephew is pretty good to him, but he'd always
wished he had kids of his own until just recently. He
changed his mind when his niece and nephew tried to
put their father in a home." Ma and Sophia glanced at
each other and shuddered in unison. Even the most
benevolent and nurturing assisted-living facilities held
no allure for these two. Then it was Sol's and my turn
to look at each other. This was the first I'd heard of
Flora's wanting to institutionalize Dom. She had never
mentioned it, and neither had Leo. My mind raced, but
I struggled to attend to what Ma said next.

    "Emilio also told me he volunteers at the homeless
shelter one night a week. That means he and two other
volunteers spend the whole night there in case there's
a problem," said Ma. "That way, Sister Roberta can go
home to sleep." Sister Roberta was well known in
Hoboken as the woman who started the town's only
homeless shelter and, through resourcefulness, hard
work, and faith, had kept it funded and staffed for more
than two decades. "Emilio's night is Monday." Even
with my brain boggled at the news that Flora had
wanted to put Dom away, I couldn't fail to grasp the
significance of Ma's last line, especially since she uttered it in the tone I imagined God used when bringing
about the creation of light. "Dom disappeared on a
Monday night. Emilio told me he hasn't missed his
night at the shelter in six months," said Ma. "Emilio
has an airtight alibi."

Ma looked so pleased with herself that I forgave her for making a shaggy-dog story out of what could have been a one-liner. "Good work, Ma," I said. "That helps a lot. It's the first break we've gotten actually."

"Think of it as an early wedding present, dear. Now go teach your next class, Bel. Sol will drive us home, right Sol?" said Ma, scooping the check off the tray before the waitress had even placed it on the table.

Sol stood to help me on with my bulky coat. Turning to face the table where Ma and Sofia still sat, he bent at the waist in an exaggerated bow and said, "At your service, ladies."

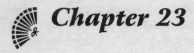 *Chapter 23*

To: Bbarrett@circle.com
From: Mbarrett@hotmail.com
Re: Good news/bad news
Date: 03/12/03 19:04:24

Yo, Ma Bel,

The good news is Aveda and I got a gig together archiving and moving the estate of a nephew of that dude we worked for before, Geraldo Figueroa. Apparently he gave us such good references that his nephew wants to hire us to archive and pack all the incredible art and antiques in his huge barn near Taos. So we get to leave the freezing forests of Maine for sunny New Mexico, all expenses paid! Aveda said we should start a business. I told her we already did. We're calling ourselves "Good to Go," and we're working on our website.

The bad news is that we'll need a lot of advance notice now to get up to your wedding. I'm sure we can get the time off, but we'll need to fly, and we'll need some lead time to get decent rates until the tourist season is over. So give us a heads-up when you and Sol set a date. And let us know what we can do to help.

Love,
Mark

I sighed as I read Mark's e-mail. When I told Sol about it that night at dinner, his response was, as usual, philosophical. "It's great that he and Aveda are trying their hand at a real business. Even if it doesn't work out, it's useful experience."

"You're probably right. But the economy's so bad right now," I said. "How many rich people are there left with collections valuable enough to archive? Or move?" I thought of all the people I knew who had lost money and jobs in the recent economic downturn.

"Bel, trust me. There are plenty of well-heeled people left. Remember those tax breaks? Who do you think got the really big ones?" Sol asked. "It's not the rich people who are hurting now. It's everybody else." Sol spoke with the authority of the economics professor he had been. "And this new client will have affluent friends who'll hire Mark and Aveda too. Just wait and see."

"I sure hope you're right," I said, pushing my beef and vegetables around in the bowl.

"What's wrong, Bel? You usually love my stew. Bad day?" Sol sipped his wine and leaned forward, ready to listen.

I nodded. "Today was the day that Marlene and Jonah Bechstein debated in my Cultures and Values class, and it was a bummer."

"What are you talking about? I got a call from Marlene, and she said it went really well. She said Bechstein was very upfront about the profit motive and the relative costs of affordable and luxury housing and the importance of adding rateables to the city's tax rolls. And you know how modest Marlene is, right?" I nodded. "Well, she said she was 'absolutely eloquent' on the impact of overdevelopment on the environment and the culture of a community, and afterwards the students asked really good questions. So what was wrong?" Sol sipped his wine and looked up at me.

I had taken a few nibbles of my stew, but before answering, I put my fork down and picked up my own wineglass. "What's wrong is that no way did Jonah Bechstein push Dom Tomaselli off the roof, that's what's wrong," I said, washing down my anger with a little more wine. "Marlene is right. The debate went very well from an educational perspective. Bechstein spoke first, and he told them all about how his father came here as an immigrant and pushed clothes around in the garment district and saved his money until he could buy a crummy little piece of property in Queens, NY. And the rest is history, the same history that produced the American dream. And my students who dream that same dream ate up every word." I put my wineglass down so hard that the few remaining sips nearly sloshed out onto the table. "Bechstein gave out business cards and told them to come and see him when they graduate. I thought he was very patronizing. And, Sol, he's a paunchy middle-aged guy—"

"Bel, it's not like you to hold a person's appearance or age against him. What happened to my PC-perfect bride?" Sol grinned. He loved it when I broke one of my own rules. "Besides, you better watch it, my love. You're treading on sensitive ground. You're about to marry a paunchy middle-aged guy." As if to emphasize his point, Sol helped himself to more stew.

"It's not the same. You're stocky or, on a dignified day, portly. Bechstein is paunchy. He reminded me of Santa Claus in a really good Italian suit. But that's not the problem. It's not his looks or even his age that disqualify him as a suspect," I said, swabbing at my stew gravy with a slice of Marie's brick-oven bread. I was starting to feel a little better.

"So, what is the problem, love?" asked Sol as he dumped a pile of greens into my now empty stew bowl. The man was a really good cook, but his presentation left something to be desired.

"Actually there are two problems. Bechstein explained the scope of his business, the developments he's built and the ones in the works. Sol, his projects are so big, and he has so many of them all over the metropolitan area that I can't believe he would care very much about whatever he could build on the site of the Hoboken Racing Pigeon Club. It would have to be a very dinky little condo. Six units would be the maximum you could squeeze into that lot with some parking," I said. "Hardly worth killing somebody over." Bitterness lent an acidic edge to my voice.

"Don't jump to conclusions, Bel. Remember, back in the seventies landlords were hiring arsonists to torch buildings so they could get rid of the tenants and develop the shells into three- and four-unit condos." As he spoke I recalled Ana Guzman's account of awakening to find her apartment transformed into an inferno. I struggled to erase that image from my mind. Sol was saying, "To a developer, a small profit is better than no profit." He was, as usual, the voice of reason. "What was the second thing you felt disqualified Bechstein from your list of suspects?"

"As a courtesy, I walked Bechstein and Marlene downstairs. He was waiting for his driver, and he happened to mention that he just got back from a month in Mexico with his wife and mother. He wasn't even here," I said. "I went to all that trouble to arrange this debate and Bechstein wasn't even in the country when Dom was killed." Sol was used to hearing me whine, so he knew how to react. He ignored my breast beating and went to the more substantive issue that, in my leap to self-deprecation, I had overlooked.

"Bel, if you were a multimillionaire developer, would you do your own laundry?" I shook my head. "Would you wash your own car?" Again, I shook my head, beginning to see where this dumbed-down version of twenty questions was leading. "So would you do your own killing? Or would you have an employee do it for you while you were out of the country? Believe me, Bel, if Jonah Bechstein wanted Dominic Tomaselli pushed off a roof, he'd have some flunky of his push him off the roof." As if to illustrate his point, Sol pushed his empty bowl away and looked smug. I nibbled at my greens and sipped my wine, now picturing the hired goons pushing Eva Marie Saint's brother off the roof in *On the Waterfront*. Sol was right on all counts.

"But Sol, remember what Ma said? Emilio told her Flora and Leo wanted to put Dom away? Doesn't that make Flora a suspect?" I asked. "That really bothers me more than anything. I mean, what if she ran up to the roof and pushed her father off?" We were both unloading clean dishes and putting them away.

"I was wondering what you made of that," said Sol. "You looked a little shell-shocked at the news."

"That's putting it mildly," I said. "But why would Flora ask me to investigate a murder she committed?"

"It's possible that she figured you'd check it out it anyway and wanted to coopt the investigation, which she very nearly has," answered Sol. "But the bottom line is that you know the woman, and I don't. Do you think she's capable of murder?" He was sliding the silverware into appropriate compartments in the drawers of our new cherry cabinets, so he did not look at me as he spoke.

I weighed the question. "She's smart, but she's very sensitive and anxious. I think she has stress-induced asthma. The poor woman has to use an inhaler to get through a bad day. She's finally begun college, so she needs time to study. Maybe she just got sick of taking care of Dom, you know? He'd started wandering off. He wasn't taking his meds. Leo did mention that before Dom enrolled in my class and began to take his pills on schedule, Flora was literally pulling her hair out and had to take anti-anxiety meds herself. She didn't tell me any of that."

"Maybe she had a midlife crisis or some kind of mood swing that threw her off track and she just lost it and . . ." To illustrate his point, Sol gave me a friendly shove with one hand and caught me with the other. "Bel, remember how you felt when your mother was living with us and hallucinating? After your dad died? You used to come home and find her talking to your dead father and your ex-husband, neither of whom was here. You came damn close to losing it yourself, and you had a caregiver coming in to help."

"True, but not once did I even consider pushing her off the roof," I said, slamming a pot into the nest of others in the cabinet. I did not like to remember that unhappy time.

"Maybe not, but you were pretty close to jumping yourself," Sol reminded me.

"But Sol, you know perfectly well that menopause does not make a woman crazy. That's an outdated stereotype," I added, my voice on the verge of shrillness.

"Okay, okay. Spare me the lecture. You're right. I know it by heart. I just don't want you to dismiss the possibility that Flora pushed her dad off that roof because she was fed up with taking care of him."

"Okay, okay yourself. You're the one who's right tonight," I said, fighting the urge to smash the pile of clean plates I was holding. "Jonah Bechstein, Santa in Armani, stays on my A list." I stacked the plates in their rightful place on the shelf and sighed when I added, "And Flora Giglio, she's right up there with him."

Chapter 24

We dedicate this book to Professor Bel
Barrett who came up with the idea for
it and who has worked hard to help each
of us record our memories so that those
who come after us will know who we were
and how we lived. Thank you Professor
Barrett. We also dedicate it to the
memory of our friend and classmate Dominic Tomaselli.

Ana Guzman

Sofia Dellafemina

Hilda Fairclough

Sadie Bickoff

Ellen O'Malley

Sam Simon

No sooner had I arrived at the Senior Center class-
room than my students clustered around me and presented me with a copy of this touching dedication.
They wanted it incorporated into the publication I was

compiling for distribution at the end of the course. Each of them had chosen a favorite section of their memoir for inclusion in what, for lack of a better title, we had come to call "Our Book." I had agreed to assume responsibility for getting it printed and collated at the RECC copy shop. To that end I had persuaded the dean of continuing education to accept the inevitable charges for paper and to pay for them out of his budget. It is helpful for writers to see their work in print, and I wanted these intrepid folks to have a souvenir of what had been a productive and pleasant collaboration for us all.

"Thank you. That's very generous of you. And I'm glad you mentioned Dom. He was an important part of our group, and we all miss him. I asked his daughter to select a section of his memoir to include." Ever since Flora had become a suspect, I felt uneasy at the very thought of her. Of course my concern was not shared by anyone else in the group except, possibly, for Ma and Sofia. "Today, last but not least, we're going to hear from Sofia. Sofia, are you ready?"

"Yes, I'm ready," said Sofia, who looked not only ready, but eager to share her recollections. She had dressed for the occasion in a black knit pantsuit brightened by a black-and-white scarf looped around her neck and falling in gentle folds almost to her waist. Her platinum blond curls were lacquered into submission, and her nails and lips flashed crimson. Clearing her throat, she began to read. "My grandmother Sofia Dellafemina must have been an amazing woman. She and my grandfather had a bakery over on Jackson Street where the projects are now. The whole time I was growing up, I heard about how every single morning she got up after just a few hours of sleep to bake bread." Sofia used a singsong voice when she read of her grandmother's toil. "I also heard how, before they had all the children to help, she delivered the bread all over town even when she was pregnant." Sofia paused, taking in the nods of recognition her story provoked.

"By the time my father was six, he was helping." Sofia continued in a singsong tone as she recounted her father's Dickensian childhood. "He wasn't strong enough to lift the flour sacks or knead the dough, but he could help her deliver them, and he could sweep and clean the bakery." She paused a moment, and when she resumed reading, the rhythm of her words was once again natural. "Whenever I complained about my chores, my father would start telling me how hard he had worked in the bakery when he was just a child. When I couldn't stand listening anymore, I used to put my fingers in my ears . . ." Sofia glanced up over her paper and saw that her classmates were nodding even more emphatically and grinning too. She adjusted the black harlequin-shaped glasses that framed her eyes and continued. "That made him really mad. I swore I would never tell my children how rough I had it when I was growing up, but guess what? I did." Sofia, obviously gratified by her classmates' murmured Me-toos, realized that she had tapped into a lode of familiar experience and read on. When finished, she waited for comments. And her classmates obliged, offering kudos and posing questions. As we all left class, I marveled once again at this group's ability to make almost every moment a teachable one.

Compared to the memoir class, all my others were discouraging. Students were plagued by weather-related illness and car trouble. Their routine struggle to

work, care for their families, and go to school did not get
easier when Mother Nature turned the heat down and
produced all that white stuff. Those who actually did
make it to class were often not only unprepared but also
coughing, sneezing, and accompanied by small children
too congested themselves to go to day care. In spite of
my students' determination, I kept wondering how they
could possibly compete with their more traditional counterparts who did not have to attend classes exhausted and
encumbered by croupy kids. When not pondering this inequity, I counted the days until spring break.

After a particularly unrewarding session of Cultures
and Values had left me feeling disgruntled, Flora approached my desk. She waited while I explained to one
of her classmates that the fact that I wanted him to revise his paper did not mean that the paper was worth-
less and he should drop the course. Apparently none of
his instructors in the other three countries where he
had studied previously had ever required that he write
a paper let alone revise one, so he was unfamiliar with
the process. He was also insulted. By the time I had re-
iterated the pedagogical reasons underlying revision
and mollified his hurt feelings, students were filing
into that room ready for a class in American Govern-
ment. I was ready to collapse in my office. I wanted
only to dive into my jar of M&M's for some serious
chocolate therapy. But there was Flora, waiting patiently, her nose in a book like the model student she
was. "Professor Barrett, do you have a minute? I got
some good news."

"Yes, Flora. I'm through teaching for the day. Why
don't you join me in my office? We can talk privately
there." I shouldn't be closeting myself with a killer, but
Flora had no reason to believe that I posed a threat to

her, so I felt comfortable with the invitation I had just extended. She smiled to indicate her agreement, and, as soon as I had collected my books and papers, she accompanied me down the hall.

Ever since I had raised the possibility that Leo had killed their dad and posed a threat to her, Flora had been tightlipped and tense. The fact that Emilio had an alibi for the night of Dom's death made Leo an even more likely suspect. I expected that this would upset her anew. Or would it? If she herself was guilty, maybe her concern for her brother was a sham. At that moment, the motives and possibly murderous machinations of the Tomaselli family seemed like a hopeless muddle to me.

Once settled in my office, Flora accepted an offering of M&M's and said, "It's Leo. Last night he said he wanted to talk to me about somethin', and so I waited to have supper until he got home. Now that he's in real estate, he misses dinner a lot, so I eat with John and save Leo a plate." I nodded, aware that Flora was breathing normally. Her inhaler was nowhere in sight. "Leo said he wanted to talk about us sellin' the house," Flora announced, taking apparent pleasure in my raised eyebrows. "See, Professor, he isn't doin' it behind my back like you thought."

"Flora, he can't really sell it without your consent, can he?" I asked. "But you're right. I am relieved that he's discussing it with you. How do you feel about it?"

"I'm sad at the thought of leavin' the place where we all were together for so long, the place where my Mary grew up, where I grew up." At this point, Flora drew a deep breath before she said, "But I'm gonna agree." She straightened her shoulders and lifted her chin just a little.

"Why are you going to agree to something that sad-
dens you?" I asked, assuming she was intimidated by
Leo or putting on an Oscar-worthy performance.

"Well, here's the way Leo laid it out. We're gonna
get about $160,000 for Papa's share of the clubhouse
when that deal goes through, so each of us gets about
$80,000. Leo says Princeton costs $40,000 a year. Can
you believe that, Professor? And Mary's tuition is way
up there too," Flora said, as if these numbers explained
everything.

"But don't the kids get scholarships?" I asked, jot-
ting down the numbers she had quoted. I never failed
to be astounded by the high price Americans had to
pay for higher education today.

"That's the problem," said Flora, sounding faintly
exasperated at my lack of comprehension. She took in
some air before trying to enlighten me. "Leo talked to
one of them financial planners he just sold a condo to.
John won't get a scholarship next year because Leo's
makin' too much money now to qualify anymore."
Flora's shoulders rose another inch at the thought of
her brother's success, even though it meant the end of
tuition assistance. "Even my Mary won't get one if I
got eighty grand in the bank, unless she emancipates
herself, and even then she might just qualify for a loan,
not a grant. And I'll lose whatever aid I get. So sooner
or later, even if I get a job, them two and me will have
to take out loans to finish school. And we don't like to
owe nobody." The very thought of incurring debt
caused Flora to catch her breath. "That's what Papa always said." Pride drew Flora's shoulders up another
notch.

"Where will you live if you sell the house?" I asked,
"Have you had a chance to consider that?"

"Well, Leo and I figure we got a few options. He says the house will sell for about $700,000. He thinks we should each buy a small condo around here, maybe in Union City," Flora said. Then unable to wait for me to respond, she blurted, "But I want mine to be in some place warm, some place I never been, maybe Arizona or New Mexico. It don't have to be too big, just one bedroom with a couple of pullout sofas for when Leo and the kids come." The words were tumbling out of Flora's mouth in a stream, a stream of damning dreams. Had Flora Giglio pushed her beloved father off the roof so she could put her kid through med school, finish college herself, and begin a new life in the sunny southwest? The thought was as chilling as the weather Flora longed to escape.

"It would be easy to take care of, so I could work, and then when I graduate and get a better job, I can get a bigger place if I want." With every word she uttered, Flora made it easier for me to picture her and Leo following Dom up to the roof and nudging him over the edge. The very thought of a low-maintenance nest among the saguaros made her eyes dance, and, for a moment, the years dropped away, giving her the carefree air of the young college coed she had never been. But then I asked myself, would she tell me these plans if they were motives for murder rather than just the dreams of a woman worn down by years of caregiving and now yearning for a life of her own?

If, in fact, Flora and Leo had conspired to kill Dom, I shouldn't share with her my thoughts about Leo and the progress of the investigation. But if she is innocent . . . I decided that I had to act as if she were innocent until I had some tangible proof to the contrary. I wanted her to realize that Leo's rather belated decision to speak to her about selling the house did not eliminate him as a suspect in his father's murder. But it did make me a little less anxious about Flora's safety, which was a big relief. I decided to start by telling her about Emilio's alibi and work my way around to the fact that Leo was still a viable suspect and therefore, still a threat. "Flora, your plans are exciting. I didn't realize you had such a thirst for adventure."

"Well, while I had Papa and the kids to take care of, I didn't even think about movin'." Her eyes teared up, but she didn't cry and she was breathing regularly. If she were guilty, she was quite an actress. "But now"— she paused and shrugged—"why not? When I get homesick, I can come stay with Leo. And he says he'll visit. He don't like these winters either," Flora added.

She looked so pleased at the prospect of a bright new future. It felt wrong to say anything that would break her rare moment of optimism and excitement. But I did it anyway. I had to see if her reaction would tell me anything. I gave her no warning before I said, "Flora, Emilio says you and Leo were considering putting your Dad in a home. Is that true?" At the sound of her uncle's name, Flora inhaled deeply, and much of the glow faded from her eyes. By the time I had posed my question, she had reached into her pocket and withdrawn her inhaler. But with her other hand, she reached for the jar of M&M's and helped herself to a handful.

Her breathing was audible when she answered me. "Professor Barrett, I'd be lyin' if I said we didn't talk about it, me and Leo. I was kinda at the end of my rope there for a while when Papa was runnin' off an', you know, not takin' his pills. We talked about a home as a last resort, you know, and we talked about findin' an adult day-care center for Papa too. But when I heard about your course, we decided to try that first." Almost as an afterthought she said, "And I got some medication too for my nerves, you know, my anxiety. That helped too."

I nodded and without comment or pause gave her even more reason for discomfort. "Flora, Emilio has a very solid alibi for the night your dad died." I heard her sudden intake of breath. "He volunteers at the Hoboken Shelter for the Homeless every Monday night. He spends the whole night there with two other volunteers. I'm going to verify that he was there that night just to be sure, but I suspect that he was."

Flora's accelerated breathing was the only hint of her skepticism at this news. If she'd set Emilio up to take the blame for Dom's death so as to divert suspicion from her and Leo, she was not reacting very animatedly to the failure of her ploy. But, I reminded myself, she could be acting. "Jeez, Professor. I think the man's a killer, and now you're telling me he's like," she paused for a moment searching for the rest of her simile, "like the Saint Francis of Hoboken. Jeez." Then she added quickly, "Excuse me, Professor, but I was so sure it was Emilio, you know 'cause he owed Papa money and all that. If it's not him . . . ?" Again she sucked in air, and tears welled in the eyes she fastened on my face.

Flora hadn't completed her question, but I answered it anyway. "Well, Leo is still the likeliest suspect, but we're not through looking at other possibilities yet." Flora applied her inhaler. I continued. "I've visited the condos on the next block and talked to some of the people who live in them. We're still hoping to come up with a witness."

I threw that out as a threat or a mood elevator, but Flora was not buying it either way. "Give me a break, Professor. Nobody's gonna come out and say they saw nothin'. It's not like in the movies." Then, as if afraid she had been too dismissive of my efforts, she said, "But I do appreciate how you're tryin' to help. I really do. It's just that I can't think of nobody who wanted Papa dead, including Leo," she added with a touch of defiance after taking another sniff from her inhaler. "Like I told you, they had their fights when Leo was growin' up, but Leo was grateful to Papa for takin' him and John in. 'Better late than never,' was how Leo put it." When she sighed at this memory, her shoulders slumped.

"Did you get a chance to look through Papa's scrapbook? The stuff from the safe box? Maybe you'll see somethin' in there that I missed." Now it was Flora who was grasping at straws, but that was what you had to do when you kept turning into dead-end streets and blind alleys. To do otherwise was to give up, and Flora was not a quitter. But, I asked myself, was she a very clever killer, leading me on a wild goose chase until I gave up? Well, I wasn't a quitter either.

"I'll try to get to it this weekend," I promised. "But you know I have a lot of paperwork that has to come first, like all those revisions you and your classmates just turned in." She managed a faint smile. "And now, would you like a ride back to Hoboken? I brought the car today," I offered. As soon as I spoke, I realized that I was having a hard time distancing myself from Flora enough to believe that she might have killed her father. But I would have to try, would have to at least consider that possibility seriously.

"Thanks, but I got mine too," she said, as she put on

her her parka and picked up her book bag. "Oh here, I almost forgot!" Flora was rifling through the contents of her book bag. "Here's a copy of the chapter I picked from Papa's memoir to put in his class book. I'd of been mad if I walked outta here without givin' it to you. My memory's not what it used to be these days, that's for sure." Flora handed me a plastic folder with the excerpt I'd asked her to select neatly typed inside.

Once more, she looked to be on the verge of tears, a far cry from the ebullient woman who had entered my office looking ahead to a life of warm-weather adventure. Now she was looking back, and it made her sad. Or was she putting that on too? "Thanks for askin' me to do that. You coulda picked a chapter yourself, but it probably woulda been a different one," she said. "Night now." And she left.

Chapter 25

Dominic Tomaselli (con't)

I'll never forget the birthday present
I got from my wife in 1957, that was
the year they disbanded the headquar-
ters of my old unit the Pigeon Signal
Corps at Ft. Monmouth. Without saying
nothing she went down there by herself
on the train and tried to buy some of
the pigeons for me as like a souvenir.
(They were selling them birds at good
prices.) There was a long line and she
was number 150 or something, so when it
got to be her turn they had no birds
left, she started to cry and told them
I was a vet and a trainer from WWII and
she kept on crying and begged them to
give her an egg at least, so they did,
she held that egg in her hands to keep
it warm for the whole train ride back
to Hoboken. When she got home she gave

it to me right away and I put it in a
nest in the coop. It was band number
4416, I named it Monmouth and had it
for seven years, I raced Monmouth for
five years., and he was a winner. . . .

Poor Renata! Dom didn't even mention her by
name, but he told us the name and number of the pigeon she gave him.

While my feminist sensibilities were confronting
what I saw as irrefutable evidence of Dom's pigeon-
centered priorities, I realized that I'd forgotten to ask
Flora to make up a title for the selection. It was too late
to call her, so I decided to title it myself. I typed "Renata's Gift" after Dom's name in the table of contents
that I was putting together. My title fit in nicely with
the other titles. Ellen had called her piece simply "Reunion with Sheila." Sam had been torn between "Me
and Dino" and "Me and the Mayor" and had settled on
the latter. Ma went derivative and dubbed hers "A Girl
Grows in Brooklyn," and Sofia used the rather old-
fashioned title "A Hoboken Girlhood." Hilda chose
"Our House in the Country" and, after much thought,
Ana went with "A Better Life."

I had already Xeroxed the dedication page and the
cover, a collage of old black-and-white photos the students had provided. Underneath it was the title of the
collection, "Our Book: Telling It Like it Was." I wished
I'd thought to take a current photo of each of the authors to include, but I hadn't, and now there was no
time. The class's final session was not far off, so I
needed to get the copy to the print shop yesterday.

I proofread the front matter carefully. Then I gathered the individual selections that were spread out on

our dining-room table and arranged them in alphabetical order, leafing through them one more time to make sure all the pages were there and in the right sequence. I couldn't help but reread some of them, so it was late when I finished and followed Sol upstairs to bed. The stories still lingered in my head. Not surprisingly, I dreamed that Hilda's country home burned to the ground in a conflagration started by a baker's daughter working too close to the fire that fueled the oven. A giant pigeon flew into the inferno, plucked the child from the flames, and deposited her safely in the mayor's office where she was reunited with her long-lost best friend.

I awakened sandy-eyed and relieved that the night's surreal scenario had been only a dream. To make the transition to full wakefulness and the Friday ahead of me, I lay in bed for a few minutes running through the list of things I had to get done. "Good morning, love. Remember, we're going to Betty and Vic's late this afternoon." Sol greeted me from the opposite side of the room where he sat tying his shoes.

"Yes, I remember. But isn't it grim out? What if there's more snow? Maybe then we won't have to go until tomorrow," I said, eager to minimize the time I would spend actually scraping wallpaper and stripping paint. I got out of bed and went to the window, where I stared out at the gray sky. An hour later when I got into my office, the sky was still gray and the air raw, but there was no official word of snow. The weather forecast had been more than usually equivocal. I resigned myself to a weekend of hard labor relieved by the proximity of good friends and Betty's promise of some fancy food.

Actually the weekend would be a chance to go over

all the conflicting and confusing information I'd gathered about Dom's death. I could brainstorm not only with Betty and Illuminada, but also with Vic, Raoul, and Sol. My most recent chat with Flora had left me so bewildered that I was beginning to question whether, in fact, Dom had been murdered. Maybe the cops were right all the time. Maybe Flora was not a murderess but a grieving daughter in denial about the state of her father's mental and physical health. Maybe poor Dom really had lost his grip on reality or had a mini stroke and fallen off the roof.

These doubts dogged me through what turned out to be a quiet day. Wendy blew into the office for a few minutes in the morning and then left for a meeting, so I had the place to myself. Friday was the day I reserved for conferences, but two of the students I had scheduled failed to show up. I made good use of the extra time, reading my way through stacks of essays and quizzes and even getting the damn English Department minutes typed and a couple of letters of recommendation drafted. By the late afternoon when I left for home I was tired, but my desk was orderly and my weekend workload considerably lightened. The item *Dom's scrapbook* was the only one on my to-do list without a line through it. Maybe I could get to it on the way to Betty's. When I got home, Sol was already sorting through our collection of suitcases in search of a small duffel bag that would do for this weekend. I greeted him with a query. "Sol, would you mind driving? I want to look through Dom's scrapbook on the way down."

"Sure. Bel, do you think I need to bring anything fancy to wear out to eat?" Sol asked. "Can I go like this? After all, it's the Jersey shore in winter. Most likely none of the chi-chi places are open."

I had expected the question, a version of which he posed every time we went anywhere overnight. Without looking at him, I gave my standard answer. "Bring a sport jacket and a decent shirt. Otherwise you'll have to eat takeout in the car while the rest of us are dining inside." As I spoke, I threw a pair of black pants, a cowl-necked gray sweater, and a pair of gray-and-black macramé earrings into the duffel along with my painting clothes, an old flannel nightgown, underwear, a toothbrush and a few other toiletries.

Sol had dug our sleeping bags out of the closet. "Too bad we still don't have one of those inflatable air beds," I said. "At least then we could look forward to a comfortable rest after our drudgery." My pitch for an air bed was as predictable a precursor to any trip requiring that we camp indoors as was Sol's earlier query about what clothes to bring.

Sol offered his standard reply, "We wouldn't really use it that often." Once we had completed this ritual pre-trip call-and-response, we threw the duffel bag into the car along with Sol's bag of tools "just in case." I left a reminder on the answering machine of my friend and neighbor Felice Acquino, who had agreed to feed Virginia Woolf in our absence, put a couple of cans of cat food on the counter where she couldn't miss them, and we set out.

The sky was still gray when Sol pulled the car away from the curb. I was sipping tea and paging through Dom's scrapbook, so I was caught unaware when we turned into a gas station less than a mile from home. "You know how crazy you get when the gas gauge goes below a quarter of a tank," said Sol. "This stop is part of my meltdown avoidance program." I nodded and gave him a thumbs-up of appreciation. I did get crazy when we ended up riding on empty on some Godforsaken strip of road. Whenever that happened, Sol assured me that there really was gas in the tank, but I didn't believe him. I was relieved that he was refueling sooner rather than later.

Just before I resumed my study of Dom's endless records of pigeon genealogy, I glimpsed a flash of blond hair out of the corner of my eye. For a moment, I thought my daughter had just gotten into a car ahead of us and driven away. But there were lots of blonds in the world and my very own golden-headed girl was still three thousand miles away, apparently too busy of late even to e-mail. Retrieving his credit card from the machine, Sol got back in the car and steered us onto the spur of highway that connected Hoboken with the New Jersey Turnpike.

The ride to Ocean Grove was less than an hour, and Betty had promised us light traffic at this time of year. Sol popped in a CD, and soon the sonorous strains of a Chopin nocturne filled the car, providing a backdrop conducive to concentration. And I concentrated. Like most pigeon fanciers, Dom had kept meticulous records of his birds' parentage, their racing speeds, and their health. These records, which he had painstakingly inscribed in longhand, filled most of his scrapbook. But towards the back, he had pasted in newspaper articles, yellowed over time, recounting some of the more spectacular victories of his birds.

In a final section there was a photo of the young Dom being decorated by President Eisenhower. I found brief obituaries of Dom's parents as well as an announcement of his marriage to Renata and what looked like a smaller version of the wedding photo in his kitchen. There were also notices proclaiming the births of Flora and Leo. Between the pages were a few yellow-edged and tattered items that had not been pasted into the book. Among these I found notices of Leo and Flora's first communions and programs from their high school graduations. I was surprised not to find any articles recounting Leo's participation in high school soccer. Perhaps Renata or Leo himself had preserved those elsewhere. I went back through the loose articles carefully to see what I had missed.

That's when I found it. Adhering to the back of the notice of Leo's first communion, which had fluttered out from between the last page and the back cover of the scrapbook, was another snippet of newspaper. At first I thought it was just a scrap that hadn't been fully cut away from the article it backed. But as I gingerly unfolded the tightly pressed wafers of crumbling paper, I saw that it was a separate article, and a fairly lengthy one at that.

It had nothing to do with pigeons or even with the life-cycle events of the Tomaselli family. Rather it was an account of one of those Hoboken tenement fires that took place in 1979, the same one Ana Guzman had recalled in her memoir. I read the story over and over as our car sped farther and farther away from the spires of Manhattan and the condos of Hoboken. The elegiac themes of Chopin's nocturnes and the still gray sky provided an appropriately dark backdrop to the harrowing account. Why had Dom kept this article among his otherwise highly focused and personal mementos? What meaning had it held for him? Had the man who died been a friend of his?

Holding the fragile folds of paper, I studied the words printed on them yet again. They joined the pieces of the puzzle of Dom's death spiraling through my head. At first this piece, a singed and jagged shard, remained separate and distinct from the flying fragments of doves and boys and building deeds winging round in my brain. Only very gradually did it cohere into a pattern all its own that was at first barely discernible. But by the time Sol turned the car off the parkway, this pattern had delineated itself in my head until its outline was as clear as that of a flame silhouetted against a night sky. Carefully I refolded the thin sheets of sepia-stained paper and inserted them between two pages of pigeon genealogy. I closed the scrapbook and placed it gently in my tote bag. Turning to Sol, I said, "I think I've figured out who killed Dom. It's the opposite of what I'd thought, and it's a long shot, but it makes sense." I felt a bit deflated once I had put the puzzle together. I imagined athletes felt this way after completing a marathon. And the solution that had finally presented itself saddened me, so I was hoping Sol's feedback would provide some much needed perspective.

But Sol's reaction to my announcement was less than interested. He was studying Betty's directions, which he held in one hand while with the other he turned the car onto a side street a few blocks from the boardwalk. He didn't even answer me at first. Only after he had pulled into an empty space right in front of a large brown shingled house that I recognized from Betty's descriptions did he speak. "That's great, love. But according to these directions, we're here." He pointed at Betty's directions and Mapquest's, both of which he stashed in the space between our seats. "And don't tell Betty that I backed up her directions with Mapquest's either," he added with a grin as we got out of the car. "Seriously, why don't you save your latest notion until we're all together inside? Your theories usually go down better with a glass of wine anyway. Here, give me a hand with this, okay?" He reached into the back seat and grabbed the duffel bag and the champagne we'd brought to christen Betty and Vic's new home and handed them to me. He took the sleeping bags. As we made our way to the front door, I was annoyed. Not only had Sol put me off, but he had relegated my important discovery to a "notion" suitable for cocktail banter.

Before I could react, though, Betty threw open the door. "Took you long enough," she growled by way of welcome. "C'mon in." No sooner had Sol and I crossed the threshold, than what sounded like a million voices yelled out "Surprise!"

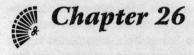

Chapter 26

Grand St. building burns
One dead eleven homeless

Fire fighters investigating
3rd tenement fire this year

Flames ravaged a four-story rent-controlled building at 215 Grand Street in the middle of the night, killing one man and leaving the remaining eleven tenants homeless. "I smelled smoke, and I ran to my daughter's room. We woke up her boys and tried to take them downstairs, but the stairs, they were on fire. We carried the two boys down the fire escape," recalled a tearful and shivering Ana Guzman, 47, who lived in an apartment on the third floor with her daughter and two grandsons, 3 and 5. The name of the tenant on the top floor who perished in bed, probably from smoke inhalation, is being withheld until his family can be notified.

"He never had a prayer. That thing went up so fast, it's a miracle there weren't more casualties," said a Weehawken firefighter who responded to a call for reinforcements from Hoboken's fire chief, Jim Corcoran. The cause of the blaze is still unknown, and the owner, Best Realty, Inc., couldn't be reached for comment. "We're going to investigate," promised Mayor Dino Sorrentino, summoned to the scene. "The boys are cordoning off the property now." Behind the yellow tape, the building has been reduced to a brick shell filled with half-burned joists, melted kitchen appliances, twisted pipe, and mounds of ash. In spite of fire fighters' efforts to drown the blaze, the fire smoldered until dawn.

This is the third fire of unknown origin in a rent-controlled building since the year began three months ago. The others are also under investigation amid rumors of arson. "If landlords can't drive 'em out, they burn 'em out," says tenant-advocate Tom Guzman, no relation to Ana Guzman. "Somebody just pours a can of kerosene on the bottom of a stairwell and throws a match, and that's it. Goodbye rent-controlled units, hello condos."

"We're doing the best we can to stay on top of this, but we got limited resources," Chief Corcoran said when queried about these allegations.

Mrs. Guzman's family and those of the other surviving tenants are being temporarily housed by the Red Cross in the Gateway Motel on Route 440. Contributions to the Hudson County Red Cross Disaster Relief Fund may be sent to Red Cross, PO BOX 4416, Jersey City, NJ 07302.

The connection between this article and Dom's death that had stunned me when I finally figured it out would remain my secret for a little longer. It was literally shocked out of my consciousness at the sight of Rebecca, Keith, Abbie J, and Aveda standing in Betty and Vic's spacious living room. Frozen open-mouthed in the doorway, I instantly assumed that Betty and Vic had masterminded a surprise shower for Sol and me, even though Sol didn't look at all surprised. I also assumed that Mark had been unable to make it, and felt a twinge of sadness.

"So, Mom, are you surprised or what?" asked Rebecca, liberating herself from the bear hug I'd given her and tossing her straight blond hair out of her face. I realized it could very well have been Rebecca I'd spotted earlier at the gas station. Abbie J stood on the stairs, a little apart, looking uncharacteristically shy. I went over to her and sank down on the step above the one on which she stood and, without a word, she positioned herself in between my knees as if she had last seen me only yesterday. Rebecca joined us. Then Mark emerged from the kitchen carrying a glass of red wine, which he handed to his sister. "Don't even think about it, Rebecca. It's for Mom," he admonished, bending over to give me a hug. Then he took the glass of wine from Rebecca and presented it to me himself.

"You both got time off from work and flew all this way to come to a shower?" I sputtered, already recovering from my initial shock and moving effortlessly into maternal mode. What if they couldn't get time off again and missed the main event? Still sputtering, I said, "How will you be able to get time off—"

"Ma, you don't get it, do you? There is no shower. This is your wedding. I mean this weekend. It's all arranged. The ceremony is tomorrow night. Right here. That is, if you're willing," said Rebecca.

I was so dumbfounded that, for the first time in

decades, I couldn't speak. When I didn't respond, Mark, sensing my confusion, said, "Rebecca's right. Let me bring you up to speed, so you're on the same page as everybody else." He spoke slowly, pronouncing every word clearly, probably the same way he used to speak to his students when he taught ESL. "Right now we're enjoying wine and cheese before the rehearsal dinner." I stared blankly at him. He pointed into the living room where Betty and Vic were, in fact, putting out cheese and crackers.

Rebecca tried again. "Drink your wine, Mom. Listen. You and Sol are getting married here tomorrow night. Lots of people are coming. Most of us out-of-towners are camping here or next door. Betty and Vic have enough room for us and the rest are bunking down over there. The folks who own that place are in the Bahamas, and Betty and Vic have the run of it." In spite of Rebecca's instructions and explanation, I was still too flabbergasted even to sip my wine. I was definitely not yet on the same page as everyone else and not even sure I was reading the same book. I looked around me. No trace of wallpaper remained on the perfectly painted off-white walls. The gleaming pine paneling bore no vestige of the brown paint Betty had complained about. Had all that talk of painting and scraping been just an elaborate ruse to get Sol and me to Ocean Grove for the weekend? My brain began to creak into action. Sol must have been party to the plan.

Letting Sol's complicity sink in, I combed Abbey J's hair with my fingers while she played with the silver bangles on my arm as Mark continued the orientation. "But you and Sol are staying at a way cool B & B across from the boardwalk. It's called Love Nest, and it's open all year round." Betty and Sol had joined us at the foot of the stairs. Seeing them, Mark said, "I better get back to the kitchen. Grandma Sadie's trying to keep Sofia and Vic from spiking the kugel with rum." He leaned down to plant a kiss on the top of my head. "C'mon, Abbie J. You can lick the tiramisu bowl. The caffeine in that espresso will keep you awake right through first grade." He grabbed Abbie J's hand, and she slipped out of my lap to join him.

"Mark," shrieked Rebecca, smacking her brother on the shoulder and taking off after the two of them. "If you get her all hyper, she's going to sleep in your room tonight. Just wait until you have a kid . . ."

"Would you listen to the two of them going at it? Don't you love how the kids regress when Mama's around?" Betty asked, with a grin. Her eyes were bright and her voice vibrant. She did not look at all like a woman whose home was overrun with guests needing to be entertained, fed, and, dare I say it, married. She was in her element, in charge. What a woman! What a friend! I blew her a kiss.

Sol echoed Rebecca's earlier request. "Have a sip of your wine, love. It's party time." He too looked remarkably calm, pleased no doubt to have executed his part of the conspiracy flawlessly. He took Mark's place on the steps and began kneading my neck. Looking up at him, I said, "You knew all the time. And you never said a word. You let me come down here thinking I was going to be slaving away. How could you keep this from me?" I didn't wait for him to answer. "And what about Sandi and Wendy?" I looked around. "And—"

"Not to worry. Almost everybody on our list who's not here tonight will be here tomorrow sometime, including Rabbi Ornstein-Klein. Sandi's driving her down after sundown to perform the ceremony.

Wendy's coming tomorrow with a few other folks from RECC," said Betty.

"Where are Illuminada and Raoul?" I asked, looking around.

"Breathe, *chiquita,* we're here. We wanted to capture your arrival on video so you too can see the look on your face when you walked in that door." Illuminada was laughing as she descended the stairs. "We shot it from the top steps and got the whole scene. You want to see?" She began to fiddle with the camera, threatening to confront me then and there with a replay of my tired Friday afternoon face contorting in shock.

"Not tonight," I said, backing away from the camera she proffered. "I'll see it another time. I'm just glad you two are here." I grabbed Illuminada's hand.

"*Dios mio,* Bel, I can't stand it when you get all mushy. Drink your wine." I thought Illuminada's eyes looked a little moist. But her next words were, "Let's have some music! Somebody put in a CD!" Someone did, and soon Frank was singing "All the Way." I sipped my wine and tried to convince myself that it didn't matter if I got married in the too-tight black pants and shapeless gray sweater I had thrown in the duffel.

After his magic fingers had kneaded the knots out of my neck and the wine had mellowed me, Sol smiled and said, "Why don't you go into the kitchen and visit with the kids? They came a long way to be here, and they're flying back Sunday night." At that moment, the front door flew open, and Sol's mother, Esther, and her current partner, Al, entered, brushing flakes of snow off their shoulders. Esther no longer rode her own bike, but she had never forsworn the biker-girl get-up she favored for travel, black leather pants and a bomber's jacket over a faux zebra sweater. Following Esther and Al were Alexis and Xhi with little Maya in tow.

We stood to embrace them. "Damn. We missed the surprise! I would've loved to have seen your face when you walked in," said Alexis. Before I could mention the video, she turned to Sol and said, "Dad was so worried that he was going to blow it. Good job, Dad." Sol acknowledged Alexis' compliment with a grin while his mother enveloped him in a hug.

Xhi stood apart from this orgy of hugging, looking a bit flummoxed until I approached him, saying, "It's an old Jewish wedding custom to hug the bride." Never one to defy what he believed to be accepted practice, Xhi enclosed me in his arms. When he let me go, I was pleased to see that he too was grinning.

And so it went all evening. We sat around sipping wine and chatting for about an hour. During this time I heard about how Betty and Illuminada had decided to fulfill my wish for a wedding planner. When they had approached Sol with their scheme, he not only went along, but joined the conspiracy. It had been his responsibility to get me to get a marriage license and to deliver me to Ocean Grove without my suspecting anything.

Betty and Illuminada, Delegating Queens, had assigned various tasks to others, all of whom had leapt at the chance to get Sol and me married sooner rather than later. Mark and Aveda had arrived the day before and taken charge of the rehearsal dinner. Aveda had rented a round table large enough to hold us all, covered it with a rented white cloth, and created a stunning centerpiece out of polished and carved fruits and vegetables, a few of which she had smuggled over the border. Ma lit the Sabbath candles and blessed the wine and challah, after which Esther read a prayer for peace

that she had written herself in our honor. Only then did
we eat, making short work of a feast of butternut
squash soup, roast turkey, kugel, and broccoli followed
by Sofia and Vic's tiramisu and decaf.

The whole weekend was like that meal, comfortable, delicious, and orchestrated with love. There was
to be no rehearsal, but Betty and Illuminada had
planned for Sol and me to write our vows over breakfast at our B & B. After a decidedly pleasant night in a
room that was only slightly too ruffled and canopied
for my taste, we lingered over scones and tea, penning
our promises to one another. We had no books or Internet, so we were forced to plight our troth in our own
words. "I bet we both have pretty much the same thing
in mind, so let's write our vows together," I suggested.
And so we did. In eight lines we stated our desire to
keep on loving and nurturing one another and support-
ing each other as we parented our adult kids and grandkids just as we had been doing for the past decade.

Then Esther, Ma, Rebecca, and Abbie J joined us for
a bracing walk on the boardwalk, admiring the towers
and turrets of Ocean Grove's restored nineteenth-
century homes. It was this felicitous combination of
unspoiled beach and boardwalk with Victorian archi-
tecture that had spurred the town's transformation
from a modest Methodist revival camp into a popular
retreat for upscale trendsetters.

After enjoying a late lunch of leftovers, Rebecca,
Ma, Esther, Alexis, and I reported to a day spa in a
nearby town, where Betty had made reservations for us
to have massages, pedicures, and manicures. During a
tête-à-tête with Rebecca while our lurid crimson toe-
nail polish was drying, I shared what, I must confess,
was most on my mind at the moment. "You know,

everything is so wonderful, but I'm going to have to get married in these." I pointed at the black pants legs protruding from beneath my smock.

Rebecca broke into a grin and said, "Chill, Mom. Felice Aquino and I e-mailed back and forth, and we came up with a way cool wedding ensemble. It's totally you, totally." In spite of the fact that my old friend and neighbor Felice owned a shop filled with highly sought after and pricey wedding gowns of her own design, this news had me worried. Rebecca's idea of "way cool" and "totally me" sounded scary even without the second "totally."

"And Mom, I know you're still wearing those striped nightshirts I had in college, so I bought you a nightgown that's a little more, you know, bridey." I pictured an EMT crew administering CPR to Sol on our wedding night. Having settled the all-important matter of my nightclothes, Rebecca added, "Felice is driving everything down later with Luci." Rebecca squeezed my hand to signal her excitement at the prospect of a reunion with her childhood friend Luci Aquino. "That's so awesome." I decided not to spoil her pleasure by raising the question of shoes. With painted toes like the ones I had just acquired, I could be a barefoot bride.

Suddenly I pictured Sol again, this time, in his jeans and khaki corduroy sport jacket with his wrinkled all-occasion soup-spotted tie. "Uh-oh," I said. "What about Sol? He's only got jeans. I better see if I can take him somewhere to get a pair of slacks at least." I reached up to untie my smock.

"Chill, Mom," ordered Rebecca. "Betty thought of that. Vic's bringing him a suit that she says is totally Sol."

First I smiled. Then I chortled. Then I laughed so hard that I had to excuse myself and walk to the bathroom on my heels, so as not to dislodge the little cubes of Styrofoam separating my enamel trimmed toes. Vic was bringing Sol a suit from the funeral home! The suit would be one of several brought there by a grieving widow for her late husband to be buried in. Another suit was selected, and, in the aftermath of the poor soul's funeral, this one had been forgotten. "He's tried to give that suit to Sol since forever," I said by way of explanation.

"Vic got one of his burial-society friends who owns a funeral home down here to lend us a lot of really nice folding chairs, too," said Ma who had joined us and overheard the last part of the conversation. "Keith, Mark, and Xhi went to pick them up."

"Who's watching the girls?" I asked, worried that Abbie J and Maya might be neglected in the excitement of the day.

"Not to worry, Bel," said Esther, who had just strolled over. I smiled to hear yet again the admonition against worrying that had become a mantra for the weekend. "Sofia and Sol have them." Styrofoam cubes separated Esther's green-nailed toes. "Eye catching aren't they?" she said as she saw me staring. "They match my sari. Besides, Al loves green." I only gaped for a moment before it was time for our massages.

Chapter 27

The family and friends of
Bel Barrett and Sol Hecht
invite you to
Bel and Sol's wedding
Saturday, March 22, 2003
at 6 o'clock
at the home of Betty Ramsey and Vic Vallone,
444 Central Avenue
Ocean Grove, New Jersey
Dinner will be served after the ceremony.

One more thing! **Not a word to Bel.** We plan to surprise her with a lovely wedding, stress free and workless. All she has to do is show up. And all you have to do is keep a secret and join us to bear witness and celebrate. RSVP to Bettyr@juno.com or 201-555-4493. We will provide directions and suggestions for accommodations if you need them. Finally, please, no gifts.

251

If you must give something, make a donation in the couple's honor to the River Edge Community College Scholarship Fund or Hoboken's Citizen's Committee to Preserve the Waterfront.

When I got back to the B & B on the afternoon of our wedding, Sol was waiting, and the fire in our room was lit. There was time for both a short nap and a long bath before dressing. When I woke up, Sol was running water in the enormous tub. We got in and sat back, enjoying a prenuptial soak. Finally, unable to contain myself any longer, I said, "But Sol, who's paying for all of this?" I gestured around me at the sumptuous terry cloth robes, the basket of fragrant emulsions, the adjacent room full of antique furniture and extravagant bedding. He splashed a little water my way and said. "This is a wedding gift from our mothers, and so was your ladies' afternoon at the spa." That made sense. I made a mental note to thank them for their generosity.

"And where is the food for tonight coming from?" I blurted. "I haven't seen Mark all day. Don't tell me he and Aveda are cooking for the wedding too? Or is there to be no food?" The last possibility was so unthinkable that I whispered it.

"Of course there's food," Sol said. "And no, Aveda and Mark are off the hook. Tonight's meal is being catered, and we're paying for it," said Sol, sending another splash my way.

"But how . . ." I sputtered, worried that catering costs would further decimate our already diminished retirement savings.

"That was the condition I put on the whole thing. Betty and Illuminada could plan the weekend, but we would pay. Raoul's keeping the books. Trust me, you'll love the caterer. Betty and Illuminada found him," Sol said with a grin. "And we're getting a real deal. Just relax." He reached over to turn on the hot water, and I melted back, grateful to be marrying such a fine man and to have such good friends.

I didn't realize how relaxed I was until I saw the video much later. My hair was still frizzy from the shower when I dressed, and the raw damp air did nothing to subdue it, so it stood out as if electrified, framing my face in zigzags of silver and brown. Although I didn't have any wine until after the ceremony, I looked as if I had been drinking all day, because my cheeks were still flushed from the hot bath. But the dark leopard-print pants of lush velvet and the simple black velvet top that hid my nonexistent waist fit perfectly, and I felt very glamorous. "Born to wear velvet," Sol had said, running his hand over my hips as I preened in front of the mirror.

"You don't look so bad yourself," I replied, relinquishing a bit of space so he could see his reflection.

"Not bad for a dead guy," he had retorted with a laugh.

Betty and Vic's first floor had been transformed. A simple *chuppah* or canopy made of two striped prayer shawls that I recognized as Sandi's and my bat mitzvah gifts to each other had been erected in front of the windows. Our colorful *tallith* were suspended from *chuppah* poles adorned by chains of greens. Rows of folding chairs with cushions of deep pink silk, undoubtedly the ones on loan from the local funeral home, filled the rest of the room. Rabbi Ornstein-Klein stood before the *chuppah,* signaling the beginning of the ceremony. People hurried to claim seats. Sol and I were seated in the front row with our mothers. The

kids and grandkids were right behind us. Mark, dapper
in a pair of tan corduroy pants and a navy blue blazer,
took a seat off to the side. I had not seen my son so
dressed up since his bar mitzvah. I cast a quick glance
at Vic to see if he had raided his supply of menswear
again. He winked.

Mark picked up his guitar, which had been propped
against his chair, and began to strum a version of "The
Way You Look Tonight," transcribed for guitar. As
soon as I recognized Sol's and my song, my eyes filled,
so that I almost missed the nod Rabbi O-K gave to
Abbie J and Maya. The two little girls, both wearing
red party dresses and white tights, and carrying bas-
kets, approached the rabbi, sprinkling rose petals on
the hardwood floor. When they got to the *chuppah,*
they stopped, looked at each other, and, flustered, ran
back to their seats and their moms.

Rabbi O-K nodded again, this time at Sol and me.
Mark stopped playing. The minute I got to my feet, my
tears began to fall. I cried all the way through the
rabbi's beautiful blessing. Rebecca had anticipated this
possibility and came forward to hand me a Kleenex. I
cried when Sandi and the other members of my adult
bat mitzvah class read a passage from the Song of
Solomon. Rebecca handed me several more Kleenex.
But I was still crying when my own dear Wendy and
Harold Markowitz, Sol's college roommate, who now
lives in London, took turns reading Emerson's "How
Do I Love Thee." I wept through Rabbi O-K's reading
of the marriage license or *ketubah,* and her inspiring
words of advice and encouragement.

And I wept as we exchanged vows, my voice blurred
by sobs and sniffles. I held the Kleenex in one hand
when Sol placed a ring on a finger of the other. I

couldn't see it through my tears. When I realized I had no ring for him, I cried even harder. Ma came forward and pushed something small and round into my hand. "I forgot to give you this before. Give it to Sol," she hissed. Without looking, I knew it was my father's wedding ring. I gushed anew. Rebecca produced yet another Kleenex. I pushed the ring onto Sol's finger, now wet with both of our tears.

Perhaps in an effort to stem the tide of my tears, Rabbi O-K shared an anecdote. "According to the Talmud, Rav Ashi was disturbed by the rowdy and drunken behavior of many of the other rabbis who were guests at his son's wedding. To get their attention, he picked up a valuable white glass and smashed it right in front of them. His gesture worked, and decorum was restored." She paused for a moment before adding, "This custom has gradually been incorporated into most Jewish wedding ceremonies but with a slightly different rationale." Sol squeezed my hand and I looked up at the rabbi through my tears. "The destruction of something valuable is a reminder that the Temple is still in ruins and that we live in an unredeemed world." At the thought of the beleaguered state of the world, I felt a weight on my heart and more tears welling in my eyes. But then the rabbi turned to me and said, "Bel, Jews have turned this rather grim ritual of stomping on the glass into a catalyst that changes the somber mood of the wedding to one of joy. Try it."

Betty and Illuminada came forward holding a white napkin–wrapped wineglass and handed it to us. At the sight of my two friends, I cried even harder and was still crying when together Sol and I stomped the glass to bits. On cue our guests began shouting "Mazeltov." I heard them through my barely stifled sobs. I was still crying when, with Rabbi O-K's final blessing, Sol kissed me as if we had never kissed before. It was only after this embrace when he brushed aside my hair and murmured in my ear, "Nothing beats kissing a woman who has lifelong health insurance," that I finally cracked a smile.

And I smiled all evening. Sol and I greeted our guests, including his old army buddy Joe Chang and Felice and Luci Aquino. Rebecca went off into a corner with Luci, leaving Abbie J to hang with Maya. While the caterers were arranging food on a buffet, Keith, Alexis, Xhi, Mark, and Aveda were making short work of setting up tables and rearranging chairs. "Are these the tables we use for the PANA block party?" I asked Charlie and Ilona Ilyssario when they approached us to offer their congratulations. "Yeah. Betty asked us to bring 'em down, so Gene threw 'em in the truck with the instruments." That's when I heard the unmistakable strains of "A Six Pack and You," muted for the occasion, but live. Gene 'D' Singing Plumber and his band had set up in the foyer and were playing just loud enough to elevate the mood but not too loud to obstruct conversation. Raoul was filming them.

Seeing that I was about to bawl again, Betty pulled me into the kitchen. Illuminada was already there, camera in hand. Betty introduced me to a tall, light-haired young man wearing the black-and-white checked pants, white jacket, and white toque that his business required. He looked familiar, but it was only when he spoke that I recognized him. "Professor B, congratulations! Long time no see. How ya doin'?" It was Oscar Beckman, the former student of mine who'd been falsely accused of poisoning RECC President Altagracia Garcia. He was catering our wedding.

I let out a whoop of recognition and threw my arms around him. "My God! It's you, Oscar! How are you?"

"Yeah, it's me." Then, all business, he said, "How is everythin'? You wanna taste the glaze for the poached salmon?" He dipped a long-handled spoon into a pan on the stove behind him and brandished it in my direction. "Look! Do we got enough shrimp?" He pointed to four huge bowls filled with shrimp. "They're puttin' out the sliced tenderloin now. And the Asian noodles." He directed his next words to Betty. "And don't worry, Miz Ramsey, we didn't forget the veggie mélange or the polenta." Then, turning back to me, he said with a smile, "And, Professor B, thanks for lettin' me try my crew out for your wedding. I just couldn't take it in the deli no more. I didn't go to culinary school so I could spend my life slicin' salami. My ol' man, he's kinda bummed, but I think my sister's boyfriend is gonna take my place behind the counter." Illuminada continued to film, now focusing on the bowls, trays, and platters of very appealing food that Oscar's helpers were carrying out to arrange on the buffet table.

The hors d'oeuvres were delicious," I said. "I could have made a meal of those chicken satays and the California rolls."

"Well, there's more to come," Oscar said. "And just wait until you see the cake, Professor B." With that he turned back to the stove, and Betty and I left with Illuminada not far behind.

While the three of us were alone in the pantry that connected the kitchen to the rest of the first floor, I said, "Really, this is the most wonderful weekend. Everything is perfect. I don't know how to . . ." I felt the tears welling.

"*Chiquita,* if you cry, I'm going to take a close-up of

you," threatened Illuminada, waving her camera in my face.

"Yeah, we've got enough footage of you bawling like a baby," said Betty. "Now go talk to your guests."

Sol and I did just that, moving from table to table, catching up with old friends and, of course, swapping school stories with our colleagues. At first I didn't recognize the couple Sarah was cornered with, but when she moved aside, I saw none other than Ron Woodman, president of RECC, and a woman whom I took to be Mrs. Woodman. It occurred to me that I had never seen the man out of his office except at graduation, so that's probably why I hadn't recognized him. It had been politic of Betty and Illuminada to add him to the guest list. I was pleased to have him there. Out of context he appeared younger, more relaxed. He planted a big kiss on my cheek and said, "Bel, I'd like you to meet my wife, Alice." The woman at his side smiled. "Sarah was just explaining how you met your husband at a meeting of that environmental group." He shook his head. "One just never knows when cupid's arrow will strike, but we're happy for you both. Thanks for including us in your big event."

"Yes, it's really a lovely affair. So . . . so . . . *heymish*," said Alice. I started, wondering if Alice Woodman was, in fact, Jewish. We chatted for a few more minutes until Sol came by and I was able to introduce him to the Woodmans. As they talked, I looked around. There was a table of young people, Sandi's son, Joel, and Wendy's entire brood along with Luci, Rebecca, and Keith. Was Joel talking mostly with Luci Aquino or was I imagining that? Mark and Aveda sat with Sadie, Sofia, and Milagros Santos, Illuminada's mother, keeping their plates filled and translating when necessary. Marlene Proletariat sat with our neighbors. Lourdes Guttierez was tending bar, and Randy Ramsey, on crutches after a skiing accident, was helping her.

Sandi Golden and Harold Markowitz were at a table with Rabbi O-K and the members of my b'nai mitzvah class and their partners. Sandi and Harold appeared to be engrossed in an intense and private conversation. Between the two of them they had suffered through at least four divorces and the breakup of several unofficial liaisons, but it looked as if each of them was making yet another try at connecting. I nudged Sol and nodded in their direction. "Don't jinx it," he said quietly. "Your old roommate and mine? It's so fifties. Do you really think it could work?" I shrugged and crossed my fingers. We hugged in tacit acknowledgment of how lucky we were to have found one another.

Later there were toasts, serious ones and silly ones. Our kids toasted us, we toasted our moms, we all toasted Betty and Vic and Illuminada and Raoul. At last, the cake arrived, a three-tiered confection in dark chocolate. Even the roses were chocolate. At that point we all toasted Oscar Beckman.

Chapter 28

To: Bettyr@juno.com, Iguttierez@IguttierezPI.com
From: Rebecca@uwash.edu
Re: Thanks
Date: 03/24/03 08:17:23

Hi Betty and Illuminada,

The weekend was totally awesome. Thanks for putting us up. And thanks for getting it together for the happy couple. Not spoiling the surprise was a challenge for our blabbermouth family, but it was worth it to see the look on Mom's face when she came in. Everything was so romantic and totally intense until Sunday when we just kicked back in front of the fire and ate leftovers. It was way cool to catch up with Lourdes and Randy. Abbie J wants to do the whole weekend again, and Keith says you two should go into the event-planning business. Hugs to Vic and Raoul. And THANK YOU!

Love,
Rebecca

PS Vic deserves an Oscar for outfitting Sol and Mark. Who knew that my grungy brother would clean up into a cute preppy dude? I'm glad Raoul preserved that on tape. We can't wait to see the whole video.

PPS Betty, your new house is incredible. We could see the ocean from our upstairs window. Keith says it would make a great B & B.

"See, *chiquita,* all that nagging worked. Your kid writes thank-you notes," said Illuminada, flipping a printout of Rebecca's e-mail message across Betty's coffee table to me.

I skimmed it, smiling. "Well, it's only e-mail, not a real note, but it's something," I acknowledged. My last words to Rebecca the night before when Sol and I had dropped her, Abbie J, and Keith off at Newark Airport were, "Don't forget to thank Betty and Illuminada." My nearly thirty-year-old daughter had wrinkled her nose at me and scowled with annoyance, but she had done it. She probably would have done it without my knee-jerk maternal nudge. As Illuminada had pointed out, years of nagging had embedded written expressions of gratitude right up there with personal hygiene as paths to godliness in my progeny's psyche.

Betty emerged from her kitchen with a tray of leftovers that she lowered to the coffee table. Even though it was Monday night, less than twenty-four hours after we had parted at Ocean Grove, Betty's voice crackled with energy, and she walked briskly back into the kitchen to get paper plates, flatware, and napkins. Illuminada practically sprang out of her chair to help and returned with several bottles of sparkling cider. They were still exhilarated by the weekend, whereas I was exhausted. My classes had all gone well, but a full day's teaching in the hallowed halls of River Edge Community College was far from my honeymoon of choice.

"So what's up, *chiquita*? Honeymoon not going well? Why else would you leave your new hubby to meet here with us?" Illuminada's voice was smooth, like that of a DJ doing a commercial, but her eyes gleamed. We all helped ourselves to tenderloin and salmon along with couscous and salad.

"Listen up, girlfriend. We married you off, but now you're on your own. Unless, of course, you want to borrow my copy of the *Kama Sutra*?" quipped Betty, while cutting her meat.

Ignoring their digs, I said, "I figured out who killed Dom Tomaselli." My voice was serious and rasping after a day deconstructing the job interview with three speech classes. But my friends were not yet, as Mark would have put it, on the same page I was. I took a bite of salmon and hoped that dinner would revive me.

"When did you do this? Was it when Sol was putting the ring on your finger, or maybe you deduced who the killer was during that x-rated kiss?" asked Betty with a chuckle.

"No. It must have been when she stomped on that poor glass. Or maybe later when Sol's mother was toasting her." Illuminada had no trouble being sarcastic while piling couscous onto her fork.

"Will you two get serious?" I directed my rejoinder to Betty. "In a few minutes, the Cubano Princess over there," I jerked my head in the direction of Illuminada,who had curled up in the corner of the sofa with her plate, "is going to be rushing me to hurry up and finish so she can go home and get her beauty sleep. And you're going to be trying to get me out of here so you can be alone with your favorite undertaker." I executed a mock shudder. We never tired of teasing Betty about having sex with a funeral director. "While Sol drove us down to Ocean Grove, I went through Dom's scrapbook, and that's when I figured it out. By the time we got to Betty's, I knew."

"You're expecting us to believe that you had this revelation on Friday afternoon and kept it to yourself all weekend?" Betty was speaking, but both of them stared at me. My friends clearly did not see discretion as a key part of my personality.

"I forgot about it when I saw Rebecca, and then, by the time I remembered, I decided to just let it go for the weekend. It didn't feel right to be talking about death and killing at such a happy time," I said. I could hear the defensive whine in my voice and felt tears welling again at the memory of the past weekend and how much it had meant to Sol and me. I tried to put it into words. "You know, when Lenny and I got married, we were very young, and our wedding was all about pleasing our parents. But the second time around is supposed to be different. It's a chance to celebrate not only with family but also with friends accumulated over a lifetime . . ." I had to interrupt myself because my tears had spilled over and I was snuffling into a Kleenex.

"*Dios mío, chiquita,* stop blubbering. Tell us. Who did it?" Illuminada's voice had lost its silky undertone, and her brusque question rang out like a challenge.

"Sam Simon." I said, my voice only slightly muffled by the Kleenex I was still using. I took advantage of the few seconds of silence that greeted this proclamation to wipe my eyes and pocket the balled up tissue.

"Remind me, *chiquita*. Who the hell is Sam Simon? I don't recall that he was even a suspect," said Illuminada. Betty shrugged, so I knew that Sam's name meant nothing to her either.

"Sam Simon is one of the seniors in my memoir-writing class," I explained. "I told you about him, remember? He used to be the ABC officer in Hoboken, but he went to jail for taking bribes. That's where he started his memoir. He's also a member of the Hoboken Racing Pigeon Club." It felt good to be back in control of my emotions again, and I welcomed the chance to elaborate on my reasons for fingering Sam. I pushed my plate away and reached for my tote beside me on the floor. "Look." I got out Dom's scrapbook and extricated duplicates of the article about the fire that I'd made on Sol's handy-dandy copier. "The original was in this scrapbook. The rest of the book is filled with things related to pigeon racing, and there are a few snippets of family memorabilia. This article didn't fit in."

Betty and Illuminada had put down their forks and were reading the article. "Sorry, Bel. I still don't get it. What has this got to do with Sam Simon? And what has it got to do with Dom Tomaselli except that the house is in his neighborhood? Do you get it?" Betty asked, turning to Illuminada, who shook her head and handed the article back to me. I put it on the coffee table.

"Okay. Here's the link. Dom Tomaselli spent a lot of time, too much time, on the roof of his house tending his pigeons. He also had very good eyesight. And you're right, Betty. The house that burned is in his neighborhood. It's next to the last one that we visited when we went door to door." I paused, letting this information sink in. "Dom Tomaselli probably saw whoever started that fire."

"*Dios mío,* Bel. That fire was over thirty years ago. Did they ever prove it was arson?" Illuminada was all over me with objections as I had anticipated.

"Today I e-mailed Sarah Wolf, asking her to comb the *Jersey City Herald*'s archives for me. I want to see all the articles relating to those fires. They will answer that question. The same articles will tell who really owned the building," I said. "Sarah is out of her office until tomorrow, so I'll have to wait for her to get back and get on it. I think she went straight from Ocean Grove to a peace demonstration in DC."

"Can't you get that information on-line?" asked Betty.

"The *Jersey City Herald,* which was the only paper serving Hoboken back then, doesn't even have its current news on-line, let alone the stuff from the seventies," I explained. "But Sarah will get it. And it will support what I'm saying." I spoke with the assurance I felt. I had wanted a witness, and now I had one, a dead one who witnessed a different crime.

"*Chiquita,* I'm still not sure what it is that you are saying," said Illuminada. "Here's what I got so far. There was a fire in a building behind Dominic Tomaselli's house. It was started by someone, and Tomaselli saw the arsonist. Is that it?" I nodded.

"How the hell would Dominic have been able to tell in the dark exactly who the person was who started the fire? His eyes couldn't have been that good." It was Betty, raising the key question, the one that had puzzled me for a moment or two.

"Sam Simon is a very big man with a war injury that left him with a noticeable and distinctive limp. Even in the dark, it would be tough to confuse him with anybody else," I said, trying not to sound too smug. I always relished the moment when I presented my two skeptical friends with irrefutable evidence in support of what they thought was a cockamamie theory. I took advantage of the silence that greeted my words to make a serious inroad into my dinner.

When I spoke again, I said, "Betty, you weren't living here in the seventies, but there were quite a few cases of arson in rent-controlled buildings in Hoboken then." Illuminada nodded, no doubt recalling the headlines. "People working in New York wanted to move here, and property values were rising, but supply didn't meet demand. The thing was there were a lot of rent-controlled buildings. Owners of those buildings couldn't evict tenants without cause. So, the landlord would arrange a fire." I snapped my fingers to show how simple and efficient this solution must have appeared to some unscrupulous property owners. Betty pursed her lips in distaste. "Of course, the tenants who survived the blaze would have to leave. Then the owner would collect insurance and deliver the building vacant to a developer. Someone even made a documentary about this called *Delivered Vacant*. The landlord and the developer made a huge profit. It's ironic, but the Guzman woman quoted in this article," I pointed at the account of the fire still on the coffee table in front of us, "she's one of my senior students. She wrote about that fire in her memoir."

"Bel's right. It's sad but true, *chiquita*," said Illuminada, flipping her hair out of her face. "There was a pretty standard MO just like it says in the article. The arsonist entered the building through the back door with a can of kerosene, and poured it in the stairwell on the ground floor. Then he tossed a couple of lit matches on the kerosene, and whoosh!" Illuminada lifted her hands suddenly in a parody of the deadly blaze she was describing. "The stairwell would act like a flue, sending the fire up and—"

"And trap the people in the building," put in Betty in a leaden voice quite unlike the brisk tone she had used earlier. "Like animals. Let me guess. The tenants in the rent-controlled buildings were mostly African American and Hispanic?" The question was purely rhetorical. The bitterness in Betty's voice was the answer to her own question.

"As I recall, one of the buildings was occupied entirely by Indians," I said with a sigh. "I'm sure glad my student lived to tell about it, but, you're right, some people didn't make it."

"Like the guy on the top floor," said Illuminada, picking up the article again and scanning it.

"Right," I said.

Now it was Illuminada's turn to sigh. "Okay, *chiquitas,* before we get so depressed we can't function, tell me this. Was Sam Simon really Best Realty? Was he the owner of that building?"

"I don't think so. I think that the articles Sarah sends me will tell us that Mayor Dino Sorrentino was Best Realty," I said.

"So if Simon didn't even own the building, why would he burn it down?" Betty's question was legitimate. I had expected it.

"He worked for Dino Sorrento. He also admired and, maybe you could say, loved him. Dino got Sam jobs, helped him buy a house, paid for his wedding. Sam sees Dino as a kind of father figure. It's thirty years later, Dino Sorrentino's been dead for a decade, and Sam is still talking about him. If Dino said, 'Burn down that building,' I'm pretty sure that Sam would have done it." I sipped my no-longer sparkling cider. I had felt tired before; now I was tired and depressed. The thought of Sam Simon as a murderer and arsonist literally turned my stomach. And recalling the sordid history of my beloved town was also painful. It was true that Dino Sorrentino had helped turn the mile-square blue-collar mill town into what some people called the Sixth Borough of Manhattan, but at whose expense?

"I still don't get it," said Betty, breaking into my funk. "Let's say Bel's right that Dominic Tomaselli witnessed Sam Simon entering and leaving the back door of that house carrying a big can on the night it burned." Betty took a swig of cider before continuing. "Why wouldn't Dominic have said something at the time? And why would Sam kill him all these years later?"

"I don't know for sure, but I knew Dom a little, and I can speculate. Shortly after this fire, Sam was indicted for selling liquor licenses to the highest bidders, and he went to jail. He was locked up for a long time." I remembered Sam sitting in my office telling me that his wife had died while he was serving his term. Banishing the flicker of sympathy this recollection inspired, I hurried on. "I suspect Dom figured Sam was being punished already." Illuminada and Betty nodded, understanding this reasoning.

"But I think Dom had another reason for keeping quiet too. Remember, Dom was a school janitor. He worked for the City of Hoboken. Of course he'd try to avoid going public with information that damned a popular and powerful mayor. Dino Sorrentino was his boss." Betty and Illuminada nodded more emphatically this time. Those of us who had lived in Hoboken during the reign of Mayor Sorrentino knew that for a municipal employee to offend the mayor was to invite dismissal.

"Okay, *chiquita,* that explains why Dom wouldn't say anything then. But if he hadn't said anything, why would Sam kill him? How would Sam even find out that Dom knew his guilty secret?" Illuminada posed her final question in the teasing tone of a soap opera narrator. I welcomed her effort to prevent us from being overwhelmed by the grimness of the crime we had revisited. Besides, this was the part of the scenario that had given Sol pause when I'd run my theory by him over breakfast early that morning.

"It's the money, stupid," said Betty. "Isn't that why his daughter suspected her uncle? Because suddenly Dom had all kinds of money?" Betty was so excited by her insight that she needed a bathroom break. Illuminada called Raoul to say she'd be a little late. I sipped cider and thought of the slab of leftover wedding cake on the kitchen counter at home. Sol had promised it all to me.

When she came back, I said, "Betty's right. I figure that when Dom couldn't get any money for his grandkids' education out of his brother-in-law Emilio without signing over his precious pigeon club, he started blackmailing Sam. At first Sam probably figured he'd pay Dom rather than go back to jail, but then when Sam saw what was left of his ill-gotten gains going bye-bye, he wacked Dom," I said.

"Will you listen to her? Girlfriend, you can't even watch a whole episode of *The Sopranos* without covering your eyes, so don't try to talk tough with us," said Betty.

"Would Simon have known how to get up to that

roof without being seen?" asked Illuminada. Leave it to her to ask the one question I hadn't had time to consider before. When I answered, I was really thinking out loud. "Sam took care of pigeons as a young man, so he's certainly familiar with the roofs. I bet he has access to one of the houses on Dom's block. I'd like you to check that out, please." Illuminada was taking out her Palm as I spoke. "The address on Grand Street is in the article. Find out who owns each house on that side of the street. And, if you can, find out who rents or owns the condos too. If Sam could get onto any one roof on that side of the street, he could easily get from there to Dom's. Remember, in *On the Waterfront,* Brando just ran from roof to roof."

"This whole thing is so way out there," said Betty. "It's eerie to be solving a crime that happened three decades ago. It's creepy."

"The cops are going to just love this one," said Illuminada, who relished one-upping her buddies in blue. "Half of them weren't even born when that fire happened. What next, Bel?"

"As soon as I get the articles from Sarah and look through them, I'll call you. We can take it from there." Betty and Illuminada nodded. "But right now, this newlywed is going home." My two friends smirked. "You have dirty minds. I'm going home to eat the last piece of wedding cake and crash."

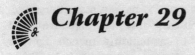

Chapter 29

Arson Investigation Burns Out
"Nothing Conclusive" Reports Chief

"Our investigation revealed nothing to indicate arson was responsible for the fire at 215 Grand Street that left 79-year-old Gustavo Maldonado dead and eleven others homeless last week. But we did find remains of a couple of space heaters. One of them probably fell over and ignited the blaze," Fire Chief Jim Corcoran speculated. "We warn tenants not to use them space heaters, and we made them illegal, but some people don't follow the rules even if we put them in the newspaper and landlords post them on the doors."

The conflagration had required the assistance of several area fire departments, and was the third such blaze in a rent-controlled building in Hoboken this year. "It's a tragedy," said Mayor Dino Sorrentino, a principal in Best Realty, Inc., the building's owner of record.

Tenant advocate Tom Guzman organized a rally

last night to request an investigation by an outside
agency. Speaking first in English and then in Spanish, Guzman said, "People are afraid to go to sleep at
night in Hoboken. We need to have a state investigation of these fires. You can't have the City Fire Chief
investigating a fire in a building owned by the
Mayor. It's called conflict of interest." Only about
twenty people braved the freezing weather to attend.
The police interrupted the rally before Mr. Guzman
had finished because of an irregularity in the permit
he had been granted to hold a public meeting.

I had faxed the article to Betty and Illuminada as
soon as I read it, so they were willing to meet for a
planning session at the end of the next work day in our
kitchen. Of course, Sol would be there, and Vic and
Raoul had agreed to join us. The men had been briefed.
In the past, they had proved useful. Besides, rather
than worry about them worrying about us, we had
found that it was easier to include them in some of our
plans. The operative word here was *plans*. I had come
up with a tentative one that I wanted to run by everybody. Raoul arrived first with two bags of Chinese
takeout, already making himself indispensable.

"The parking is worse than usual," he said. "Illuminada and I had to come separately. If Betty and Vic do
that, we have to wait for three more people to find
parking spaces. . . ." Few of our visitors who arrived by
car failed to complain about their struggle to find a
parking space on Hoboken's car-lined streets.

Sol took the bags of Chinese food from Raoul and
gestured for him to throw his coat on the sofa. "Let's
have a beer while we wait," said Sol. "My wife has
come up with a doozy of a scheme this time, and I

think it'll go down better if we're a little lubricated when she reveals it." Raoul and I grinned to hear Sol refer to me as his wife.

"My husband's right," I said, batting my eyelashes at both men. Sol produced a couple of bottles of Tsing Tao and poured them into three glasses. By the time the others had arrived, we three were sitting around the sink island speculating on whether or not Raoul and Illuminada's daughter, Lourdes, and Betty's son, Randy, had been looking at each other in a new and different way over the past weekend. "I don't think Randy is much of a drinker, but he hung around the bar where Lourdes was handing out drinks all evening," I said.

"Lourdes and Randy hung out together the next day, too," said Raoul.

"Wouldn't it be just too perfect if they got together?" I asked. "Talk about picking your in-laws, Raoul. You and Illuminada would be related to Betty—"

"Bel, get a grip," said Sol. "If it happens, fine, but don't go writing invitations yet."

"Your hubby's right, Bel. Lourdes will probably marry some guy with a family right out of the Simpsons, or worse, just to drive us crazy. Randy is such a good kid. And he has a real job. She would never go for him," said Raoul, rubbing his chin. Lourdes had been dating a string of losers recently.

By the time the others arrived and we had all settled around the table, I was more than ready to explain the scheme to entrap Sam Simon that I'd cooked up that afternoon during an endless faculty meeting. I couldn't even wait until we had helped ourselves to the takeout, so I started talking while Betty and Raoul were opening the bags and passing the containers around. "The problem is we have to get Sam to confess to the arson. And we also have to get him to confess to killing Dom," I began.

"Which he is not going to do," said Betty, just a little too emphatically. I could tell she was still upset about having had to drive around for twenty-five minutes looking for a parking space.

"No, he's not," I said. "You're right. So we have to entrap him. Here's the tricky part. Flora and Leo, Dom's kids, have to get word to Sam that Dom left them a letter to be opened at the time of his death. In this letter Dom tells them how years ago he witnessed Sam enter the building with the kerosene can and that he recently began to blackmail him." I looked around the table to find all eyes on me, which I interpreted as an invitation to continue. "In this same letter Dom instructs Flora and Leo to continue the scam. So they tell Sam to come to the roof with the next payment, or they will go to the cops with Dom's letter and accuse him of arson and murder." I took a deep breath and continued. "Meanwhile, we hide on the roof, maybe in the empty lofts, or just inside the opening to the roof hatch and tape what is said when Sam shows up with the money, thus admitting his guilt. We make a citizens' arrest. What do you think?" I paused for breath and feedback. While I waited, I began to eat.

"Flora and Leo?" said Betty. "From what you say, I get the impression that she's kind of wimpy, and he's a flake. Can they pull this off?"

"She's got asthma, and stress makes it hard for her to breathe sometimes, but she's not a wimp. She's smart, and, after all, she is the one who wanted to find out who killed her beloved father," I said. "I just don't know how she's going to take it when she learns that her dad was a blackmailer." I paused for a moment, picturing Flora's dismay at confronting her idol's feet of clay. "And Leo should be real good at this sort of thing. He's a good talker, an athlete, and he's smart too. As long as we don't drag his ex-wife into the conversation, he should be fine." I smiled. "Besides, he's still got a kid in college, and putting Sam in jail will make one less person that Leo and Flora have to split the proceeds from the sale of the pigeon club with."

Illuminada, who was sitting next to me, flashed me a grin. I knew she appreciated my ability to put myself in the head of a guy like Leo. Betty's question about Flora and Leo's roles in our scheme had pleased me, because it was not a dismissal of my plan but rather an effort to refine it. Raoul's comment was similar. "How they communicate this to Sam will be critical. Can they tell him in person? Or by e-mail?"

"He doesn't do e-mail," I said. "He predates it."

"I think the rooftop scenario should include a few cops around to witness the whole thing as well as to protect us all," said Sol. "I know this Simon guy is eighty-something, but he could show up at that rendezvous with a gun." Sol was right. After he spoke, I realized that Sam might very well decide to kill Flora and Leo rather than give up any more of his swag. After all, he'd killed Dom.

"That makes sense, but why would Flora and Leo meet this psycho on the roof anyway? Especially in this weather?" Vic asked. "I mean, it made sense for the old pigeon racer to meet him up there because he lived in that house and it was private, but wouldn't his kids want to meet somewhere safer or at least warmer?" Silence greeted Vic's question as we all

sought the answer in our plates of chicken with eggplant and twice-cooked pork.

"Yeah, why not have Sam come to their home?
That's private, warm, and makes more sense," Raoul
asked.

"I don't know. I just pictured us all up on that roof,
but maybe you're right," I said.

"You pictured us all up there on the roof, with
Brando and Karl Malden and Eva Marie Saint," said
Sol. "My wife watches too many movies. I'm with
Raoul. They should meet in Flora's and Leo's house.
We can all hide in there without freezing our buns off."

I nodded, not able to think of anything wrong with
abandoning the rooftop for the warmth of the
Tomaselli living room. "So how are we going to get
this information to Sam? By phone? Letter? Pigeon?"
asked Betty. We all smiled at the reference to the passion that had gotten poor Dom involved in all this in
the first place.

"If we do it by letter, we can enclose a copy of
Dom's letter to Leo and Flora. That could be very convincing. I have Dom's journals. I know how he wrote,"
I said, downing the last of my beer and reaching for a
cup of green tea that had magically appeared on the
table.

"That would be good because if he's hard of hearing, he just might miss the whole point on the phone,"
said Illuminada. "My mom has a really hard time with
the phone now."

"I think he does wear a hearing aid, now that you
mention it," I replied. "A lot of the people in that class
do. You're right. We're safer going with a letter and an
enclosure. That way, Flora and Leo can tell him when
and where to meet also. A letter precludes negotiating.

And controlling where and when they are meeting will make it easier for us to set him up."

"So, Bel, you'll talk to Flora and Leo and get them to agree to participate in this wild scheme?" Betty was not really posing a question. Vic and I exchanged glances as we recognized that, once again, she had taken charge. "And you'll write the message to Sam and the enclosure as well?" I accompanied my nod with a mock salute, a gesture I often made when Betty's inner commandant took over. "Illuminada, can you get the police in line on this one? It's going to be a reach." Betty paused, waiting for Illuminada to respond.

Illuminada enjoyed very cordial relationships with the local police, even though she often out-investigated them. She provided evidence that got them convictions, and more than a few officers had used her office to handle delicate personal matters for them. "I think that will be a piece of cake." We all looked puzzled until she explained. "Well, Sorrentino's dead. And I asked around today, and I learned that Jim Corcoran is in a nursing home. All the other firemen who investigated are probably retired or dead. This will be a chance for the current new mayor to make a lot of points without really stepping on any toes. I suspect the mayor may even tell the police to back us up."

"But what about the fact that the cops wrote off Dom's death as accidental without really checking into it?" I asked.

Illuminada nodded. "That's a wrinkle, *chiquita,* but I think it will be overshadowed by the chance to solve the earlier crime. You know, PBS is doing a special, a walking tour of Hoboken. The mayor wants everything to be shipshape when the photographers get here. He'll

want this to be out of the headlines and back under the
rug again."

"Well, now that we've got all that settled," said Vic,
"tell me you two lovebirds, how's married life treating
you?"

Chapter 30

To: Bettyr@juno.com, lguttierez@lguttierezPI.com
Re: Wedding for the ages
Date: 3/27/04 01:18:45

Hi Betty and Illuminada,

Mom and Sol's wedding rocked, man! In fact, the whole week-end was way cool. Thanks for putting Aveda and me up and for letting us help. We were in the kitchen when the happy couple arrived, so we didn't catch the look on Mom's face when she came in and eyeballed Rebecca. Can't wait to see that on the video. How did you get my motor-mouthed sister to keep a secret from mom? Seriously, I have to admit that Rebecca did a good job of transforming Ma Bel from a prof at AARP Academy into a totally hip bride. And speaking of transformations, thanks to Vic for bringing that blazer and tie for me. Mom really goes for that retro bar mitzvah boy look. So thanks from me and Aveda for a totally happening experience. If we ever need a wedding planner, we know who to ask.

Mark

I recalled the royal battle Mark and I had had after his Bar Mitzvah when he had resisted writing thank-you notes. It was no small satisfaction to see that he'd finally stopped resisting and started writing. Was this due to Aveda's influence or had my years of conditioning finally sunk in? Or did e-mail just make it so easy that he didn't mind? Or, good grief, had he grown up? And, even more interesting, what was this about a wedding planner? Were he and Aveda finally considering getting married?

I didn't have time to speculate on the last line of Mark's thank-you note, though, because I had some letter writing of my own to do. Illuminada had called to say that Sam Simon was the owner of record of a condo in a building two doors down from the Tomaselli's. He rented the unit out, but, as the owner, he had the keys and would have been able to access its roof and, from there, the Tomaselli's roof. Now I had to talk with Flora and Leo.

I called Flora and arranged to meet with her and her brother at their home that very night. Sol walked over with me, and we took a half-block detour to pass the scene of Sam's first crime. "Just the brick shell was left, and it's been completely rebuilt. See?" I pointed to the four doorbells at the front door and the one below for the basement apartment. "It's got five condos. If each one sold for . . . well, you were the economics prof, you do the math."

"I get it," said Sol. "I get it. The whole arson scenario seems more plausible when you actually see the house."

"Wait until you see it from behind, from the Tomasellis' roof," I said.

"I can wait. Don't you think it's a little cold for the

roof tour?" he asked, putting his arm around me. "Will you keep me warm up there?"

We got to the Tomasellis', where Leo and Flora greeted us and ushered us into the kitchen of Flora's apartment. I introduced them to Sol, and we settled around the table. Flora, clearly apprehensive, was serving tea and coffee and biscotti. "Flora, why don't you sit down for a minute. We've got some interesting and rather surprising news to share," I said.

"Yeah. Do what the Professor says, Flo. Park it." said Leo, pulling out a chair for his sister and guiding her into it. His affectionate gesture was at odds with his gruff words. He had greeted us politely, probably because I had told Flora it was finally okay to tell him that I was investigating their father's death. This suspicion was confirmed when he said, "Professor, I'm sorry I lost my cool the other day when I was showing you that house. I still go ballistic on the subject of my ex-wife." He looked to Sol for support. Sol nodded, no stranger to the ex-wife as witch syndrome himself. "And I promise you, Professor, this is the last time I'm gonna have to apologize to you for actin' like a jerk." Leo flashed me a high-wattage smile that was probably not unlike the one that had once captivated Sofia's daughter when she and Leo were both in high school.

"Apology accepted, Leo," I said. "Now let's get down to business because we have a lot to talk about tonight. First, I'd like to tell you both who I think murdered your dad." Flora gasped audibly. Leo pulled his chair over to hers and put his arm around her. "Do you remember back in the seventies there was a fire in that building behind this house?" I gestured toward the backyard. Flora nodded. Leo shrugged.

Flora turned to Leo and said, "You were young, in

middle school, I think. Papa heard the fire engines and got us all out of bed. We went up on the roof and watched it. Remember?" Leo looked puzzled. "Papa was very upset. You were half asleep." She turned to me and said, "My brother could sleep through Christmas when he was a kid." Flora's voice was lower when she continued, "We found out the next day some old man died."

The fact that Flora had such a vivid memory of the fire just might make it easier for her to see how it related to Dom's death. Encouraged, I went on. "Well, that was a rent-controlled building, and some people think the fire was started deliberately to force the tenants out, even though they never proved it." Leo straightened in his chair as my story began to engage his professional interest in real estate. "Let's go upstairs for just a second. I want to show you something." At the prospect of braving the cold, Sol groaned. I nudged him sharply. Marriage had not dulled my elbow.

It took a few minutes for us to bundle up and clamber up the stairs. We emerged from the roof hatch into a Van Gogh-worthy skyscape aswarm with stars. A crescent moon was partly obscured by a sliver of cloud, the only one visible. I led the way over to the edge of the roof, to the very place where Dom had stood just before his death. "Look," I insisted. Up there in the dark I heard Flora's intake of breath as she and Leo reflexively peered down at the spot where Leo had found Dom's body. "No," I said, trying to keep my voice gentle. "Look over at the house that burned. Over there." I pointed. They refocused, and the three of us stared at the rear of the rebuilt house. "Notice how easy it is to see the back door from here."

Without waiting for a response, I went on. "Let's suppose your dad was standing here, scanning the sky, maybe waiting for a bird to fly in." In the starlight I saw Leo and Flora look at each other and nod. Clearly I was describing a scenario familiar to them both. "But let's say something else caught his eye, like that peeping tom you told me about, Flora." I didn't turn my head to see if she had made the association or not. "Let's say your father saw a big man with a limp and carrying a can enter that back door and then come running out. And let's say a few minutes later that house went up in flames."

The cloud had drifted past the moon, so when I turned, I could see Flora's face contort in the moonlight. For a brief moment she had the wild-eyed look of someone who realizes suddenly that she has boarded the wrong bus, and it's too late to get off. It was Leo who spoke first. "You're telling us that you think our old man saw somebody burn down that house?" I nodded.

"Could we finish this discussion downstairs?" Sol asked. "We're really done up here now, aren't we, Bel?"

We trooped downstairs, took off our coats, and reassembled around the kitchen table. This time it was Leo who poured the tea. Flora still looked stunned, but her breathing was even, and when she spoke, I knew that her mind was racing. "Are you sayin' that papa's old friend Sam Simon burned down that house?"

Now it was Leo's face that blanched as he connected the name and the description. "Sam Simon? The excon? The old dude who used to work for Mayor Sorrentino? Man, that's incredible. You're saying he pushed our old man off the roof?" Leo leaned back in his chair as if to distance himself from this ghoulish view of a person he'd thought he knew.

"He may have knocked him out first," Sol added. "The autopsy was inconclusive as to whether your father's death resulted from the fall or whether he had received a blow to the head before he fell." Leo lowered his own head as if to ward off a blow himself.

Flora took his hand in hers and shuddered, but she still did not reach into her pocket for her inhaler. Instead she said, "But why? Why would Sam Simon hit Papa or push him off the roof? If what you say is true, Papa never went to the cops." She shook her head.

"And why wouldn't he go to the cops? My old man was strictly a law-and-order type of guy," said Leo, his voice strained. "He practically turned me in a couple a times for a lot less than burning down a building."

"The building was owned by the mayor and your father worked for the city. He might have lost his job," I said. "Also, he soon learned that Sam Simon was going to prison anyway for another crime, so perhaps your dad justified keeping quiet about what he saw because he knew Simon was going to do time anyway." Leo and Flora sat quietly, each taking in this new perspective on their father. When Flora spoke, it was to say, "I remember how upset Papa was that night, the night of the fire. I thought it was because it was so close to our house. . . ."

"If he hadn't spent so much time on that damn roof, maybe he'd still be alive," was Leo's take. Flora used what we had said to explain her father's righteous dismay while Leo used it to criticize his parent for neglecting him. In time each of them would, perhaps, develop a more complex view of Dom. I hoped so.

"Flora asked me to look into Dom's death because

he had come into possession of large sums of money that she couldn't account for, and given it to each of his grandchildren to help with their college expenses," I said in an effort to bring Leo up to speed. "I know your Uncle Emilio owes your dad money, but I do not think Emilio has come through with it. I think your dad tried to collect and Emilio said he would only pay his debt if your dad signed off on the sale of the pigeon club to a developer. As you both know, your dad refused to do that." Flora and Leo nodded.

"So I think your dad told Sam Simon that he saw him start the fire and that if Sam didn't pay him off, your dad would tell the cops. With no Dino Sorrentino to protect him, Sam went along with this because he doesn't want to return to jail. But I think he got tired of giving away his ill-gotten gains, and so he hit your father over the head and pushed him off the roof." Now Flora reached for her inhaler.

Again Leo spoke first. His voice was thick with unshed tears. "Who would've thought the old man had it in him to do something like that? He was such a straight arrow. I used to think he didn't know me very well. Now I realize that I never knew him at all." Sol reached over and poured a round of tea for everybody.

Leo struggled to come to terms with his altered perception of their father, but Flora appeared to have regained her composure. She put away her inhaler and sipped her tea. "Professor, this is gonna take a little gettin' used to, you know? It's a lot to take in. Have you gone to the police yet?"

"It's unlikely that the police will accept our word against Sam Simon's, especially after all these years. We need some evidence or a confession. And I think we can get a confession." Leo's shoulders squared, and

he leaned closer. "Here's what I think we have to do."
I walked them through the plan to entrap Sam that we
had honed the night before, ending with, "All we really
have to do is get him to show up with the money."

Neither Leo nor Flora responded for what seemed
like an eternity. Then I heard a familiar intake of breath
and Flora, her hand on her brother's shoulder, said,
"Okay. Leo, I think we can do this. But there's one
thing." Leo looked up. "It's John, Leo's boy. I don't
want him involved in any way. Leo, can you make sure
John stays downstairs that night? I don't want him in
the same room with Simon. It's not safe." Flora had resumed her role as family caregiver, slipping back into
it automatically when she perceived a threat.

"Right, Flo. I'll see to it that he's out of the house for
the night. I sure don't want my boy in harm's way. Or
my sister either," he said, looking at Flora.

"Give it up, Leo. I'm not goin' nowhere. I need to do
this for Papa. Once in awhile John tutors some kid in
his class in physics, so maybe he can do that for an hour
or two that night and then go to Uncle Emilio's. What
do you think?" Flora spoke directly to her brother, but
her decisive and problem-solving style registered with
Sol and me. That's why we weren't too surprised when
she continued. "We can all write the letter tonight. It
shouldn't take that long. Leo and I know how Papa
wrote," said Flora. Her voice was energetic and dismissive at the same time. She made it sound as if forging a
blackmail note was just another assignment, something
to be tackled and completed in a timely way, something
she had been doing all her life.

"Good idea," said Sol. "Bel was going to do it herself, but your idea is better. The note will be much
more authentic if you two help write it."

Flora was already opening and shutting drawers in search of paper and pens. When she found them, she threw a couple of note pads on the table. "Here, but maybe we should use my computer to do a draft," she said, still standing. "That might be a lot faster. Then we can copy it in Papa's handwritin'."

"Yeah. I got the old man's writing down when I was in high school," Leo said with an unrepentant grin. "I used to skip school and then forge notes from him to get excused. Nobody ever questioned them." Even Flora smiled at the retro confession. "What're you laughing about, Flo? I could do your handwriting too," Leo teased. Flora smiled for the second time that evening. We all agreed to do the first draft on the PC.

Flora's computer was in her daughter Mary's old room. Sol and I sat on Mary's bed, trying not to muss the cabbage rose–covered spread. Flora sat at the desk and typed while Leo paced back and forth on the deep pink carpet. The walls were decorated with the many certificates and diplomas that attested to Mary's impressive academic accomplishments. Photos of friends and family had been crammed under the edges of the mirror over the maple dresser. On the wall at the head of Mary's bed hung a painting of the Madonna and Child.

It was an unlikely setting in which to be forging a blackmail note, and we four were odd collaborators, but in less than an hour, we had composed what we all agreed was a credible document. Leo unseated a few stuffed animals from the maple rocker, took a clipboard that Flora handed him, sat down, and, in about ten minutes, transcribed the letter from Dom onto a blank sheet of paper. Leo's handwriting was so similar to Dom's that had I not sat there and watched while

Leo counterfeited the letter, I'd have thought Dom had written it. "Now you two have to sign off on your note, and we have to make a copy of this letter," I said.

"I have a copier on my printer," said Sol, always eager to use his new toy.

"No problem," said Leo. "I've got one on mine downstairs. I work from home sometimes now, and John uses it a lot, especially for those damn college applications." He shook his head at the complexity of the process of applying to college. "It's just easier to be able to run stuff off at home. Be right back."

We all trooped downstairs after him and waited in the kitchen for a few minutes until he returned with a copy for each of us. "This part was easy," said Sol. "I just hope Simon takes the bait and shows up."

"It's a little like waitin' for a bird to return to the loft after a race," said Flora, taking a deep breath and letting it out before going on, "Like Papa always said, 'Sooner or later he'll show up.' "

"Yeah, but even the old man sometimes needed to use a *chico* to bring in a bird that wasn't ready to fly into the loft on his own," said Leo.

"This letter from Papa is the *chico,*" said Flora. "Sam Simon will show."

"And let's hope that he brings the money," said Leo. "That will really clinch it. Let's just hope that Simon shows *and* brings the money."

"Amen," Sol and I chorused. "And let's hope that we're ready for him when he does," I added silently.

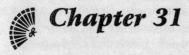

Chapter 31

Sam,

If you don't come up with $30,000, we will see to it that the cops get the enclosed letter our father left for us. If anything happens to either of us, we have arranged for a copy of the enclosed letter to be delivered to the Hoboken Police and the County Prosecutor's Office. Bring the money in cash to Dom's house, 1st floor, at 8 on Monday, March 31.

> *Come alone.*
> *Flora Giglio and Leo Tomaselli*

Dear Flora and Leo,

I'm old now and I could die anytime. Here's what you got to know. The money for the kids schooling I get from Sam Simon. I meet him up on the roof and he pays me not to tell the cops that back in the 70s he started the fire that burned down

*one of the houses behind ours. I was up on the
roof that night and I saw Simon go in there with
a can of something and then come running out.
You can't miss him with that gimpy leg, next thing
the building goes up in flames. I kept an article
about it in my scrapbook. Simon will keep paying
if you show him this letter. He don't want to go
back to jail. This is the best I could do for now.*

*Your father,
Dominic Tomaselli*

As we had agreed, Flora and Leo themselves put the
envelope containing the two letters under Sam Simon's
door the night before they hoped to meet with him. On
the appointed evening, the six of us arrived at the
Tomaselli house separately so as not to attract attention. I had suggested that each couple carry a casserole, albeit an empty one, so that if we were spotted
going in, we'd appear to be well-meaning friends
showing up with food, not exactly an unusual sight at
a home where there has been a recent death. Once we
got inside, we piled our empty dishes on a kitchen
counter and checked out the vantage points where
Flora and Leo suggested we position ourselves.

Betty and Vic drew the unenviable job of staking out
the back entrance to the house from the roof because,
as Betty reminded us, we were dealing with an arsonist who, if desperate enough, might very well stage a
repeat of his original crime. "Maybe he'll think you're
bluffing and just torch the whole house" was how
she'd put it to Flora and Leo. I thought this was unlikely, but not impossible, so we agreed that she and
Vic would hunker down in one of Dom's old lofts.

From there they could see anyone who entered the yard or who climbed the fire escape. And, of course, they would also see anybody who tried to enter the house via the roof hatch. They had dressed for the job in multiple layers of warm, dark clothing.

Because she was the only one of us who carried a gun, Illuminada had to be able to enter the living room immediately if Flora signaled her. So Illuminada was to station herself on the top step of the stairway leading from the living room to the basement behind the slightly open door. Raoul would be a few feet away in the hall coat closet. From there he could tape the conversation Leo and Flora would have with Sam, which we hoped would include a confession. He was using a super sensitive surveillance recorder that Illuminada had provided from her office. Without the sanction of the court, we might not be able to use this tape as evidence, but she wanted him to make it anyway in case the rest of us had trouble hearing Sam's conversation with Leo and Flora.

Illuminada was a little jittery because Hoboken's police chief, whom she had hoped the mayor could cajole into providing on-site back up, had only agreed to have a patrol car cruise the neighborhood. "Sorry, Illuminada, we lost five officers in the latest round of budget cuts, and we're short of manpower. You tell the mayor this is the best I can do. Radio the patrol car if it turns out you get some action," he'd said. "But just between you and me, why not let sleepin' dogs lie?" I knew this unusual lack of cooperation would only inspire Illuminada to try harder to show the cops up.

Even so, as Sol and I took our places behind the old-fashioned pocket door to the pantry just off the dining room, I shared Illuminada's concern. And in spite of the anti-anxiety meds he'd been on since 9/11, Sol too was worried. I tried to concentrate on logistics as a way of ensuring that we had thought through our plan and to dispel the tension that was making me sweat. "Please, be sure you speak up," I called to Flora and Leo. "Otherwise we won't be able to hear you."

"Not a problem, Professor," said Flora. "Remember, you said Sam Simon wears a hearin' aid, so we'll have to talk loud so he can hear us." I was relieved to see that Flora appeared calm, her breathing regular, and her voice steady. Leo, unshaven, tousled, and dressed in sweats, looked a bit less composed. When I first saw him that evening, I wondered if he had been drinking. But he put that concern to rest when, noting the once over I gave him, he said, "I thought I'd try to look the part of somebody desperate enough to resort to blackmail, somebody a little wacko."

Like poor Dom, I thought. The full extent of Dom's folly struck me as I stood there talking with Leo. To think he could successfully blackmail somebody as hardnosed as Sam Simon was definitely more than a little wacko. Had Dom lost touch with reality as he aged? Or had he, perhaps, always been a little out of it? Maybe that's why he had focused so single-mindedly on his precious pigeons. Or maybe he got disconnected from how things work by spending so much time with the birds. I did not share my speculations with Dom's children. They had been saddened by his death, and sorely troubled by the way he died. My amateur attempt to analyze their father's psychological underpinnings offered neither comfort nor clarity. Besides, we had a killer to catch.

Flora and Leo rehearsed their lines. They had obviously gone over them before, so their final practice

session went off smoothly. Then at a few minutes before eight, we all assumed our hiding places. Leo
turned the TV on, and he and Flora settled themselves
in front of it, she in an easy chair and he sprawled on
the sofa. News of the invasion of Iraq drowned out the
beating of our hearts as Sol and I huddled in the dark,
our ears to the pantry door. As we waited, my mind
raced from conjecture to catastrophe, causing me to
break into a sweat again. What if the whole script I'd
reconstructed in the car on the drive to Ocean Grove
was wrong? What if Sam Simon hadn't started that long-
ago fire? What if Dom hadn't blackmailed him? What if
Sam took Flora and Leo's letter to the police? Would Leo
and Flora be found guilty of extortion? Would Leo lose
his license to practice real estate? Would he and Flora
have to go to jail? Would Sol and I be arrested for con-
spiring to commit blackmail? After all, we'd helped
write the letter. Would I lose my job?

I tried to rein in these fantasies by studying the illu-
minated hands of my watch. They seemed to have
stopped. If I forced myself to look away and counted
to one hundred, and then checked my watch again, I
could see that the minute hand had, in fact, moved a
hair's width to the right. I repeated this ritual three
times, and then a car door slammed shut. I started and
grabbed Sol's arm. Even after I realized that the sound
I had heard was part of a car commercial on the TV, my
heart continued to beat furiously and sweat trickled
down my neck.

Again, questions ran wild in my burning brain. What
if Sam Simon did, in fact, show up at the front door as
we had planned, and Flora and Leo let him in? But instead of being duped into confessing, what if the canny
old man called their bluff? What if he didn't believe

that a letter would go to the authorities if something happened to Flora and Leo? What if before Flora could say the word gun, Illuminada's cue to come out with her own weapon drawn, Sam shot his blackmailers? And what if he then set fire to the house to destroy the evidence of his evil act and left the way he came? I could smell the smoke and feel the heat from the flames licking at the pantry door. . . .

Next to me, Sol straightened up to stretch his lower back. The familiar feel of his body next to mine was enough to extinguish my imaginary inferno. I peeked at my watch. Two minutes had elapsed. Following Sol's example, I straightened and saw stars when my head collided with a pantry shelf. Fortunately it held only cookbooks, so the clink of china did not betray our whereabouts. I swallowed a yelp of pain, and there in the dark, Sol tried to massage the hurt away.

Near tears, I cursed myself for my hubris in ever devising such a flawed scheme. What had I been thinking? Why hadn't I just gone to the police with my suspicions and left it to them to follow through? And where the hell was Sam Simon? Had he come across the roof and been accosted by Betty and Vic? Was he now holding them at gunpoint and making them open the roof hatch? Would he force them to reenter the building and then torch it? Just as I was picturing Illuminada trying to radio the patrol car before she succumbed to smoke inhalation, I heard her familiar voice. Her words drowned out the drone of the TV anchorman. "Raoul! Bel! Sol! All clear! Come on out!"

Chapter 32

To whom it may concern,

For the record, I never meant no harm by that fire.
I just wanted to do the mayor a favor to repay him
for all the favors he done for me over the years. Believe me, we never meant for nobody to get hurt. It's
like Dino always said, sometimes you got to give
people incentive to get them to do the right thing
and those tenants got paid good money from the city
to relocate after the fire. I tried explaining all this to
Dom, but he wouldn't listen. I reminded him how I
paid my dues to society for taking a few bucks for a
couple of liquor licenses when I was head of ABC
in Hoboken. I tried telling him what I went through
in jail with all those criminal types, and I never even
told Minny or Dino about that. I told Dom I wasn't
never going back to jail. But you know, Dom could
be very stubborn, and he was bleeding me. But I
could be stubborn too. I still ain't going back to jail.

Sam Simon

At least an hour and a half passed before we read
Sam's note. As soon as Illuminada called us back into
the living room, I made a beeline for the bathroom.
Raoul went up to the roof to get Betty and Vic. By the
time we all reassembled in the living room, I had assumed that by not showing up, Sam Simon had proved
his innocence and our plan had failed. After all, an innocent man has nothing to fear from blackmail. We all
looked to Illuminada for an explanation of what had
made her put an end to our pointless vigil. She obliged.
"I had my cell set to vibrate, and when it did, it was Police Chief Amatruda." She paused for a moment, and
we all stared, waiting for her to continue. "He said to
relax. Sam Simon would not be coming over tonight.
Then he said he had some mail for me. He said he'd get
a copy of it over here as soon as he got the original
processed. He hung up before I got to say a word." Illuminada shrugged, and we all looked at each other.

"Do you think they picked up Sam for something
else?" asked Leo. "Maybe they've got something else
on him."

"Maybe he left the country," speculated Flora. "You
know, liquidated his assets and took off like that other
Jewish crook did. You remember, the one who disappeared from a yacht and turned up years later scuba
divin' and livin' high off the hog on some island. Near
India I think it was." She shook her head at the sheer
bravado of this notorious New Jersey fugitive.

"Sam's too old to scuba dive," I said in an ill-timed
attempt at humor. I made that feeble joke in an effort
to conceal how upset I was at Flora's labeling Sam
Jewish. But he was Jewish. And so was David Fried-
land, the other man she mentioned. Why did Flora's
offhand reference to their Jewishness bother me? I

knew the answer to that. I cringed when forced to confront the fact that Jews, like other humans, could be criminal. Maybe that's why I still felt conflicted about the way I thought the evening had turned out. I was upset to have my theory disproved by Sam's failure to show. But inside me there was a tiny voice that said, Good. Sam Simon didn't set the fire that killed that old man and made all those people homeless. And he didn't murder his friend Dom either. Hooray!

While these opposing reactions were vying for supremacy in my head, I noted that Flora, for once, was not making any effort to entertain us. It was as if the abrupt end to our scheme had drained her of both energy and obligation. She sat with us, talking quietly, until we heard the knock on the door. Then she came to life and opened it to none other than Hoboken Police Chief Amatruda himself and another uniformed officer. The chief, his hat in one hand, greeted Flora with a nod, and walked over to where Illuminada sat next to the sofa. He executed a mock bow and held out an envelope. "I came to deliver your mail along with an apology. You were a hundred percent on the mark. I don't know how the hell you do it, Illuminada," he said, scratching the back of his head.

"So tell us, what happened?" Illuminada asked, trying not to look smug since the Chief was being so conciliatory.

"At about eight o'clock tonight, we get a 911 from a guy says he's a tenant of Sam Simon's. He said he was late with this month's rent, so he called Simon this afternoon and promised to bring a check to Simon's house at eight tonight. He walked over there and saw lights on in the house, but nobody answered the door. Then he heard a sound coming from the garage and smelled gas, so he called 911 right away."

Flora gestured for the chief and the other officer to take a seat. "No, thanks, we can't stay. I just wanted to fill you in and drop that letter off." He nodded at the envelope he'd already handed to Illuminada. "Like I was saying', Officer Damrosh here," this time he nodded at the other cop, "he was in the area, so the dispatcher sent him and his partner to check out the scene. They forced open Simon's garage door and found Simon dead in his vehicle with the gas still on and this note next to him on the front seat. It's a pretty incriminatin' document," said Chief Amatruda. He scratched his head again. "To come up with a firebug so many years after the fire and nail the killer of a guy we didn't even have down as a homicide both in one night . . . wait till they hear about this at the County. They'll think we tried to keep it from 'em." He laughed at the reaction he expected from his colleagues at County Homicide, the team to which individual municipalities referred murders.

"So give us a chance to notify next of kin before you go public with that, Illuminada," he said. "Good night, all. And remember, give us twenty-four hours, okay?"

"There are no next of kin, really," I said, quietly, wondering who would say Kaddish, the Jewish prayer for the dead, for Sam. Nobody was really listening, though, because everybody was waiting for Illuminada to open the letter. When she did, she read it aloud. When she got to Sam's first reference to Dom, Flora's eyes filled, and then overflowed. By the time Illuminada finished reading, Flora was sobbing, and Leo, looking dazed and incredulous, was patting her shoulder.

Again Leo was the first to speak. "It's like he doesn't get it. There's no remorse, no nothing."

"You're right. He makes it sound like he had no choice," said Raoul.

"The man acknowledges no responsibility for those two deaths let alone for displacing all those people." Betty's voice was an angry indictment.

Flora, reviving for the second time that evening, looked up red-eyed and said, "I could make some coffee and tea. . . ."

"Thanks, Flora, but we're going to head home," Sol said, taking me by the arm. "I've had enough for one night." The others made ready to leave also. We got our coats from the hall closet where Raoul had been hiding just a few minutes earlier and put them on. I ran back into the kitchen and retrieved my empty casserole dish, which now seemed like the prop in a high school play. "Good night, all," Sol called over his shoulder. Only when we had refused a ride home and walked a block did he turn to me and say, "Well, you called that one, Bel. Chief Amatruda may never know, but I do. And, frankly, I'm amazed." He was grinning now. "I really thought you were way off base this time."

"Well, I had my own doubts," I said. "When we were stuck in that pantry waiting for Sam to show up, I was beginning to wonder myself."

"As a reward, you get to start planning our honeymoon. I'm thinking Maine or Paris. What do you think?" Sol squeezed my arm as we walked.

"Paris," I said without inquiring as to how we were going to pay for a trip to Paris. "But not until summer. I have to get through the semester first."

Getting through that semester was easier said than done, especially for my memoirists. The final session of their ten-week course coincided with the publication

of the newspaper article declaring Dom's death a
homicide and Sam Simon his killer as well as an arsonist and a suicide. They entered the room shocked
and so, although I had brought refreshments and
copies of their books to distribute, the class was more
post mortem than party. The missing men left a jagged
tear in the fabric of the group. I hoped we women
could patch, embroider, or darn it together somehow.

"I don't know whether to mourn Sam or celebrate
with you, Ana," said Sofia, clearly articulating the
dilemma that most of us recognized.

"Yes, you must be so relieved to have closure. Isn't
that what they say?" asked Ellen. "After all these years,
you now know who burned down your home."

"I no celebrating. Only on TV ees there closure,"
said Ana. "I always wonder who did it. I never teenk
eet would be Sam. I like Sam. He always make us to
smile. Now he ees dead. He keel himself." She shuddered. "And he keel Dom? No, ees too much." She
covered her face with her hands as if in prayer.

"Dom must have been losing his marbles to resort to
blackmail," said Sofia, mincing no words. "Blackmail
doesn't even work on TV." She spoke with authority,
but I could tell she was upset by this revelation about
Dom. She would rather believe he was crazy than corrupt. I didn't blame her.

"The paper said Dom was trying to get money for
his grandkids' schooling. But he wouldn't sell his
share in the pigeon club. I don't get that," said Hilda.
"I mean, one has to make choices, doesn't one?"
Clearly no one in Hilda's world had ever had skewed
priorities.

"Sam seemed like such a cheerful person," said Ma.
"To think he carried around all that guilt for nearly

thirty years." Of course, Ma, no novice herself in the guilt game, was projecting. If she had done what Sam did, she would feel guilty.

"I didn't get the impression from his note that he felt much guilt," said Ellen, her voice getting louder as she went on. "That's what's so hard for me to fathom. Remember when Ana read her piece about that fire, and he just sat here and listened like the rest of us? He pretended to be horrified, but he knew all the time that he himself had deliberately set that fire and caused a man to die and nearly killed several others including Ana." There was no arguing with her. We'd all been here that day.

"Maybe Sam's loss of his son made him a little crazy," I offered by way of explaining the man's behavior, not excusing it.

"Just like maybe Dom was a little crazy." Sofia nodded.

"I lost my husband and my sister and a daughter, Professor," said Hilda, her voice smooth as steel. "We've all had losses." It was my turn to nod. Hilda's point was irrefutable.

"Do you think women are stronger than men?" asked Ellen, speaking softly once more. None of us seemed surprised by her question. "Look at us. We're all still here and those two are dead. Ana survived the fire, and the man who set it is dead."

"Well, we do live longer than men," said Sofia. "Seven years, isn't it?" She turned to me to corroborate her statistic.

"It's tempting to explain what happened in terms of the superiority of our gender," I said with a smile, "but I don't buy that as an explanation for what happened to Sam and Dom. I don't think there's any one explanation. But we owe it to ourselves as writers to treat this series of events we've borne witness to as another chapter in our memoirs. Even though the course is officially over, we could meet once more in about a month and share what we have written. How do you feel about that?"

Everyone nodded. At that point, I distributed paper cups and opened a bottle of apple juice and a box of Pepperidge Farm cookies. I got out the anthologies I'd had Xeroxed and distributed them. The six of us spent the rest of the hour examining and autographing one another's books. No one of us said anything about Sam's and Dom's pieces, preserved there among ours for posterity.

The rest of the semester passed, summer came, and finally Sol and I spent a blissful week honeymooning in Paris. It wasn't until we returned that I read Flora's e-mail.

To: Bbarrett@circle.com
From: Florag@juno.com
Re: Thanks
Date: 07/07/03 12:04:36

Hi Professor Barrett,

It's been awhile since I been in touch, but I enrolled in classes full-time down here and I'm working part-time at an adult Day Care Center, so I've been pretty busy. I finally found a really nice condo right outside of Tuscon. You can download some pictures of it if you want. Leo, Mary, and John helped me load the U-Haul and me and Leo drove down in June. Boy was it hot. But it's great for me here because guess what? My asthma's almost completely gone. I feel like a new woman. I'm going to spend Thanksgiving in Union City with the kids at Leo's new place, and then we'll all be down here for Christmas.

I miss Papa a lot. But me and Leo, we got a good idea. We told Mr. Bechstein that we wouldn't sign over Papa's share of the pigeon club unless he gave us a room off the lobby of whatever he builds there for an exhibit space for the Hoboken Racing Pigeon Club. And he said yes! So Papa gets his museum after all, and Leo and me and the others get our money. And Uncle Emilio is paying me and Leo back now too, so the kids and my schooling is all set just like Papa wanted.

Like I told you, I can't thank you enough for helping me and Leo through that mess with Papa. It all seems like a bad dream now, but I'd still be having it if it weren't for you. And I learned a lot in your class too.

Sincerely,
Flora Giglio

The World of Bel Barrett

The "M" Word

The very first Bel Barrett Mystery, The "M" Word, *introduces us to the smart and sassy midlife professor and part-time sleuth. With a sensibility shaped in the sixties and kids born in the seventies, Bel hit the big five-O in the nineties. In Bel's first case, it's hot flashes and a fancy fundraiser that really turn the heat on when Bel's boss, college president Dr. Altagracia Garcia, is poisoned. When the police suspect one of Bel's students of murder, she sets out in search of the real killer, before she becomes his next victim . . .*

We entered and seated ourselves in a corner booth. I ordered a cup of hot water into which I dropped an herbal tea bag from a stash in my purse, and Illuminada ordered black coffee. I looked straight at her across the table and made my move. In the special voice that I use to cajole potential drop-outs to stay in school, speech-phobic students to address the class, and blocked writers to compose research papers, I said, "Illuminada, I just know Oscar Beckman didn't kill Dr. G. And the more I think about her being murdered, the more I want to figure out who really did do it and why. And now here you are, a bone fide private eye sitting right across the table from me. I just have to ask. Will you help me?"

"You mean pro bono?" Illuminada screwed her delicate features into a grimace. "I do this sort of thing for a living. But . . ." she grinned as I whipped out my fan and began to circulate the air around my face, "for the mother of all mentors. To vindicate our shared heritage, mine and Dr. G's," she added hastily as it was my turn to look quizzical, "and finally, because if we do unravel this, it'll be good for business. I'll make a deal. If you let me observe a few of your classes, I'll do a little poking around." Laughing, Illuminada raised her coffee cup in a toast and then we awkwardly clinked cups, sealing our compact.

Still fanning, I said, "I'm going to find out everything I can on my own. Then we'll know where to look further."

"You better be careful, Professor. Like it or not, somebody did poison Dr. Garcia and that somebody is not going to appreciate your curiosity. This is not exactly library research." When had this role reversal happened? Now who was mentoring whom?

I responded to her warning with more confidence than I felt. "Oh, I'm just going to chat up people the way I always do. One of the advantages of being the faculty yenta-in-residence is that people are used to me having my nose in everybody's business. No one takes me very seriously. I'll start with Betty Ramsey. She was very close to Dr. Garcia. She'll help us. Don't worry about me."

Death in a Hot Flash

In Death in a Hot Flash, *Professor Bel Barrett's colleague, popular local undertaker Vinny Valone, shows up dead. Many suspect suicide, but when the police accuse one of Bel's students of the crime, Bel knows that she's the only one who can clear his name. With loads of leads and phony clues that challenge her midlife memory, Bel must face her toughest case yet.*

Just then Gilberto Hernandez arrived, nodding politely at me as if to apologize for his tardiness, but not actually saying anything. Gilberto had been doing an externship at Vallone and Sons, so I assumed that he had known Vinny better than the others. Because he wasn't usually late, I decided not to make an issue of it. There were clearly extenuating circumstances that day.

Gilbert had flashing dark eyes and an easy grin and was handsome in a male-model sort of way. But as he took his seat that day, his eyes were still and his lips were a straight slash across his face.

I resolved to do more listening than speaking, since I had no insight to offer and since the students clearly wanted to talk. "Please take one of these and pass the rest," I said, handing Alan a sheaf of announcements about Vinny's wake and funeral. The familiar class-room routine of passing around printed material occu-pied us for a moment or two.

Then, while she was stuffing the handout into her book bag, Joevelyn blurted out, "You know, maybe he got bad news or somethin', like, you know, his health . . ." Her words hung suspended in the room, catching all of us off guard. Of course, she could be right. How much did any of us know about Vinny, really? Vinny had never mentioned a word to me about being sick, but would he have? For all his chattiness, Vinny had always kept his private life private. It was awful to think of him hiding a serious health problem behind a facade of bad puns. Poor soul. Joevelyn must have been think-ing the same thing, because her eyes were tearing up again.

"Maybe he was worried about somethin', like, you know, maybe somebody had somethin' on him." It was Henry Granger, speculating so matter-of-factly in his deep voice that Joevelyn stopped blowing her nose and, along with the rest of us, turned toward Henry, a dark face in our circle.

As usual, Alan required more information. "You mean you think somebody might have been threaten-ing to blackmail Professor Vallone?" Alan's voice ap-proached a squeak when he got to Vinny's name. "So instead of calling the cops or paying the blackmailer, he jumped in the river? Is that what you *really* think?" Alan looked incredulous. In his own carefully ordered version of the universe, such a series of events was out of the question.

"Yeah man. Somethin' like that. You know everybody got secrets. And Professor Vallone, he like a walkin' secret," said Henry. Just then Gilberto rose, gathered his books, and left the room as quietly as he had come. He hadn't been in class more than five minutes. He must have been taking Vinny's death especially hard. Henry paused for a moment and then went on. "And not just his own secret. Folks tell things to undertakers. I bet that dude heard a lot of other folks' secrets when he was helpin' them bury their dead." Henry still sounded matter-of-fact, as if he were droning on about the weather. But suddenly I found it impossible to ignore the two tattoos that hung below his eye like tiny daggers. Today they made everything he said sound ominous. Clearly, Henry knew from secrets.

I reminded them of their assignment and promised that there would be a replacement teacher before too long. "I'm planning to attend Professor Vallone's viewing and funeral. If anyone here would like to go . . ." I wondered if anyone else appreciated the irony of funeral-service education students attending their prof's wake and funeral.

No one smiled when Alan Weiner interjected, "If we go, do we have to take notes?"

Gilberto had not returned by the time I dismissed the class.

Mood Swings to Murder

Bel Barrett is once again on the case in Mood Swings to Murder, *when local Frank Sinatra impersonator, Louie Palumbo, turns up dead. When the bogus Blue Eyes' fiancée Toni pleads for help in solving the crime, how can Bel say no? In her own unique style, Bel plunges estrogen-patch-first into the strange world of obsessive Sinatra worship—a move that could prove to be something stupid . . . maybe even fatal!*

"You met while you were doing your research, right? In the Sinatra archives?" I knew she was going to want to tell her tale from the beginning, so I tried to cue her.

"Yes. It was in the archives. Louie knew everything about the Sinatras. It was awesome how much he knew. And he was so helpful." A new teardrop was forming in the corner of her reddened eye.

At the sight of this harbinger of yet another parox-ysm of sobs, I quickly interjected a question, "I guess it was love at first sight, wasn't it?"

Big mistake. I could read Sol's critique of my ill-chosen line of inquiry when I saw him shaking his head.

We waited for Toni to regain control of herself. "No, actually, I was engaged to someone else when I met Louie. A really awesome guy I've known for years, the boy next door actually." Toni smiled at the absurdity of this cliche, and a wayward teardrop slipped from her lash and splattered on the counter. After swiping at the tiny puddle with a Kleenex, she took a sip of her lemonade and continued. "Well, anyway, my former fiancé—John is his name—is a law student. One night last December, he was studying for finals, so he couldn't go to a concert at city hall in Hoboken that this other Frank Sinatra impersonator, somebody new in town, was giving. It was to celebrate Frank's eighty-second birthday. Louie wanted to go to check out the competition, you know? He was a little surprised not to be asked to do that gig himself, or at least to share it." Toni shook her head, recalling the logic of the dead man, and forged ahead with her story. "So I invited him to use John's ticket, and we went together. It was there, that night, listening to Luke Jonas singing 'All the Way,' that Louie and I fell in love." For a second my eyes glazed over, and once again I was in the backseat of Teddy Lichenstein's father's new T-bird with Frank crooning over the radio about how glad he was to be near me.

Neither Toni nor Sol had noticed my moment of private tribute to The Voice. When I tuned them in again, Toni was saying, "So right after that I, you know, I broke off my engagement to John. It was only right." For a moment I felt a pang of empathy with the Demaios, who had probably had some difficulty understanding why their bright and lovely twenty-two-year-old daughter would prefer a thirty-something tone-deaf Frank Sinatra wanna-be to a future lawyer. But had the future lawyer been so unhinged by the loss of his ladylove that he had stabbed his rival in the back several times and then pushed him over the palisade? Apparently Toni didn't think so.

"But, look." Toni had reached for the tiny shoulder bag she had hung over the back of the stool and was rooting about in it. "This is terrible. It just makes everything worse." She pulled out a creased copy of a newspaper article, the same one that Wendy had shown me earlier. "Look. They actually think John killed Louie."

"What do you think?" It was Sol's first contribution to what had been a dialogue between Toni and me. I was surprised to hear his deep voice enter the conversation. "It wouldn't be the first time the green-eyed monster got some guy in over his head."

Toni looked at me, puzzlement clouding her tear-blotched features. "Huh? What are you trying to say? John's not a monster."

"It's a metaphor," I offered, "for jealousy. That's the green-eyed monster. Sol's suggesting that maybe jealousy drove John to murder Louie."

"But John would never ever do that. Not in a million years. And that's why I came here tonight. The police questioned him for hours. John's parents look at me like I'm dirt now, and even my own mother says everything's my fault. Louie's parents too. They looked at me tonight like I wasn't really there. And his brother, Danny, too. It's bad enough I lost Louie, but I can't stand to see poor John blamed for something he would never do." Toni's head went down again onto the cradle of her arms, her glasses found their way back onto the counter, and her gulping sobs rasped loud in the quiet kitchen.

When she finally looked up, she said only, "Please

help me, Professor Barrett, please. Just help me to prove to them that it wasn't John. I know it was you who really solved the murder of that part-time professor, the undertaker. Everybody at RECC knows that. Please."

Midlife Can Be Murder

Professor Bel Barett is in hot water again in Midlife Can Be Murder, *when she agrees to help one of her former students prove that a friend's freakish rock-climbing death was no accident. But the only way to find some answers is to go undercover as a housekeeper at a suspect's office and look for clues. Too tired to moonlight, and to feisty to give up without a fight, Bel won't stop until she finds the killer.*

"Hey! How'd you get in here?" It was Greg himself who had glided silently into the doorway on his Rollerblades. Holding onto a doorjamb with each hand for balance and leaning into the room, he filled the doorway, making escape impossible. "What're you doing here, huh? Calling your relatives all over the Caribbean like the last one? You people never learn, do you?"

I realized that he thought I'd been using the phone to place long-distance calls. This was a fairly common practice among homesick evening maintenance workers and even security personnel in Jersey City, who couldn't resist making "free" calls to relatives, friends, and lovers they had left behind in places like Miami, Dominica, Haiti, and Ecuador. At RECC this unauthorized activity had resulted in some pretty high phone bills, so the administration had blocked long-distance access on most of the college's phones. "What's your name? Answer me?"

I smiled idiotically. I did not have to mimic fear. I was terrified. What I had to mimic was Spanish, so I kept muttering, *"No comprende"* and then, in a desperate imitation of Illuminada's accent, I whispered, *"Dios mío,"* lowered my head as if awaiting the guillotine, and crossed myself. Gliding over to the other side of the desk, he picked up the phone and punched a number. "Jack, send someone from security up here to escort one of Delores's girls downstairs. She can wait for Delores outside. I don't want her in the building. I'll call Delores myself and tell her I caught her girl using the phone in my office." I struggled not to let my face show that I understood what he was saying as I moved tentatively from behind the desk in the direction of the doorway.

It took a few minutes for the security guard to get upstairs, so I was able to hear Greg bark into Delores's message machine. "Delores, Greg, CEO at e-media.com here. I just caught one of your girls using the phone in my office tonight. Those offices are off limits. I don't want to see her here again." I was livid. This underaged and underbred techno tycoon had pushed most of my buttons. He'd called me a girl. My blond wig and uniform did not mask the obvious fact that I was, literally, old enough to be his mother. He'd referred to non-native speakers as "you people," lumping all immigrants together as, at the very least, petty criminals.

And finally, he'd lied about me using the phone, and his lie would have gotten me fired if I'd been a real employee of Delores Does Dusting.

By the time the security guard arrived, Betty and Illuminada had finished the basketball area without me and were putting away their equipment. I pantomimed to my keeper that I too wanted to stash my maid props, and I did. As I walked out, my escort and I went downstairs in the same elevator as Betty and Illuminada. But there was no question about it. For me it was a one-way ride. From now on Delores would be dusting without me. I had been canned.

Out of Hormone's Way

Bel Barrett already has enough to worry about with her busy teaching schedule, not to mention dealing with the annoying challenges of midlife and menopause. So when she agrees to head up the Urban Kayaking Club, it's just one more thing to add to her already full plate. And when a sweet, shy fellow kayaker is found floating in the water, Bel once again puts her sleuthing skills to the test to find the killer, before she gets sunk as well.

Politicians weren't the only headliners though. There was an equally predictable population of psychopaths who routinely and fatally shot, strangled, stabbed, poisoned, and suffocated their hapless victims. That's why I hadn't really been surprised earlier by Gina's account of a murder at the Outlets. Nor was I surprised now to see that it had made the front page. The victim, a young Colombian-American woman, Maria Mejia, had been found stabbed to death in the parking lot of her place of employment, His 'n' Hers Shoes, presumably on the way to her car after work. Because her

purse was missing, the local police officer summoned
to the scene assumed that she had died resisting a thief.
There were no suspects or witnesses yet. I wouldn't
have paid too much attention to poor Maria Mejia's un-
timely demise had it not been for Gina's heads-up. But
now, reading about it in the paper, I felt a chill.

I poked Sol, who was holding the *Times* with one
hand and his head with the other, distressed by events
in Washington, the Middle East, Africa, and Asia. "Sol,
look, some poor young woman was just murdered at
His 'n' Hers Shoes. That's the outlet where I bought
the black flats I wore to Rebecca's wedding," I added,
hoping that if I put this killing in a personal context, he
would pay attention. "Right in the parking lot. In Secaucus. At the Outlets. Betty said Gina was there when
it happened," I added, trying harder to interest him in
this odd confluence of conversation, shopping, and
death. "Look," I insisted, finally placing my copy of
the *Jersey City Herald* over his *New York Times* so he
couldn't help but eyeball a headshot of the late Ms.
Mejia.

"What the hell did she do? Shop till she dropped?" I
winced as the familiar bad joke rang out for the second
time that day. "Jesus, Bel, she's not the first and she
won't be the last. The Meadowlands has been a body
drop since forever. Before Jimmy Hoffa." Even as he
spoke, Sol gently but firmly pushed my paper out of
his way and immersed himself once again in The Big
Picture.

I didn't bother explaining that Maria had not been a
shopper but an employee. Nor did I say how discom-
fiting it was to read about this murder on the same day
I'd been reminiscing about shopping at His 'n' Hers
Shoes in Secaucus. Sure, it was just a coincidence, but

an eerie one. I was chilled by the killing itself and by the fact that the killer was still out there somewhere. *Not at Laurel Hill Park, I hope*, I muttered to myself as I moved closer to Sol.

Hot and Bothered

The work of a full-time professor and part-time sleuth is never done. As Bel Barrett tries to cope with the effect that September 11 had on her hometown of Hoboken, New Jersey, one of her colleagues turns up dead. But things aren't always as they appear. The victim led a double life—academic by day, stripper by night—and Bel must discover which of those lives attracted the murderer. Education and titillation could prove a most volatile mix, and a murderer may be closer than she thinks . . .

The block party fell on one of those perfect Indian summer days that we had been perversely gifted with during that cataclysmic fall. The bright sunshine and unseasonable warmth brought out the neighborhood neatniks all ready to sweep early in the morning. I was not among them. Since the terrorist attack on the World Trade Center, I'd resumed attending synagogue on Sabbath mornings. Sabbath worship, a habit I'd only begun cultivating when preparing for my adult bat mitzvah, had been a casualty of the Saturday mornings

I'd spent as faculty advisor to the RECC Urban Kayaking Club the previous spring. I shuddered, recalling the grisly murders that had become indistinguishable from that experience and blighted it in my memory.

The sight of Sol brandishing a broom delivered me back to the present. Unfortunately, since September 11 the present had been blighted as well, and Sol was living testimony to that fact. His stocky frame appeared less substantial and his eyes, normally mischievous, were now more often wary. I was worried about him. Like Betty's son, Sol had been enroute to the WTC on the morning of September 11 and had witnessed the buildings' destruction. But whereas Betty's son had been on the subway, Sol had been aboard the ferry. Badly shaken by what he had seen, he feared more terrorist attacks.

But that morning he had joined our neighbors to prepare for the block party. He was sweeping fallen leaves and scraps of litter from our gate, the vernacular term for the concrete area in front of a row house. As soon as the street was completely cleared of cars, Sol and the other gate sweepers would turn their attention to what was to be our communal patio for the next fifteen hours.

Sol and I were sharing a good-morning hug when Joey P came rushing over to us looking flustered. His simple words would have sounded ordinary a year earlier. That year they had the ominous ring of prophecy. "Jeez. I was tryin' ta move my car but they got cops all over the Avenue." For reasons lost in local lore, Hoboken's main drag, Washington Street, is always referred to as "the Avenue." "Traffic's backed up for blocks."

Delphine, Felice, and Tony, all engaged in sweeping their gates, put down their brooms and gathered around the tall gray-haired man. Sol, his brow suddenly rutted with worry lines, asked, "What's going on?" I resolved to try not to focus on Sol's anxiety. I wanted to believe that, given time, this retired economics prof would re-cover the self-possession and wry sense of humor that had attracted me to him when we first met. That had been years before, when we were both active in the Citizens Committee to Preserve the Waterfront, a group determined to stave off those developers hoping to play high-stakes Monopoly along Hoboken's strip of riverbank.

"A cop told me," Joey P wheezed, "that there was an unmarked package delivered to Swift Savings this morning. They don't know what's in it. The cops are waiting for the bomb dogs and then if it's not a bomb, they'll take it to examine for traces of . . ."

"Anthrax . . ." everybody intoned in unison, a Greek chorus articulating one of our newest and worst fears.

A hefty woman with tufts of red-orange hair and the social style of an antebellum plantation overseer showed up just then. It was Ilona Illysario, and she spoke with her usual authority, an authority derived largely from being married to the PANA president and mother of last year's PANA scholarship winner. "It's not a bomb and they've already taken it away for test-ing. So let's get this place cleaned up. Remember, the kids gotta make chalk drawings on that concrete. Move it guys!" She grabbed her broom and headed for the street to begin sweeping the gutters where earlier the cars had obscured the week's accumulation of litter and leaves. Sol looked only slightly relieved, but by the time I left, he had finished sweeping our gate, bagged the debris, and joined several others in the now nearly carless street.

Coming soon!

Eye of the Needle: For the first time in trade paperback, comes one of legendary suspense author Ken Follett's most compelling classics.
0-06-074815-X • **On Sale January 2005**

More Than They Could Chew: Rob Roberge tells the story of Nick Ray, a man whose addictions (alcohol, kinky sex, questionable friends) might only be cured by weaning him from oxygen.
0-06-074280-1 • **On Sale February 2005**

Men from Boys: A short story collection featuring some of the true masters of crime fiction, including Dennis Lehane, Lawrence Block, and Michael Connelly. These stories examine what it means to be a man amid cardsharks, revolvers, and shallow graves.
0-06-076285-3 • **On Sale April 2005**

Now Available:

Kinki Lullaby: The latest suspenseful, rapid-fire installment of Isaac Adamson's Billy Chaka series finds Billy in Osaka, investigating a murder and the career of a young puppetry prodigy. 0-06-051624-0

First Cut: Award-winning author Peter Robinson probes the darkest regions of the human mind and soul in this clever, twisting tale of crime and revenge. 0-06-073535-X

Night Visions: A young lawyer's shocking dreams become terribly real in this chilling, beautifully written debut thriller by Thomas Fahy. 0-06-059462-4

Get Shorty: Elmore Leonard takes a mobster to Hollywood—where the women are gorgeous, the men are corrupt, and making it big isn't all that different from making your bones. 0-06-077709-5

Be Cool: Elmore Leonard takes Chili Palmer into the world of rock stars, pop divas, and hip-hop gangsters—all the stuff that makes big box office.
0-06-077706-0

Available wherever books are sold, or call 1-800-331-3761.

AuthorTracker
Don't miss the next book by your favorite author.
Sign up now for AuthorTracker by visiting
www.AuthorTracker.com

PERENNIAL
DARK ALLEY
An Imprint of HarperCollinsPublishers
www.harpercollins.com

DKA 1104